For Roy Plomley, who has so long thrilled listeners with *Desert Island Discs*, and because I wrote the first few lines of this novel 'off the cuff' during my appearance on his programme.

DARK CORRIDOR

Denise Robins

CHIVERS

British Library Cataloguing in Publication Data available

This Large Print edition published by AudioGo Ltd, Bath, 2011.
Published by arrangement with the Author's Estate.

U.K. Hardcover ISBN 978 1 445 83730 7
U.K. Softcover   ISBN 978 1 445 83731 4

Printed and bound in Great Britain by
MPG Books Group Limited

CONTENTS

Part One

CHAPTER ONE

She was in the middle of the dreaded nightmare again. She called it the Long Dark Corridor. Usually she woke up bathed in sweat and crying out, yet she knew perfectly well, when she grew calmer, that even a recurrent bad dream has no real significance and she mustn't take it seriously.

She had been christened Corisande Gilroy, but from childhood they had called her Corrie. She couldn't think why she should have ever suffered from this sinister nightmare— particularly not last night when she was so happy, and had so much to look forward to.

She was going to be married very soon to Martin Ashley—the most marvellous man in the world in her estimation. She was very much in love. For the last two years she had worked in *Green Fingers,* a florist shop in Hampstead, where she also shared a flat with the owner, Christine Taylor. Now, for good, she had left that life and was down in the country at Brabett's Farm with her aunt, Ann, where she spent most of her weekends. She loved Brabett's and meant to stay there until her life changed dramatically—starting with her wedding day.

Martin wanted her to have three months of freedom now, which is why she had said

3

"goodbye" to Christine and her job, and moved from London to the little Sussex farmhouse in Nutley. Since the death of her parents, Corrie had made Ann's house her home. And Miss Williams, who had never married, appreciated the company of her delightful niece. They got on well together.

Last night Corrie had spent some time sorting out old clothes and finding things for Ann's next local jumble sale. They had a light supper, looked at TV for an hour, then gone early to bed. Corrie had not even read a book. which was her custom. She had quickly fallen asleep, first giving a long blissful look at Martin's photograph on the table beside her bed.

'Good night, my darling dear,' she had whispered, 'I do love you so much.'

Why couldn't she have had a lovely dream about him? Why did she have to dive headlong into a grim nightmare, and find herself moving down that mysterious corridor, trembling, terrified, knowing that it always ended with the icy hand reaching out from some invisible doorway, dragging her into a fearful void of nothingness. It reduced her to utter despair—as black as it was inexplicable. Then she would hear herself scream, wake up, and dissolve into the customary storm of tears.

After such occasions, Corrie became nervous and unlike herself and was ashamed of the fact.

When first she had told Martin about it, he had laughed, kissed the tip of her nose, and said, 'You're adorable, but quite idiotic, my love. Nightmares don't mean a thing. Indigestion probably, poor sweet! I wish I could go to sleep too and find myself in the same nightmare with you. Then I could reach out my hand and pull you into that room which seems so awful and you would find it full of light and you'd be in my arms. And whether the ring was on your finger or not, I'd make mad love to you and you'd be wholly mine and you'd never be afraid again.' That was comfort indeed.

Corrie had noticed a change last night in the usual pattern. She distinctly remembered hearing somebody call to her at the end of that corridor, and it was *Martin* speaking—sharply. It was unlike his usual low-pitched lazy voice which she found so attractive. He called her by name, her full name for once: *'Corisande!'* She tried to answer but couldn't, then she was dragged into that dreaded room. After that, the awakening.

She wept as she sat up and realised that the night had gone. Faint light filtered through the window panes. Her bedside clock told her that it was seven o'clock. She was at least glad she would not have to try to get to sleep again. That was always difficult.

She got out of bed, went into the bathroom and sluiced her tear-wet face in cold water.

5

Looking into the mirror she shuddered. What a sight! Haggard and pale, and hair damp with sweat. Fortunately she was having her hair done in East Grinstead this morning.

She and Ann had planned a morning's shopping.

Corrie attended to her make-up until she was satisfied that she looked more herself. Martin would have a fit if he could see her so changed—so disturbed. She must get a grip on her emotions.

Hastily she finished making up her face and brushed back the splendid hair which almost matched the warm golden-brown of her eyes. Martin in one of his poetic moods, once described them as the eyes of an enchantress. Sometimes he teased her. 'You know perfectly well when you flick your long black lashes, you enchant and confuse me until I haven't a clue how to cope with you.' Which extravagance made her laugh but she was secretly pleased.

She couldn't deny that the gods had given her the gift of beauty. A slim, graceful figure, a delightful tip-tilted nose and a wide sweet mouth made for loving and kissing (as Martin frequently reminded her). She was a sensitive, artistic sort of girl but far from weak or shy. She had an unusually strong will—even a streak of obstinacy. She was certainly not one to give in easily where her principles were concerned.

'You know, Corrie, you have *everything,*'

Martin had told her when he first asked her to marry him, 'absolutely everything a man could want. Why should you want to marry *me?*'

In his arms she had answered, 'Because *you've* got everything I want and I don't know why *you* want to marry *me!* So we're quits.'

Now on this cold morning, she rapidly recovered from the effects of the tantalising nightmare. She fully expected a letter from Martin this morning and looked forward to its arrival eagerly.

Martin worked for Horton & Mullins, the publishers. At the early age of twenty-five he had already been promoted to European sales manager. A well-paid and creditable position for a young man who had only been with the firm four years. He was dedicated to his job, and ambitious. It seemed to Corrie that he was bound to succeed.

At present he was in Lisbon, attending the Book Fair which was held there every year in the early spring. While she thought only of Martin, she relived a few of her special moments with him.

For instance, the dinner at Mariota's, an Italian restaurant in Chelsea which had become a favourite. Corrie had no need to look at the menu, that particular night. In advance, Martin had ordered her favourite food—pasta, followed by *truite almondine,* and a special chocolate gâteau topped with whipped cream and flavoured with Grand

Marnier.

Corrie had become engaged to Martin during a dinner in this very restaurant. Mario, the proprietor, had been delighted and brought them a special bottle of wine. They had all three toasted the great event. She had been blissfully happy. Martin had seemed so utterly right for her.

It was at Mariota's they dined just before Martin flew to his job in Lisbon. Mario, sentimental and perceptive, saw that evening neither of his young clients seemed to laugh as much as usual. But Corrie smiled at the anxious little Italian as he poured out their wine, 'Nothing is wrong. It's just that we can't bear to be parted, can we?' She turned to Martin.

He reached for her hand, kissed it, and answered, 'Darling, you really have got a super nose, the way it tilts just a *fraction* upwards.'

'I like your big boney nose,' she joked back. 'Oh, darling, won't it be marvellous when you get back from Lisbon and we can be together again!'

Three weeks ago he had thought up the plan for her to meet him in Madeira on the return journey.

'Even for a few days—let's have a sort of pre-honeymoon holiday.'

At once Corrie agreed. 'Super idea. I'll be waiting for you. People may think us mad but meeting you like that sounds so heavenly, I can't resist it. It'll be madly extravagant too.'

'Then madly extravagant we'll be,' he said. 'And everyone will think we're an old married couple.'

Then he had given her a wicked look from those sleepy handsome eyes of his—grey and darkly lashed. But the sleepy look was deceptive. Martin, as they all told Corrie at his office, was right on the ball. And so very good-looking with his thick fair hair, not too short, not too long, his attractive mouth and boyish gay smile. He was not tall. Of medium height and with the broad, strong shoulders of an athlete. He played excellent tennis when he got the chance. Corrie played less well but they enjoyed a set or two together.

Thinking of their plans for Madeira she said, 'The only thing I have against all this gorgeous madness is that I'm not allowed to pay for my ticket. I've saved up quite a bit, you know.'

He smiled. 'My precious. You must get used to me spending what money I have on you, and only you. In any case, my grandmother is financing us as one of our wedding presents.'

'You don't think it will spoil the thrill—staying at Reid's? I mean, we intend to have our real honeymoon there,' Corrie ventured a protest.

'I do not. It will increase the thrill of anticipation,' he answered.

Her pulses quickened and her cheeks

9

burned.

'Oh, I love you so, Martin! I hate you going to Lisbon without me. I shall miss you so much.'

'I shall miss *you*. But look what we've got to look forward to!'

She laughed softly. 'We're old-fashioned really, don't you agree we are? And romantic—more so than a lot of our friends? Some say today that romance is just an illusion.'

He gave her another all-embracing look and lifted his wine-glass.

'I give you a toast. To illusions!—may ours never be shattered.'

They drank deeply to that.

It was a tender, happy yearning kind of evening ending in the sitting room of the flat Corrie shared with her employer during the week. There Martin had held her tightly against him and they exchanged those long breathless kisses which at times he jokingly told her were bad for his nerves.

The next day he flew to Lisbon.

On this cold bright March morning, Corrie finished dressing, added a touch of coral-pink to her lips, and looking through the casement windows was glad to see that the frost was rapidly vanishing. The pale weak sunlight made her think with fresh longing of the golden sun that would shine on her once she landed at Madeira. It would be like early June over there, warm enough for them to swim in the heated pool at their hotel, if not in the sea.

She tidied her room feeling more cheerful. She would have a happy day with Ann—who had been less of an aunt than a friend or sister. Miss Williams was a delightful woman, fond of the young and particularly of Corrie.

The girl heard Ann's pet—a Schnauzer, barking in the bedroom and called out, 'Morning, Ann.'

'Morning, dear,' Miss Williams called back. 'Let Zena out for me.'

The door opened and Zena the grey, soft-eyed Schnauzer bitch bounded out still barking.

Corrie took her downstairs.

CHAPTER TWO

The telephone bell was ringing. Corrie ran to the hall and answered the call. The rich throaty voice at the other end of the line was familiar. It was Martin's much-loved grandmother.

'Good morning, pet.'

Lady Grey-Ewing, once-famous actress and dancer, was known to thousands in the thirties as Violetta Maye—leading lady in many successful musicals. Violetta had retired from the stage ten years ago. Now she was a widow of eighty, still sparkling, still attractive. At first meeting Corrie had quite fallen in love with her. Silver-haired, with her lined pretty little face, eyes as blue as forget-me-nots and petite figure—she wore up-to-date clothes and prided herself on being "with it".

Martin had lived with his grandmother since her daughter, Vanessa—Martin's mother—had married for the second time, a man Martin did not care for. They had gone to live permanently in Australia.

Violetta this morning was asking for news of her adored grandson.

'Did he phone you and are you still planning to meet him in Madeira?'

'Yes, darling, it's booked, signed and sealed—thanks to your generosity. We'll have at least three super days together.'

Violetta gave one of her chuckles. Corrie could visualise those incredibly blue eyes dancing with mischief behind the big horn-rimmed glasses.

'Permissive pair! Shame on you! I oughtn't to countenance it. Staying in Reid's Hotel and not even married.'

Corrie's cheeks burned but her own eyes sparkled. She laughed. 'I don't think we'll actually spoil the Great Day, dearest, and we *are* in separate rooms—but we can't miss this opportunity. Martin so rarely gets any time off except his normal three weeks' holiday. But the firm's allowed him extra time, and thanks

12

to you, darling, we're able to afford it. Reid's Hotel sounds so gorgeous.'

Now Corrie heard a sigh from Martin's grandmother. 'It is—and so nostalgic for me. I can hardly bear to think of me not being there with you. It was Bill's and my honeymoon hotel!'

Hastily Corrie looked at the grandfather clock just behind her. Much as she adored Violetta, she couldn't afford the time this morning to listen to a tale about the once-famous actress and the late Lord William Grey-Ewing when in Madeira. She had heard it so many times.

'Do forgive me, but I've got to get on, darling. I'm late with Ann's breakfast—' Then as she heard the slither of envelopes through the letter box, 'Hang on, I've just seen a telegram being pushed through the box. It must be from Martin. I'll open it and see if there is any news.'

There were three lines. Enough to make her heart beat fast.

'All set for Sunday, 19th March. Meet me at Reid's. I love you. Martin.'

Corrie repeated this to Violetta.

Lady Grey-Ewing squealed delightedly. 'Terrific, my pet. Oh, how I envy you! Come up and have lunch—or dinner—before you go.'

'I will but I'll have to hustle. He's only given me forty-eight hours' grace to get myself ready.'

'But you've got your ticket. I booked the 19th for you. Remember?'

'Yes, and you gave me the escudoes, darling. You've been angelic.'

'I remember—' began Violetta but Corrie broke in.

'Oh, *darling,* forgive me, but I must go.'

As soon as Violetta rang off, Corrie telephoned her answer, addressing the wire to Martin's hotel in Lisbon.

'I'll be there. I love you.'

She felt light-hearted with happiness. Her next act was to go to her aunt's room to tell her the exciting news. She found Miss Williams just coming out of her bath. 'Going to be a good day, Corrie. Let's get into East Grinstead before the crowds spoil the field.'

'I'm ready now. I'll go down and make the coffee,' said Corrie.

Miss Williams buttoned up her shirt. A cigarette hung from her lower lip. She was a tall thin woman in her middle age. The reverse of Martin's grandmother. There was very little of the feminine about Ann. She had large hands and feet and a bony face redeemed only by a pair of fine hazel eyes. She didn't wear glasses. She boasted that she could see anything, any distance. She had all her own teeth, thick curly hair, and was rarely ill. An excellent sportswoman, she trained her horses with the help of a girl assistant and a stableboy. Her foals were in great demand.

Since her childhood when she first came to live with her aunt, Corrie had rarely seen Ann (she was never allowed to call her aunt) wear anything but trouser-suits and polo-necked sweaters. There had been a time, once Martin came on the scene when Corrie wondered whether his grandmother and her aunt would "get on". But once they met, the two women— so unalike—seemed to take to each other. Violetta warmly admired any woman who could do what Ann Williams had done. On very little capital she had made a fine business of her stables, and sent her orphaned niece to school on the proceeds. She had lost the only man she had ever cared for, through polio, and since then had cared for nothing but her horses. But Ann, secretly, envied Lady Grey-Ewing her beauty—faded though it was—her tiny figure, her wit and her charm. They became firm friends.

Corrie was devoted to her aunt. The "horsey" atmosphere of Brabett's Farm had never succeeded in destroying the girl's natural femininity. And she had accepted the fact that Ann had little interest in pretty clothes or romance or other things the average woman enjoyed. Ann was just "a good sort".

Usually she was already down in the stables at this hour but today her assistant was on duty. Ann could relax. She put on a blue tweed trouser-suit as she chatted to her niece. She was pleased the girl had heard from Martin. She knew Corrie had been on tenterhooks, waiting for this summons. Being of a more thrifty disposition than Lady Grey-Ewing, Ann had protested at first against the "ridiculous extravagance" as she called it, of an expensive flight for only three days' holiday. But Lord Grey-Ewing had left his wife plenty of money. Martin would inherit it, so Miss Williams had no worries about her niece's future.

She couldn't help noticing this morning how really beautiful Corrie looked. Excitement made her eyes brilliant. She was glowing.

True to type, Ann never flattered. With a grin, she scowled at the girl, 'Now, now, don't get the bit between your teeth. It never pays to bolt. Easy does it.'

'You can't damp my spirits, you misery!' Corrie tossed her head.

'And you remind me of old Firelight,' grunted Miss Williams, 'forever tossing her head and champing at the bit! Don't get so het up.'

'Why shouldn't I?' Corrie laughed. 'It's all terrific. The day *after* tomorrow, I'll be off on my pre-honeymoon holiday—Martin and Madeira. The two big M's in my life.'

'Okay, now let's get breakfast and get the car out,' said the practical Miss Williams, but under her toughness there lay an enduring affection for her niece.

She just didn't believe anyone should be too

16

sentimental and show it. Corrie's effervescing spirits reminded Ann of her sister, Corrie's mother. She had been just as beautiful and excitable. Poor pet—happily married, everything to live for and she and her husband had to go and die in a car-smash. Rotten luck. Enough to make one harden up. All a long time ago now, of course. Ann had looked after Corrie since she was seven. She had been a happy, friendly child and never looked back. Ann had no need to worry about the man she'd chosen. Martin Ashley was a good boy.

Corrie resigned herself to what she called "*a* lot of horsey talk", and good-naturedly listened to her aunt rambling on about her stables during breakfast. Corrie knew all the names—*Firelight—Chestnut King—Ebony Boy,* the beautiful black horse she had just bought in Ireland. *And* the rest! Corrie liked them but in one way she knew she had disappointed Ann. She had never cared for riding.

This morning her thoughts circled like restless birds round and round Martin. She could not imagine any sort of life without *him* now. *If he were to die* suddenly, unexpectedly . . . people did . . . if she were to find herself alone forever in that long corridor of her nightmare—*God!* what a horrible idea. She wouldn't be able to *endure* it, and she certainly would never find a substitute for him. She would want to die, too.

Corrie drank two cups of strong coffee and

shut her mind to any such possibility.

Once in the car, on the way to East Grinstead, she cheered up, remembering Martin's telegram. All was well. In forty-eight hours' time they would be together.

She parked her aunt's mini-van in East Grinstead. Ann went off to see a friend. Corrie walked to her hairdresser's.

Zena, the Schnauzer, lay obediently on her rug on the back seat of the car. She had been trained to wait.

When Corrie left the shop, her long tawny hair was smooth as satin, curving down to her shoulders. It had the glow of a ripe chestnut, and there was a glow on her face and in her eyes. She had blotted out all dark reflections, and once more her mind was filled with the exciting prospect of her journey to Madeira.

After lunch she would start thinking about her packing. Life was good. Zena barked excitedly and welcomed her back to the car. When Ann rejoined them, it was to say that she had been invited by her friend to spend the evening with her.

'Okay by me,' said Corrie. 'You'll have the car. I'll go up to town to see Violetta.'

She took a train to Victoria after tea. A few hours with Martin's grandmother would be bliss. She was so amusing—more worldly and sophisticated, of course, than Ann. And because of Martin, Corrie felt close to his grandmother.

Another twenty-four hours passed. Then came the day of departure.

A fine March morning. Corrie wasted no more time worrying about nightmares or possible disasters. As she flew from Heathrow to Madeira, she felt that she must surely be the happiest girl in the world.

Once she landed in Madeira she was taken by motor coach to Funchal—the famous little port where she expected to find Reid's Hotel and Martin.

They passed through fabulous scenery and she looked with breathless admiration at the magnificent mountains rising up on the left-hand side and to the right, hundreds of feet below, she could see the blue creamy sea.

Even now in March it was hot and sunny and there seemed a never-ending glory of flowering bushes and exotic trees. Already the avocados were laden with rich green fruit and the small golden bananas were ripening.

Half an hour of this, then some distance beyond the centre of the charming little town they came to Reid's Hotel.

Corrie's heart beat faster.

Martin would already be here. He had only to fly from Lisbon.

'Oh Martin, my love!' She whispered the words, her whole mind and body vibrant with anticipation.

A dark-eyed courteous porter took her suitcase. She stopped a moment to smile at an old peasant woman, wearing a straw hat with a scarf over her white head, who sat hunched near the entrance beside an enormous basket of flowers.

Corrie was fascinated by the sight of the magnificent orchids which grew so plentifully on this island and which the old woman had arranged in tall cellophane funnels, and by the glorious multi-coloured freesias.

But she did not stop to buy flowers now. Madly excited, she followed the boy and her case into the hotel and asked the hall-porter if Mr. Ashley had arrived.

He examined the list then gave Corrie that warm pleasant smile with which all Portuguese greet the tourists.

'Yes, mam'selle. He came this morning. You are Miss Gilroy, yes? Mr. Ashley's room is 91X on the top floor-the ninth. Somebody in Reception will take you up. You are on the same floor as Mr. Ashley.'

CHAPTER THREE

Now all the world seemed to be singing for Corrie. She looked around her with wide happy eyes, examining the big vestibule—finding it splendid. She was enthralled by the sight of the enormous white jar of lilies on the marble table facing the entrance. Then, longing to see Martin, she hurried on to the reception desk. Here a nice-looking young man gave her a form to fill up after which he offered to take her up in the lift.

'Please, no, do you mind if I take myself,' Corrie said breathlessly. 'I can find my way. And I have only this one small case with me. I don't need a page. No—really I don't need anybody to conduct me. Just give me the key.'

Perhaps the young clerk was himself a romantic, but he understood. The couple wanted to be reunited in great privacy. It was he who had taken the fair-haired. Englishman, Mr. Ashley, up to his room earlier this morning. The receptionist decided that it was undoubtedly more than friendship that had brought these two to Reid's. They made a wonderful couple—indeed yes. He had seldom seen a more beautiful girl than Miss Gilroy. How graceful and charming! Such glorious hair and eyes!—he was sorry that he would not have the privilege of taking her up in the lift, but he must respect her wish to be alone.

There were a lot of elderly people in the hotel. It was a pleasure to see one as young and ravishing as Miss Gilroy. Like so many English and American visitors she wore a smart trouser-suit and it was right for her slenderness; blue, with gilt buttons, and a crisp white bow at the throat. The sentimental clerk sighed as he handed Miss Gilroy the key.

So Corrie went up in the lift—got out on the

ninth floor—and quickly found her way to the number marked on the key. Martin's room was two doors farther along the corridor.

First she examined her own room and put her case on her bed, then opened the shutters. The view was exciting. Immediately below lay two bright blue swimming pools, surrounded by green palm trees and fringed with scarlet flowers. Corrie could see a small crowd of swimmers in the water. Other guests lay supine on their floral mattresses, sunbathing. The whole lido appeared to have been built on a terrace halfway up the cliffside. Farther down she could see the glistening rocks and the smooth blue sea.

Blissfully, Corrie stretched her arms above her head. She breathed in the fresh salt air. The sun was warm upon her face She had never felt happier.

It was only ten days since she had last seen Martin. It might have been ten years, she had missed him so badly. She wouldn't wait to unpack her case. She hurried to Room 91X. *His* room. She knocked several times but there was no reply—only silence. She felt absurdly disappointed but presumed Martin must have gone out.

A plump little Portuguese chambermaid wearing a tiny crisp white apron over her short black dress, came down the corridor and spoke to Corrie in halting English.

'Want . . . *in* . . . .?' She pointed to Martin's

door.

Yes, thought Corrie, I will go in and wait for him, and when he opens his door he'll find me there. It'll be terribly exciting.

The little maid said, 'Me—Carmela—for *you*.'

Corrie, understanding that this girl was to be her chambermaid as well as Martin's, thanked her. Then she was let into Martin's bedroom. As expected, she found nobody there. She telephoned down to the hall-porter. He said that he, personally, had not seen Mr. Ashley go out but his key was not on its hook. Perhaps he had taken it out with him. Some of the guests did this. His absence had not been noted.

'What sort of time did he arrive?' Corrie asked.

'Before midday,' was the reply. 'He may, of course, be down by the swimming pools or in the gardens. I will have him paged, Miss Gilroy.'

Corrie put down the telephone. Her brows contracted. For her, it was a sudden depressing drop from the romantic heights to reality. Her adored Martin wasn't here to welcome her.

Yet he had booked in! Oh, well, she told herself, why should he wait in the hotel? He was probably down on the lido, or as the porter said, in the garden. This was a momentary setback.

But ten minutes later the hall-porter

23

telephoned back to tell her that Mr. Ashley was nowhere to be found, and that nobody had seen him leave the hotel. Unfortunately, he could give her no further information.

Corrie stayed awhile, looking disconsolately out of Martin's window. Like hers, it had a splendid view of the swimming pools and sea. To the right lay the harbour. Funchal was a favourite place for cruise-ships. A P & O boat was anchored there at this very moment. It all looked interesting. How strange to think that two thousand years ago this enchanting island had been shot out of the Atlantic Ocean by volcanic action and, over the years, grown and flourished and become the Madeira of today.

Turning, Corrie noted with satisfaction Martin's suitcase open on the bed, his blue pyjamas and dressing-gown thrown on top. He hadn't really unpacked. She saw too a half-opened packet of cigarettes on the dressing-table. Beside it, a silver lighter. Why, Corrie thought, it's the rather special one she herself had given him for Christmas. Oh, where *had* he gone? And without taking his 'smokes'—unusual for Martin.

Now Corrie took a cigarette from the packet, murmuring, 'Thank you, my darling,' and began to walk up and down the room. She liked the polished decorated woodwork of the furniture—all made by hand on this busy island where the natives were never idle. The curtains and covers were palest yellow—all very fresh and attractive.

Peering into the bathroom, she saw a crumpled shirt and a pair of light blue trousers, lying in a heap on the floor. Martin must have bathed and changed. Untidy Martin! So like a man to let his things lie where he throws them. Corrie smiled and decided it was high time Martin had a wife to look after him.

Neatly she folded his clothes then seated herself beside the open window—to wait.

Soon with one of the rapid changes often experienced on this coast, the sun went in. A cool wind blew on Corrie. Enough to make her close the windows again, and sit there whilst she watched the clouds billow from the southwest. The line of coast with the tall hotels began to look less inviting.

Corrie shivered suddenly.

'Don't be too long, Martin,' she said the words aloud, *'Oh, please don't be too long, my love!'*

In this hour she realised more intensely than ever how deeply and absolutely she loved him. He was the one and only man for her. She loved him more than anything in the world.

An hour passed. Still he did not come.

Corrie put her watch to her ear to make sure it was going. It was. She had wound it as they touched down. It was over an hour and a half now since she had arrived at Reid's. *Had* Martin gone on a shopping expedition? Or had he run into someone he knew and was still chatting. Many English people came to Madeira and Martin had many friends.

After another hour alone, Corrie grew restless and more than a little puzzled. It was so odd. Surely he had known what time her plane was due to land? He must realise that she had arrived by now. Of course he had warned her before he left her that he wouldn't be able to meet her at the airport. He was flying from Lisbon. They would not arrive at the same time. But he had already booked in at Reid's. It was now quarter past six. It didn't make sense.

Then she saw a black attaché case on an armchair. She had seen it many times before. The strap was fastened. Obviously, it was full of papers. He had, after all, gone to Lisbon on business for his publishers.

She felt fidgety—unable to settle down. She went to her own room and found a paperback she had bought at Heathrow. A reprint of short stories by Somerset Maugham. She enjoyed Maugham.

She tried to read. But she couldn't concentrate and soon closed the book.

Every time she looked at her watch, time seemed to have raced on by leaps and bounds. It seemed so long since she had first entered this room, so full of excitement, of joyous anticipation. Surely he *couldn't* be touring Funchal without her, and *this* long!

26

The sun did not come out again. The wind dropped but the sky remained cloudy. The sunlight seemed to have gone out of her life, she thought with exaggerated emotion.

Carmela, the Portuguese maid, knocked on the door—came in, pointing with a smile at the bed.

'Me do—for sleep?'

'Yes, of course,' said Corrie and watched the little maid remove the spread and deftly turn down the sheets.

On the plane Corrie had been studying a little book of Portuguese phrases. She remembered how to say thank you.

She smiled at the girl.

'*Obrigada.*'

'Ah! You speaka!' began the little maid delighted but as she broke into a flood of unintelligible Portuguese, Corrie speedily denied her ability to understand.

The little maid looked admiringly at the lovely bronze-haired young English lady, said good night and departed.

Corrie felt suddenly overwhelmingly tired. It was sheer exhaustion she supposed after the flight, the drive to Funchal, and then this bitter disappointment and restlessness.

She leaned back and closed her eyes. Almost immediately she fell asleep. When she awoke it was dark. She realised with quite a sense of shock that night had fallen.

She got up and peered through the window.

She could see thousands of lights twinkling in the harbour and town and all up the mountainside. A beautiful sight. She remembered that Violetta had told her Madeira looked like Hong Kong at night.

'It's fabulous,' the old actress had said. 'So romantic.'

It *was* fabulous, but the beauty meant little to Corrie this evening. She was too upset. She switched on a lamp, then went back to Martin's room, still hoping, stupidly, to find him there. But everything was unchanged. The open case on the bed, the attaché case—the blue pyjamas and dressing-gown. The brush and comb on the table. *But no Martin.*

Where was he? Feeling suddenly sick and even scared, Corrie returned to her own room. It looked bare and unfriendly. She picked up the telephone.

'I suppose you haven't seen or heard anything of Mr. Ashley?' she asked the head-porter. 'There's been no phone message or anything?'

She was told courteously that there was no message for her and as far as they knew, the gentleman had not returned to the hotel.

Corrie began to walk up and down, up and down. She did not want to go into Martin's room again.

She unpacked—trying not to feel disturbed and anxious. Eventually she had a hot bath and changed from her trouser-suit into a

28

dinner-dress. Violetta had told her that even in these days they changed for dinner at Reid's, because it was proud of its "old-world" atmosphere. But Corrie dressed without enthusiasm. She had brought a long jersey dress—black with a white floral design and a wide black belt which suited the slenderness of her waist. Martin had seen her in it and liked it. With it she wore black shoes with platform heels and gold buckles. But as she sat down to put the finishing touches to hair and face, a gloom spread over her that she found difficult to overcome. It was now eight o'clock. She was frankly frightened. Perhaps Martin had met with an accident. But how—when—where?

'Oh, I can't bear it!' Corrie said the words aloud.

She picked up her evening-bag and with a white, light wool coat under one arm she took the lift downstairs with a young couple—an attractive girl and a good-looking man. Corrie noticed that their fingers were linked. They chatted and laughed. She felt a surge of envy. Martin should have been with her in this same lift going down to dinner and they too would have laughed together.

A fourth passenger entered the lift from the next floor down—a tall man, dark-haired and dark-eyed. He had a young but pale face. He leaned on a stick and was lame and he looked as though he had been ill. He caught Corrie's eye for a moment and kept glancing in her direction. She looked back and vaguely thought she knew him.

After they reached the sixth floor they all got out. Even in her state of misery, Corrie noted what an extraordinary thing it was that in this hotel one went up three floors to the bedrooms, down three to the lounge and bar, then down again in another lift to the lido, and the sea.

Once away from the other couple, the young man who had been staring at Corrie, spoke. 'We've met before, haven't we?' he asked.

His voice was attractive. She told him her name and his eyes brightened. A smile transformed his face.

'But, of course. My sister was at school with you. I'm Hugh Aylmer.'

'Oh, *of course!*' echoed Corrie, 'Liz Aylmer's brother. Gosh! That takes me back. Believe it or not, she and I once played tennis for our school—and won the Doubles. I think I did actually meet you on one of our Sports Days. You would have been about eighteen or nineteen. I seem to remember Liz telling me you were just going to Cambridge.'

'Right.' Hugh Aylmer flushed with pleasure at Corrie's recognition of him.

She really was lovely. He could only remember her as a thin schoolgirl with short curly hair which, even then, he had noticed was the most attractive russet colour. He

30

remembered, too, that Liz used to say Corrie was much nicer than the other girls because she was so kind and generous. They had been firm friends.

Huge spoke again. 'Are you by yourself? If so, come into the bar and have a drink with me.'

The colour rushed to her cheeks. 'I'm not actually alone. I am here with my fiancé—but I'd like to talk to you, as a matter of fact, because I am rather worried about him.'

Hugh raised his brows. This sounded interesting. He gave her a friendly smile. 'I think I am rather good at sorting out problems. Come and be sorted out on a sherry or gin-and-French—or whatever you suggest.'

'I'd like that,' she nodded.

Leaning on his stick, Hugh walked with her to the bar, which was not far from the dining room.

A waiter led them across a small dance-floor to a row of tables beside long windows that looked down on the harbour, and up the mountainside where a million lights glittered in the purple dusk. The sky was luminous with stars.

'A lovely night,' Hugh remarked.

It should have been marvellous, Corrie thought miserably, it should have been the *greatest*.

She stayed silent while Hugh Aylmer ordered the sherry chosen by them both. Then,

31

with all her anxiety welling up from her very heart, she poured out her story. Soon Hugh knew all about Martin Ashley's failure to come back to the hotel.

He lit a cigarette for Corrie and one for himself, then sat frowning, pondering.

'Odd, I must say. Don't understand it.'

'Nor do I,' she said. He saw that the slender hand holding her sherry glass was shaking. The poor girl was all nerves, he thought and was full of sympathy for her.

'As I understand it,' he said, 'you and your fiancé arranged to meet here. He arrived first. You know he did because he has booked in, also you have seen his luggage in his room. You, yourself, turned up a bit later. How long ago?'

'Oh, ages! It's half past eight, isn't it? I was here by four fifteen.'

'I'm sure nothing very serious has happened to him. Why should it?'

She wrinkled her forehead.

'Well, there are all kinds of possibilities.'

'Not necessarily sinister ones. He just went out for a walk and perhaps lost his way or met someone he knows, and who is in Madeira, and has got a bit tied up.'

'But he wouldn't have stayed out so long when he must have known I'd be here by now. He would have been in a hurry to meet me.'

Trying to comfort her, Hugh said, 'You know what men are like. They get talking,

32

having a couple of drinks. I am sure your Martin will come walking through the door at any moment and have a plausible explanation.'

She tried to smile but still felt uneasy. It was as though a cold hand had gripped her heart. Mentally and physically she felt no warmth and saw no light.

'You agreed with me just now that it seems a bit odd,' at length she reminded Hugh.

'Yes, I did, didn't I? Perhaps it is. But let's enumerate some of the things that *could* have happened.'

'An accident, he could have had an accident.'

'Hardly likely. And unless he was struck down and killed outright, which God forbid, he would have told the police or hospital or wherever he was by now, to get in touch with Reid's.'

'I suppose so.'

He watched the colour come into her cheeks and ebb again. And he could see that she was still shaking. She must be very much in love with this fellow. Hugh felt a sudden envy of Martin Ashley.

Now he tried to joke, and help in that way to ease some of her tension.

'*I* know what's happened. He has met up with a smashing Portuguese girl with huge black eyes and she's cast a spell on him and he's completely forgotten his date with you.'

She gave a weak laugh. 'Yes, that's it! I've

33

been jilted.'

'You haven't, you know!'

'No,' she agreed with another laugh.

'Seriously, Corrie, he just must be somewhere on the island and hasn't noticed the time.'

Ashamed of the acute anxiety which was increasing every moment that passed, Corrie tried to agree.

'Yes, that's undoubtedly what's happened.'

But she knew deep down within that it was not the answer. First of all, Martin was the exact opposite of a man who lets time run away with him. He was, in fact, an extremely punctual person. He had a habit of looking rather too often at his wristwatch.

No—he certainly wouldn't have forgotten the time, *or* that she was here, waiting for him.

Grateful for Hugh Aylmer's company and the efforts he made to chase her fears away, she changed the conversation and asked for news of Liz and said she would like to know about him, too. Now she learned the meaning of the limp and the stick. She also learned that young though he was—Hugh was only twenty-five—he had already faced personal tragedy.

Liz had been lucky—married a man older than herself and gone to live in Nairobi where she had found complete happiness. This, of course, Corrie already knew. She had kept in touch with her old school friend until she settled in East Africa, but since then their correspondence had grown more infrequent and Corrie had not heard what Hugh Aylmer had to tell her now.

Corrie did remember that Hugh had not been at his sister's wedding.

A month ago, Hugh told her, he had been on a ski holiday in Switzerland with a party of young people which included Juliet Burton— the beautiful girl he was going to marry. They were all driving back from the Jura mountains. Four of them. There had been an accident on the French-Swiss border. The other man was driving at the time. They met a French lorry on the wrong side of the road. In the crash, Juliet was killed instantly. But Hugh who was sitting beside her, was thrown clear.

He finished the sad story, 'I left the hospital in the village of Lons-le-Saunier where we crashed, with a fractured femur, and was taken back to London on a stretcher. My leg's okay but I'm still a bit lame; however I am assured by one of the best orthopaedic surgeons in London that I will be able to throw away my stick any moment now.'

'Oh, I'm glad!' Corrie exclaimed.

He looked down into her eyes which were beautiful and soft with compassion. She really was 'something', he thought, and he was grateful for her sympathy. He had had a rough time, physically and mentally, since that crash. His poor Juliet—to die so young!

He spoke again. 'I don't know what I would

have done without my Mama this last couple of months. She is a very special person. Much too good for my father who left us for another younger woman. Liz must have been at school with you at the time and I was at Brighton College. We were pretty hard-up but Mama managed. Father cleared off to America with his new American wife and prospered and sent funds for me from time to time. However, my mother was an extraordinary woman—had almost a masculine mind so far as business went, and got herself a super job in a firm of accountants. She worked and saved until I went to university. I owe a helluva lot to her.'

'She sounds terrific,' said Corrie. 'I remember Liz telling me how clever and attractive she was and now I remember seeing her on Parents' Day. Tell me more, Hugh.'

He was glad he could take her mind off her troubles if only for a brief while.

He went on with his story. Long days in hospital and the shock of his fiancée's death had taken the zest out of his life. Corrie could believe that. She sat silent, listening. It was as though he suddenly needed to pour out his repressed feelings.

She heard, too, how with the passing years things had improved for the Aylmer family. Hugh's father went through a second divorce. He had done well in his business in New York and when he died suddenly of a coronary, he left his son and daughter a handsome legacy.

'Surprising, because he had never bothered to see either of us,' Hugh told Corrie, 'but he seems to have developed a conscience about us in the end. He left Mama a bit, too. No. 2 wife was not a success, apparently.'

Mrs. Aylmer had then been able to afford to buy the country house in Sussex which she had always wanted, and there was no further need for her to work.

After his accident, Hugh spent most of his convalescence with his mother but by then Liz was expecting her first baby and once the day drew near, Mrs. Aylmer flew out to Nairobi. She was still there—an enthusiastic grandmother.

'And I've become an uncle,' Hugh smiled at Corrie.

'Oh. I must write to Liz. I just can't believe she's a mum!' Corrie shook her head. 'Oh! Isn't she lucky! Was it a boy or a girl?'

'A boy who Mama tells me is exactly like I was at the same age—poor little devil!'

He went on talking. Neither of them seemed aware that most of the guests who had been drinking cocktails in the bar had long since gone into dinner.

Corrie learned more about Hugh's boyhood and how he read History at Cambridge.

Once he got his degree, luck had come his way. His newly acquired private income enabled him to start work on the one thing he wanted most to do—write an historical novel.

The first, entitled *England and St. George,* with the reign of Henry V as a background, had been an instant success.

He bought a small but attractive flat at the top of one of the period houses in Little Venice and enjoyed life immensely. When he first met and became engaged to Juliet Burton it had seemed to set the seal on his good fortune. He hadn't written a line since she had died although he knew this was a state of mind he must conquer and that he would get back to his new novel once his convalescence ended.

He went on chatting to Corrie but made no further reference to the girl he had loved and lost so tragically.

Corrie began to feel she knew him quite well. The link with Liz particularly, established a friendship between them.

She tried to sit on her personal troubles and through the confusion in her mind to concentrate on Hugh and forget Martin for a moment. She said suddenly, 'The penny has just dropped. What an idiot I am! I have just realised *who* you are I didn't connect it up. You are H. G. Aylmer and you have written a marvellous book, *England and St. George.* It had super notices. I'm not very good at history but the one thing I did remember was that quotation: *"Cry God for Harry, England and St. George."'*

Hugh grinned at her, 'Splendid!'

'And you realise, don't you,' she went on,

'that you and Martin are both in the book world? He flew out to Lisbon for Horton & Mullins.'

'Very good publishers. Mine are Garfield & Spence. Incidentally, I remember meeting Sir Paul Mullins who I think is head of Martin's firm, at one of the Foyle lunches.'

Another link, thought Corrie. And then, thinking of Martin, she said under her breath, 'Oh God! I have just realised it's past nine and still not a word from Martin. Something *must* have happened to him.'

CHAPTER FOUR

Still later that same night the situation remained unchanged. Watching Corrie it seemed to Hugh Aylmer that her beautiful face almost underwent a physical change. Hour by hour it grew smaller, paler, more desperate. She kept looking at a little enamel watch on a brooch which was pinned to her dress. She said nothing. She was obviously trying to control her feelings. But normal anxiety was fast giving place to an overwhelming fear coupled, of course, with bafflement. She didn't—couldn't—understand what had happened to Martin. And Hugh was not surprised. He was beginning to be more than a little puzzled himself.

For some time he went on talking to Corrie hoping to divert her attention. Only once or twice he tried to joke—told her not to worry—that at any moment her fiance would walk into the lounge. But he did not come and after they had finished coffee Hugh insisted on taking Corrie out into the mild starlit night. The fresh air would do her good, he said. They went for a stroll along the tree-lined avenue beyond the hotel, but after a few moments she wanted to turn back. She couldn't keep away from Reid's—Reid's where she had arranged to meet Martin. He *must* return there, wherever he had been. And she must be there to welcome him.

Only once she tried to make light of the situation.

'I believe you've got it,' she said to Hugh with a slightly hysterical laugh, 'he's met a devastating island beauty, and she's drugged his wine or something.'

Hugh gallantly remarked that no man would be all that easily beguiled away from *her.* But he could see for himself that the compliment meant nothing to Corrie. Her entire being was concentrated upon the missing man.

She intrigued Hugh. He had never come across a girl quite so intense and single-hearted as Corisande Gilroy. In this hour, he had a sudden mental flashback to a moment—years ago—when his sister was in her last year at school—and had showed him a snapshot of

40

Corrie. 'Isn't she gorgeous, Hugh?' Liz had said, 'I'll always adore Corrie. She really is my best friend. But sometimes I wish she wasn't so sensitive. She's awfully easily hurt. When she falls in love I bet it won't be an ordinary affair. She never does anything by halves.'

Those words coming from his cheerful, happy-go-lucky little sister had impressed Hugh at the time. He'd wanted to see more of Corisande Gilroy. But Fate decreed otherwise once the two girls finished their schooling. Now, on this unhappy night, he could *see* what Liz had meant. Corrie certainly wasn't a type to take things lightly. When they returned to the hotel after their brief stroll she said, 'Martin's had an accident. I know it now . . . *oh God, I know it!'*

Hugh was half-inclined to agree. It seemed no longer possible that Martin had just run into friends and been kept by them. Nor did any of the other explanations they had considered—or he would be here by now. There were all those things of his up in his room. The fellow just hadn't shown up and it could be for no ordinary reason. From everything that Corrie had told him, Hugh was quite sure Martin had meant to keep his date with her. And that he was as much in love with her as she was with him. Damn it all, they were going to be married soon after they got back to England and he had cabled her to meet him here today. This couldn't be accounted for

41

because he had suddenly experienced a change of heart.

Hugh took Corrie's arm—he could feel her trembling. Poor little thing—she was in a state all right. He said, 'The time has come for us to do something a bit more positive. We'll have a chat with the hall-porter and get him to phone up the local hospital—and the police.'

Corrie's golden hazel eyes looked suddenly stricken. The *police!*

'Then you do think something awful has happened to him?'

'Not necessarily awful. Although I don't understand it. Why hasn't someone let the hotel know? He must have gone out carrying a wallet—some identification on him—even if he'd been picked up unconscious.'

'Oh, I don't know, *I don't know!*' she whispered.

By now she was feeling as though the whole weight of the world had descended on her, and not a very nice world, at that. It certainly seemed that she had lived in a much happier one before arriving in Funchal. She thought of this time last night—chatting with Ann about her forthcoming journey—then lying in bed smiling at Martin's photograph—imagining their blissful reunion here, in Madeira.

Hugh decided that the thing to do was to approach the manager of Reid's himself.

He was at once available and talked to them in the writing-room which was unoccupied at this hour. He was a charming Frenchman, sympathetic and helpful. He could see that the attractive young English girl was labouring under a great strain and he was full of sympathy. By the time he had talked things over with her and with Hugh Aylmer, he was as baffled as they were.

'It seems incredible,' he said 'Are you quite sure that you have all the facts right?'

He looked at Corrie. The hand that carried the cigarette to her lips was shaking. She assured him that every word she had told him about the meeting arranged here between Martin and herself was true.

'You've only to go to his room. His case is open on his bed—his things just as he left them—half-unpacked.'

The manager nodded. 'Then he must have gone out soon after he arrived.'

'That's all we do know. The hall-porter made a thorough search of the hotel and grounds. Nobody saw Martin go out or come back.'

The manager exchanged glances with Hugh. 'And *you* have no idea what can have happened, monsieur?'

'None. Actually I don't know Mr. Ashley. Miss Gilroy is an old friend of my sister's and we met here this evening at Reid's quite by chance.'

The manager put out the cigarette he had been smoking and rose to his feet.

43

'I shall now follow your suggestion. I will first get in touch with the local hospital to see if they have had anybody brought in whose name they do not know. I will also notify the *Policia de Segurança Publica.*'

Hugh looked at Corrie. 'The Portuguese for Security Police, I presume.'

Corrie stood up. She looked very white. The very word *police* made her feel sick. The whole situation was beginning to appear a lot more dangerous. But she dared think no further.

Now the manager took them to his private office. Hugh asked Corrie if she would rather be alone but she wanted him to stay with her. Liz's brother—so kind and gentle—gave her some kind of confidence, and she had never needed it more.

She sat by the manager's desk, her hands tightly locked in her lap. He asked for a description of Martin and wrote down her replies. *Of medium height, well-built, fairish hair—dark grey eyes. Unusually dark thick lashes and brows.* Rather strong features, boney nose—a little on the big side, clean-shaven and, like so many fair-haired men, he had a reddish tinge to his complexion.

'I have a photograph of him with me—if it is any use to you,' Corrie added.

'It might well be.' The manager nodded. 'We will see. I would just like to tell the hospital if he has any particular mark, something that would pick him out, as you

English say.'

Corrie put her fingertips against her forehead. Strange, she had to think about this although she had always imagined she knew everything about Martin. *Yes,* she could tell the manager about the mole on the right side of Martin's mouth. He was always grumbling about it. He said that it was a nuisance when he shaved. Her heart seemed to plunge lower at the memory, but she went on answering the manager's questions.

Now he telephoned the hospital. He spoke in Portuguese. When he put down the receiver, he turned to Corrie.

'Nobody has been brought in—no one who has not been named. So that should reassure you.'

Corrie flushed and her eyes widened. 'But it doesn't. He could have met with a terrible accident—fallen over a cliff etc—and not been found yet.'

The manager nodded. 'I will speak to the police.'

'I am sorry,' Corrie said suddenly in a voice that was not quite steady, 'This must be very disturbing for you, monsieur. Oh!—I am *so* sorry!'

He reassured her with a smile and a shake of the head. 'Please—I am glad to do anything I can, mademoiselle. It is my pleasure. I am only too sorry that this should have happened to spoil your holiday with us.'

Now he spoke rapidly in Portuguese to an inspector at the police station. Afterwards he turned to Corrie again.

'Nothing—not a thing. There has been no report of any kind—no body has been found of any unidentified person here in Funchal since this morning, mademoiselle.'

'Body!' Corrie gulped and looked so ghastly that Hugh reached out and took her hand.

'Okay, Corrie, don't let the word upset you. It's just routine questioning. After all, they have got to consider every eventuality.'

She nodded, speechless and despairing.

'It might be a good thing,' said the manager, 'if I ordered a cognac for mademoiselle.'

But Corrie swiftly recovered herself. She accepted a cigarette from Hugh, pressed his kindly hand then relinquished it again. 'I'm all right. Please do what you think best, monsieur.'

'I spoke to my friend at the police station and he will send an officer to talk to you tomorrow morning if Mr.—' he glanced down at his pad, 'Mr. Ashley has not returned by then.'

It was all that could be done tonight. Corrie realised it. She was now in a fever of anxiety— so beset with fears that she found it difficult to keep an even keel. This last hour of interrogation and the manager's unavailing efforts to help left her without hope.

Before the manager bade Corrie good

46

night, he reaffirmed his intention of doing all he could to help her, tomorrow. He even added a few words of comfort which in fact he didn't really believe himself.

'Monsieur will come back, mademoiselle. You will see. There will be some simple explanation.'

Hugh Aylmer also tried to give her hope but by this time Corrie was in no mood to be comforted. It was half past eleven. There seemed no object in them staying up any longer. Any further discussion only meant going over and over the old ground.

Hugh took her upstairs in the lift and said good night outside her door.

He had an extraordinary longing to gather her up in his arms and kiss that pale strained young face. *Poor darling!* She *was* in a state! His heart bled for her. What a Goddamned awful thing to have happened—fantastic that anyone could arrive at Reid's then disappear completely.

Once alone, Corrie faced the worst night of her life.

She did not go to bed. She knew she would not sleep. She had both keys so wandered between the two bedrooms, finally settling in an armchair in Martin's room. Here, at least were his things. With heavy tired eyes she looked at them—his case—his clothes—staring at them as though their very existence kept her in some way in touch with him.

She closed her eyes a moment, then opened the window and looked out.

'*Martin, Martin,* where are you?' she groaned the words.

It was such a beautiful night. The clouds had lifted and the purple sea was lumious with starlight. The lights in the harbour and up the mountainside still twinkled gaily. She could hear the swish of the sea on the rocks below. She stared desolately into the distance, and now the tears began to run down her cheeks. She threw herself on the bed, and crushing Martin's silk dressing-gown against her breast began to cry in earnest.

After the long hours of worry and effort she was so exhausted that at last she returned to her own room and drifted into sleep.

Inevitably the old dreaded nightmare pursued her. But this time it was a little different. She gasped her way down the long dim corridor which had grown so familiar, and was pulled into that dark, sinister room. She heard a voice calling her name. It was a man who spoke but it was not Martin. And it was not Martin's hands that gripped hers. Then she heard a low mocking laugh. A horrible laugh that echoed down the corridor.

She woke screaming and did not sleep again that night.

CHAPTER FIVE

At half past six in the morning Corrie stopped even trying to sleep, put on a dressing-gown and drew her curtains. She caught sight of her face as she passed a mirror and shivered at the sight. She had never looked worse, she thought. And who cared? She cared about nothing except that Martin had not come back to the hotel and for the moment he seemed to be inexplicably, hopelessly lost to her.

Nothing could comfort her or allay her anxiety. She shivered even though she felt the warmth of the early sun on her face. Below, the two swimming pools gleamed like blue mirrors reflecting the light, and the blue of the sky. It was a brilliant morning and going to be as warm as an English summer's day.

She wondered if she ought to telephone Martin's grandmother and break the news to her. But no, not yet—why worry the poor old lady and rub the happiness from her slate? At the moment she was blissfully unconscious of catastrophe and fondly imagining that the 'young lovers' as she liked to call them, had had a glorious reunion and were thoroughly enjoying life.

Let her remain ignorant until she, Corrie, was quite certain Martin was irrevocably lost. Despite her nightmares and her terrors she could not yet be sure of *that.* Fate couldn't be so hideously cruel.

She bathed, put on white slacks and shirt and with a yellow cardigan over her shoulders unlocked the door of Martin's bedroom. The shutters were drawn. It was still dark in here. She felt a great lump in her throat. How empty and desolate it seemed!

Once she had let in the light, she turned to the bed, stared for a moment at the open suitcase and wondered if she ought to go through it—just to see if she could find the smallest clue to Martin's extraordinary disappearance.

But there was a cautious streak in Corrie, sensitive and emotional though she was. She decided that it might not be the thing for her to touch his case before the Chief Inspector from the *Policia de Segurança Publica,* arrived to take control.

She thought gratefully of Hugh and how helpful he was being. It was a relief to have him by her side and strange that he should have come into her life after all these years.

It was too early for her breakfast. She went downstairs and walked out into the sunshine and along the road in the direction of the town. Two Portuguese labourers working on the new big hotel and casino noticed the slim girl with her beautiful flowing hair. They eyed her out of the corners of their eyes and shouted something to each other in their own language, then smiled and waved at Corrie.

She knew that they meant no harm, and that it was a tribute to her rather than an impertinence. She waved back. Somehow this gay appreciation only made her remember Martin.

The early morning wind was a little too cool. She soon returned to the hotel where there was now more activity carpets being hoovered, furniture polished. She asked if her breakfast could be served to her downstairs. If so she would have it in the sun on the sheltered terrace. They assured her it would be no trouble. It arrived with a big basket of fruit—a pineapple, custard-apples, the little local bananas, passion-fruit and small golden mandarins. Typical fruits of Madeira, she supposed. She read the card that came with them. *'With the manager's compliments.'* The ready tears came to her eyes. Everybody was being so kind.

Before she finished breakfast, Hugh Aylmer joined her.

'I'm not going to ask if you slept well, I'm sure you didn't,' he said, and putting his stick down, sat in a basket chair beside her. 'But I hope you had some sort of rest.'

'I'm okay.'

He knew that was not true. He could read the denial in those remarkable eyes. He said, 'I dare say the police will turn up fairly early. Would you like me to be with you during the

51

interview?'

'Oh I would! I feel sort of better—I mean less lonely and lost—if you're around. Incidentally, I must write to Liz and tell her about our meeting and how marvellous you've been to me.'

'I've done nothing. I feel helpless,' he said sadly.

'Nevertheless, you help.'

'Liz will be glad to hear from you.'

'I feel guilty for having neglected her so long but I didn't know about the baby.'

'I see you have half-finished your breakfast. I'll order mine and eat it quickly. Do sit with me.'

Suddenly, pathetically she said, 'Martin *could* walk in at any moment—couldn't he?'

'Yes, he could,' said Hugh.

But he wasn't in the least happy about it. He, himself, had done a lot of thinking last night once he left Corrie. They had so little to go on. Martin's disappearance seemed so unreal—like something from one of the paperback 'whodunnits' he had brought with him. Yet what possible reason had they to suppose Martin had been the victim of a crime?

It all seemed even more unreal once the Portuguese Inspector of Police arrived on the scene. He was courteous and out to help, even if a little on the officious side. But he was enthusiastic and thorough. Obviously there were few mysteries of this kind to solve on this tranquil island and he was welcoming an interlude from boredom.

He was a handsome youngish man—rather like Omar Sharif. His huge dark eyes looked with undisguised admiration at the lovely English girl while he questioned her. He spoke very good English. He accepted a cigarette from Hugh, and tapping his foot gently with a silver-headed cane, concentrated on Corrie.

'Please tell me everything you can of this unfortunate matter, Mees—er—Gilroy,' he said.

She answered his questions. When and why she and her fiancé had arranged to meet at Reid's—what business he had in Lisbon—what plans they had made—when they had arranged to leave Madeira again. He even asked (first apologising) if there had been any kind of quarrel or misunderstanding when she had last seen him that could account for his reluctance to meet her now—despite their so-called 'date'. This she hotly repudiated. On the contrary, she said, they were deeply devoted and had expected to be married after they returned to London. The Inspector jotted down notes then asked if he might be taken up to Martin's bedroom.

'If you do not mind, Mees Gilroy, I would like to go through his luggage. We might discover some leetle thing to enlighten us. I will also have with us my assistant, who is waiting in the lounge.'

Corrie exchanged glances with Hugh who said, 'That would be in order.'

The handsome Policia eyed Hugh, then Corrie.

'Can I know please, who is the *Senhor?*' he asked politely.

'He is Mr. Aylmer, an old family friend,' said Corrie.

The Inspector gave a stiff little bow. Hugh acknowledged it. They were joined now by the second officer—a young man who was small and less spectacular than the Chief Inspector. They all went up in the lift to the ninth floor.

Corrie unlocked the door of Martin's bedroom.

'Please be seated,' the Inspector bade the English couple. Corrie sat down. Her head had begun to ache. Hugh remained standing, leaning on his stick. It made Corrie feel slightly sick to watch the Inspector sifting through Martin's suitcase. As expected, he found nothing but Martin's dark suit, obviously meant to be worn for dinner, some underwear, socks and handkerchiefs and two pairs of shoes—one black patent, one dark blue canvas. Also a pair of blue-and-white striped bathing trunks. These the Inspector pulled out and showed to Corrie.

'So! We did not go for a swim or he would have had these with him.'

'True,' she nodded.

'So—forgive me if I speak brutally—he is not likely to be found drowned unless he had an accident and fell from the cliff.'

Corrie changed colour. She caught her breath.

The Inspector added, 'There are, of course, occasional bathing fatalities. The currents around this coast are negligible, but if anything did happen, the body would be washed up in time and so eventually found.'

Hugh Aylmer clenched his hands. Fool of a man, frightening Corrie like this. But that thought was followed by another. The Inspector was here to try and unravel the mystery of Martin's disappearance. He had to consider all eventualities.

Corrie's face looked pinched but she remained poised. She tried to be sensible. 'I understand,' she said in a low voice.

The Inspector found nothing belonging to Martin that was of any interest to him. He noted the shaving-gear in the bathroom—his sponge-bag and the few clothes Martin had already unpacked. Then turned his attention to the black attaché case on the armchair.

This was locked.

The Inspector said something in rapid Portuguese to his assistant who had been taking down notes, even though there was nothing much of importance to write. The Inspector then turned to Corrie.

'With your permission, Mees Gilroy—we

shall have to break the lock. There could be something in this case to help us with our enquiries. Yes?'

'Yes,' she nodded, 'but it seems all wrong to break the lock. They are my fiancé's private papers.'

'Your extreme pardon, Mees Gilroy, but as I have already explained to the manager downstairs, if I am to be of help to you I must leave no stone unturned. If we find nothing of use, I will, myself, arrange to have the lock mended immediately.'

Hugh bent down to Corrie. 'Fair enough, don't you think?'

She answered under her breath, 'I suppose so.'

But she hated to watch the Inspector break that lock. Standing by the window, the Inspector went through the various papers and pamphlets he pulled from the case.

They confirmed the fact that the missing man was an employee in a firm of some well-known London book publishers known as Horton & Mullins. There were several printed leaflets, some notepaper with the publisher's address a few bills and receipts. Also an order book, the contents of which suggested that Martin had not been idle in Lisbon. He must have sold quite a few English novels to two of the biggest firms in Lisbon.

The Inspector also examined a canvas bag with a zip-fastener, full of those books which

Martin had brought over from London.

He confessed himself as baffled. He could find absolutely nothing that gave him a clue as to where Mr. Ashley could have gone, or could be at this moment. Or why he had not returned to his hotel yesterday.

Corrie looked at the Inspector with big bewildered eyes. 'What are we going to do?' she asked.

The Inspector handed the broken attaché case to his assistant.

'He will take it now for the lock to be mended, Mees Gilroy, and it will be returned to you. We will leave the rest of your fiancé's possessions in this room. You have absolutely nothing else belonging to Mr. Ashley, Mees Gilroy?'

Corrie shook her head. 'Nothing. Only this—you can read it,' and she handed the Inspector the telegram she had received at Ann's cottage telling her that Martin would meet her here.

The Inspector shrugged, pursed his full red lips and smoothed a little black line of moustache.

'H'm. Very curious. I will question all the staff—especially any who spoke to Mr. Ashley yesterday. More here I cannot do. There is definitely no evidence whatsoever of foul play in the hotel.'

'That's for sure,' cut in Hugh. 'Anyhow, who would want to murder Mr. Ashley? And having done so, how would they have disposed of the body so speedily and without leaving a trace? It's a laughable idea.'

Corrie thought, *It isn't laughable. Nothing is. Even that. Something quite terrible has happened to Martin, whatever they say.*

'What can you do now? Oh, *please* do something,' she appealed to the Inspector.

He bowed from the waist. 'All shall be done, Mees Gilroy. You have my word. But it is early days, you know. For instance, the hospital you telephoned is not the only one. There are a few more little places on the outskirts of the town where they take in sick people—invalids, etc. If Mr. Ashley was in a street accident he could have been taken in one of these and perhaps is not yet conscious. I will send enquiries to them all. And to all pharmacies. Funchal shall be searched. Indeed, the whole island of Madeira shall be alerted with a description of your fiancé. If you have a photograph, might I have it, please?'

'Yes,' she said.

She felt utterly miserable as she went into her own room and took the familiar photograph of Martin out of its little frame. She brought it back to the Inspector.

He looked at it and nodded.

'A very delightful face, if I may say so—truly English. Have courage, Mees Gilroy. Every day in this world there are missing persons, most of whom turn up—isn't that the English expression? Mr. Ashley will turn up. Somehow, I feel this.'

She bit her lip. If only she could feel it, too. But she was weighed down in her mind, and in her spirits.

This was veritably the long corridor of her horrible nightmare, and she was walking farther and farther into the darkness. She wanted to scream the name *Martin* and make him hear it—wherever he was. She controlled herself and thanked the Inspector politely for his kindness and sympathy. As he went towards the door, he turned back to her and said, 'Forgive me if I am brutal—' it was obviously a favourite word with him—'but something quite ridiculous might have happened to your fiancé. There are many places where tourists can find wine, perhaps too much—too intoxicating. Maybe he lies somewhere not yet quite himself, and will return to us during the day.'

Corrie broke into a laugh that had a touch of hysteria. 'Unlikely, Inspector. My fiancé is not much of a drinker, but of course it could have happened, couldn't it?' she turned to Hugh.

He gave a faint smile. 'Could, my dear. Let's snatch at any straw.'

'I will report now to my station and alert my men,' said the Inspector grandly. 'We will leave no stone unturned.'

With this, he clicked his heels together and

made a splendid exit followed by his assistant.

Corrie momentarily relaxed. She sat down on the edge of Martin's bed, and burst into tears, hiding her face with her hands.

In ordinary circumstances, Hugh Aylmer might have felt embarrassed and uncertain what to do, but somehow the sight of this girl whom he thought so sweet, so delightfully sincere in her love for the missing man, completely touched his heart. He felt as though it were Liz, his sister, sitting there weeping. He sat down beside Corrie and put an arm around her shoulders.

'Don't—*don't* cry! You've been so wonderful. Don't lose heart. I admit that it's all very odd and rather frightening but it's really early days. Martin has only been missing about twenty-four hours, you know.'

Corrie was the one to feel embarrassed. She drew away from Hugh's comforting arm and gave a laugh and a sob together, then walked to the window and stared out blindly.

'Sorry. I'm being very stupid.'

'You are not at all,' he said gently, 'I don't wonder you're terribly distressed.'

She walked into Martin's bathroom. Reaching for a hand-towel she dried her face. Then she turned back into the bedroom again.

'You are most awfully kind to me. I can't tell you what a lot of support you give me.'

He sighed and stood up, tapping his stick on the floor, shaking his head thoughtfully.

60

'I feel pretty helpless to give you the sort you really need. I am as baffled as you are and apparently that spectacular policeman is just as clueless as we are.'

Corrie looked round Martin's bedroom. She shivered although the sun was shining warmly now on this perfect morning. Oh God, she thought, how perfect it would have been if *he* had been here.

'I think we will get out of this room,' she said. 'And if you will forgive me, I'll just go to my own room and put a phone call through to London. Martin lives there with his grandmother. I ought to let her know what's happened.'

'By all means. I'll go downstairs to the main lounge. Do join me and we'll see what next we could do. You might like to take a walk through the town. We could do a bit of detective work ourselves. Go for instance, into some of the tobacconist's or men's shop—any place you think might have interested him. Just ask if he was noticed by anybody. What do you think?'

'Great! But I haven't got his photograph now to show anybody. I gave it to the Inspector.'

Hugh frowned. 'That's true but they're getting it photostated so we'll have one later on today, I expect. Anyhow, come down soon and sit in the sun somewhere. It'll do you good.'

61

Nothing will do me good, she thought, nothing except to see Martin walk into the hotel.

There was a two-hour delay before she got the call through to Violetta. During this time she washed her tear-stained face, made up again and brushed back her hair. She thought she looked awful but she didn't care. When at last she spoke to Martin's grandmother it was scarcely a happy conversation.

Lady Grey-Ewing—as was to be expected—put up a good show after receiving the news but obviously was horrified. But she was a practical old lady and tried to be helpful.

'I feel sure nothing awful has happened to him, darling. Perhaps a little accident and he is still unconscious. I can't believe he has fallen over a cliff and got drowned or anything ghastly. Martin's not the sort of person to walk on the edge of cliffs or climb dangerous rocks, now *is* he?'

'No,' said Corrie in a choked voice. 'I'm sure he isn't. And it wouldn't be easy to do it either. The coast in Funchal isn't like that—I mean there are houses and hotels built all the way along the coast—and I can't believe he would have started exploring a few hours after he had got here.'

'He'd have wanted to have a look round Funchal, I daresay,' said Violetta, 'and to buy you some flowers or a present.'

I thought of that,' Corrie said, and the tears

62

started to her eyes again.

'Take his photograph and go into all the shops where he might buy flowers, etc.,' suggested Violetta.

'Yes, I will,' said Corrie without bothering to tell Violetta that she had already decided to do that, too.

Violetta asked a dozen more questions. Corrie tried to answer them. But it all seemed such a muddle in her mind and so absolutely inexplicable. She got rather tied up, added to which this, she realised, would be an expensive call and if allowed, dear Violetta would talk forever. She had absolutely no sense of time— or economy.

Finally, after saying everything she could to comfort Corrie, Violetta added, 'I must admit I'm terribly shaken and I'm too sorry for you, my poor, *poor* darling. What a miserable welcome for you! But don't despair.'

'Thank you—I really must go now,' said Corrie and shut her aching eyes.

Violetta added, 'One moment, darling. Shall I ring Ann up for you? And tell her the news?'

'Yes, please. She'd better know. I can't face another call.'

'You don't have to. I'll phone her and I'll phone you again tonight to see if there is any news of our boy. If necessary I'll get into a plane and fly out and join you, my darling.'

'Thank you,' said Corrie. 'You're always so wonderful to me,' and put down the receiver.

She knew Violetta. Despite her age—she would do as she said and rush over to Madeira. Corrie told herself to get a firm grip on her emotions. It was no time for a display of weakness. She ought to have more 'guts', anyhow. Any moment now something might happen to solve the mystery, and it was wrong to anticipate the worst. Of *course* Martin hadn't fallen down a cliff, or been drowned!

Later Corrie went downstairs to join Hugh again.

During the time he had been away from her, he had not wasted time. He had personally questioned every one of the porters, page-boys, barmen, waiters or waitresses and chambermaids, trying to get some line on Martin's movements. But only one porter had noticed Mr. Ashley leave the hotel yesterday morning—no more. George, the genial barman, said Mr. Ashley hadn't been in there for a drink. He had a keen memory and would have noticed a new face, anyhow. Neither had Martin been seen by the two swimming pool attendants.

'I gave them all down there a good description,' Hugh told Corrie, 'remembering what you've told me about Martin. But the boys who clean out the pool and arrange the chairs assured me nobody like him had appeared at the lido and, they'd have noticed if he was fully dressed. Most gentlemen, they said, came down there ready for swimming and

64

sunbathing.'

Hugh had even questioned the old woman with the basket who sold flowers outside the hotel entrance. The porter there had also talked to her in her own language but she was quite adamant that she had not seen the English gentlemen, nor had anyone ordered flowers to be sent to a Miss Gilroy.

'So you see, if Martin had any idea of sending you flowers and I'm sure he had—he must have decided to go into the town and choose them.'

Corrie shook her head. She was speechless. There was nothing she could say.

Gratefully she accepted a cigarette from Hugh. They sat smoking and talking a while longer out on the terrace. Corrie began to feel strangely removed from her surroundings— hardly a part of the scene at all. This might not have been Reid's Hotel in Madeira. The whole place seemed unreal, and she felt almost confused. Only Liz's brother, sitting here beside her, cool, quiet and resourceful, was substantial—factual—and reassuring.

She did not really want to leave the hotel but after another hour or two she agreed to walk with Hugh into the town.

Before they left the hotel, the manager appeared. He told them he had just received word from the Bureau of the Policia . . . the Inspector wished Miss Gilroy to know that he had not remained idle and that everything possible was being done. Already he had alerted all police stations on the island—even the small villages outside Funchal would know that Mr. Ashley was missing. Also the Inspector had been in touch with the airport authorities. There they had stamped his passport on arrival but they were quite definite that nobody with this passport or any man who bore a resemblance to him, had left Madeira since then.

Now it remained for the local police to make their searches. Already they had photostats of Mr. Ashley, and the Inspector said he was returning the original to Miss Gilroy's hotel later this morning.

Corrie schooled herself to smile and thank him.

The main hall was full of people at this hour. Some newly arrived guests were just checking in. Corrie's tired eyes examined them with painful intensity. Yet why, she asked herself, drearily? How mad to suppose that he could be amongst these people.

She spoke to the head-porter. 'I am going out for short walk. Please take all messages carefully—particularly if anybody telephones—' She stopped as though the words were difficult to express.

The entire staff at the hotel had, of course, been briefed by now about the extraordinary disappearance of the gentleman in Room 91X. The hall-porter looked at the lovely, sad-eyed girl with sympathy.

'You can be sure all messages will be taken, Miss Gilroy, and I hope that there will very soon be good news for you.'

'I hope so,' Corrie said under her breath and walked with Hugh into the sunshine.

CHAPTER SIX

Two weeks later Lady Grey-Ewing arrived at Reid's Hotel.

She had come to Madeira by boat and drove to the hotel from the harbour. She had wanted to fly but her doctor wouldn't allow it. This had annoyed her. She did not like any reference to the fact that now, because she was in her eighties, she had to take care of her health. But after her beloved grandson had been missing for fourteen whole days and there was still no sign of him, nothing could keep her away from joining Corrie despite the girl's assurance that she would be all right alone.

'So you may be,' Violetta had said over the telephone, 'but as you have made up your mind to stay out there until you *do* find out what has happened to our darling Martin— and I agree with you—I wouldn't have left the place either, if it had been my Bill—I feel you need someone to support you, darling, and I'm coming.'

'It will be wonderful to have you,' Corrie had answered.

Violetta telephoned to Ann.

'I can't let Corrie stay out there alone and I know you can't leave your horses so I'm off. I'll take care of her. And as you know, my dear, I've a lot of money and nothing to do with it and I might just as well spend it and give that poor pet the chance to stay on at Reid's till she finds Martin. She won't borrow from me so I'll just arrive and organise the whole thing. Do you agree?'

Ann had agreed only too gladly. The shocking news about Martin had distressed her just as it did all those who knew him. And still more so Ann who knew how much he meant to her niece. It seemed so awful that this should have happened, especially just before their intended marriage. Lady Grey-Ewing, who was in constant telephonic communication with Corrie, had told her that everyone on the island remained baffled. In addition to the police investigation, Sir Paul Mullins, the chairman of Martin's publishing firm, had flown out there himself a week ago and after interviewing the *Policia de Segurança Publica* returned to London and consulted Scotland Yard.

At the Yard they were sympathetic but not too helpful. It had not been established that a crime had been committed. London and

Interpol were interested in crime. If a body had been found and murder established— there would have been a lot of publicity and plenty of communication between the English and the Portuguese. However, Martin Ashley was only listed as a 'missing person'. There were thousands of missing persons every year. Sir Paul got little satisfaction from his repeated efforts to trace the young man who was such an excellent salesman and member of the staff and much liked by all of them.

So Violetta came to Madeira with Ann's blessing and many tender messages for Corrie, plus a suitcase full of her clothes. Corrie hadn't taken nearly enough things out with her. She had only meant to stay at Reid's for a few days.

When Lady Grey-Ewing arrived she had the sort of reception to which she was accustomed. Everybody rushed to be of service to the charming little old lady who looked at least twenty years younger than she was, made up to the eyes, exquisitely dressed in navy blue and white (the latest model from Paris) and wearing a white hat and exaggeratedly large dark glasses which she took off as she entered the lounge. A page-boy followed with what seemed to the hall-porter a great deal of luggage. Obviously her ladyship meant to make a long stay. And quite apart from the personal aura of glamour that always hung around the once-famous actress, Violetta was a figure of interest on account of her association with poor Miss Gilroy. The word 'poor' had now been affixed to Corrie's name whenever she was spoken of. Those among the guests who learned about the strange disappearance of Martin Ashley were not only intrigued but sincerely sorry for the young girl. She was so beautiful and she looked so tragic and what *could* have happened to the young man?

That was, of course, the salient question in the minds of both Corrie and Martin's grandmother as they met in the lounge and fell into each other's arms.

Once up in the big double room which Violetta, extravagant as usual, had taken for a fortnight, she looked more serious than Corrie had ever seen her. She had removed her smart little hat. In the bright light her face was haggard and she seemed unusually tired.

Against her doctor's warnings Violetta had continued to smoke after her eightieth birthday. She lit one now, using the long holder which made her look like a woman who had stepped straight out of the twenties. And having listened to all that Corrie had to tell her—adding quite a number of details that she had not included during their long-distance calls—Violetta drew a deep breath of her cigarette and shook her head.

'Oh my! oh *my!*' she exclaimed, 'it just doesn't seem possible. One reads about these things—one knows they happen, and yet one never dreams they are going to happen to someone as close as Martin is to us. My poor darling Corrie, what you must have suffered!'

Violetta seated herself in an armchair by the open windows with Corrie beside her It was such a glorious afternoon. The weather was warming up. The swimmers and sunbathers down on the lido were at this hour enjoying their buffet lunch.

Violetta had ordered a meal to be sent up here. For all her youthful appearance and bravado she had found the long journey trying. And she and poor Corrie wanted to be alone, to talk.

A week ago Corrie would possibly have burst into tears on receiving Violetta's sympathy but now she had reached a pitch when she could talk about Martin without crying. She just sat dry-eyed and tense. There were deep purple shadows under her eyes. She was finding it hard to sleep. It wasn't that she had had as many as usual of the old nightmares, but even when she did fall asleep she kept waking up—looking around—listening—as though she expected someone to come in and tell her that Martin had been found.

'It's been grim,' she admitted, 'and it's so *unbelievable.* How can a man just walk out of an hotel and disappear?'

'You are quite sure the local police have

done everything possible?'

'Quite sure. The Inspector has been most helpful. He's right on the ball. And as I told you over the phone, Sir Paul Mullins came out himself and spent the night here, while he made investigations.'

'He must have been very shocked about Martin.'

'He was. Martin was very well thought of by the whole firm and the contents of his attaché case, which incidentally Sir Paul took back with him, as the police had no use for it, proved that he'd roped in quite a bit of new business in Lisbon.'

Violetta sat back and shut her eyes a moment. She smoked in silence. It was obvious to Corrie that the old lady was unnerved—quite unlike her usual cheerful amusing self. Corrie forgot her own grief and concentrated on Martin's grandmother. She knew that Martin meant all the world to Violetta. She, Corrie, was his fiancée but Violetta had nobody in her life but her 'boy' as she still called him. Having lost her husband, and as her only daughter lived in Australia, Martin had become not only her heir but her dear companion. She ran her home for him. They were very close.

'Every kind of enquiry has been made.' Corrie continued to put Violetta in the picture. 'Every nursing home or rest house or hotel he can have gone to has been visited and searched, in case he was in an accident that affected his memory.'

Violetta's big blue eyes now stared at Corrie over her horn-rimmed glasses. 'Anyhow, my dear darling girl, he's been gone two whole weeks. By now were he in this town and suffering from concussion somebody would have reported it.'

Corrie nodded.

'Quite so. That's what makes it doubly mysterious. Sir Paul told me that the Inspector said himself that Martin is the strangest "missing person" they have ever dealt with. He arrived here, he half-unpacked and changed—someone saw him leave the hotel—and after that—' Corrie shrugged her shoulders speechlessly.

Violetta smoked furiously, searching her own lively mind for some kind of feasible explanation for the affair, and failing. It infuriated as well as saddened her. She had always been able to help solve people's problems and did so constantly. She was famous among her friends for finding remedies for this or that, where others failed. But what remedy was there for the complete disappearance of her adored boy? What could it mean? If it was anybody but Martin she might have said the boy had had a change of mind about marrying his Corisande and just walked out. But this, as an idea, seemed too ludicrous. When Violetta had said goodbye to her grandson before he flew to Lisbon he had been full of joyous anticipation of a future to be shared with Corrie. They were so well matched, so deeply in love. Violetta in the past had sometimes disliked, or been indifferent to the one or two girls Martin brought home to her. But from the start his grandmother had known that his golden-eyed tawny-haired Corrie was for *him*.

Now she spoke her thoughts aloud.

'One thing is for sure. He hasn't gone because he couldn't face marrying *you*, my pet!'

For the first time Corrie's lips curved into a wan smile.

'No, I don't think that's the explanation.'

'I'm quite sure it isn't. What else can we think of?'

'Well, it's been accepted now, officially, that he never left Madeira either by boat or air. The seaport and the air terminus are both sure of that. Neither can he have been forcibly kidnapped and held as a hostage or anything so sensational, or we would have heard.' Again Corrie gave a smile. 'The police took that into consideration but ruled it out. This isn't the island for hijackers or kidnappers or any desperate criminals, and if a gang were holding Martin for money, they'd have contacted me by now so as to get the ransom.'

Violetta took a half-finished cigarette from the long ebony holder and stubbed it in an ashtray. 'Of *course*. It's out of the question.'

So, thought Corrie desolately, we are back to square one. There was, of course, that other awful possibility that Martin—unseen, unheard—might have met with some fearful accident and that his body was still to be found. This was in Violetta's mind, as well as in Corrie's but neither of them could voice it.

Lady Grey-Ewing was a born optimist. She never believed that the worst could happen *until* it did. Corrie, with her deep emotional temperament, was a little more pessimistic— perhaps more imaginative than Martin's grandmother. But she deliberately cast that sinister thought from her whenever it rose to the forefront of her mind. In any case, the Chief Inspector had assured her that his men had combed Funchal and the rest of the island without success. What was there left to do except to sit and wait—and go on hoping for a miracle—for some explanation they had none of them thought of.

Suddenly Corrie got up, put an arm around Violetta's frail shoulders and kissed one of her delicate-powdered cheeks. She always smelt delicious, *dear* Violetta.

'You don't know how I appreciate you coming out here like this,' Corrie whispered and they clung together for a moment, sharing their grief, their terrible anxiety.

'I'm going to stay on at Reid's until Martin is found,' Violetta declared, and blew her little retroussé nose. 'We'll neither of us go back to England without him. We'll just live here where his things are and where he arranged to meet you.'

Corrie felt the ice around her heart suddenly thaw. With tears in her eyes, she said, 'It does me so much good to hear you say that. I've been feeling so depressed. Thank you again for coming all this way, *dear* Violetta.'

Her whole family called her by her Christian name. She liked it that way. Eighty she might be, but those large blue eyes still held the secret of eternal youth. Corrie remembered Martin once saying, 'You know, my grandmother is much more a friend to me than one of these grannies you've got to tip-toe around and mind what you say. Violetta's unique and quite unshockable, bless her!'

And he had added that Violetta was closer to him than Vanessa—his own mother. She, so Corrie gathered, was a complete contrast. Handsome—a head taller than her mother and with bigger bones. Martin had inherited her grey eyes and the thick fairness of his hair, but little of her nature. She had always been selfish—turning all things towards herself. Inordinately vain, she lapped up admiration and received plenty on account of her good looks and her distinction in the world of sport. She had meant to become a Wimbledon champion before she married Martin's father, then temporarily gave it up for marriage. But as a wife and mother, she failed. She hadn't even wanted children. Once Martin arrived she gave him all the material things he needed, with occasional spurts of affection. She had also quickly grown tired of the man she had married. He was too quiet and too artistic for her. She had fallen in love but regretted the marriage, and when he died ten years after their marriage, she almost immediately married again. This time an Australian tennis champion who was obviously better equipped to give her the life she had always wanted. And when Vanessa's mother had offered to keep young Martin in England and bring him up, Vanessa made little or no objection. Particularly since Martin, even as a child, did not get on with his step-father.

Now that Martin was a grown man and leading his own life, Corrie knew he bore no grudge against his famous mother who had made such a success in Sydney. Very occasionally she came over to England. She and her son got on quite well but there was never any real warmth between them. Vanessa liked to be thought younger than she was. A grown-up son was an embarrassment. Besides, although he was moderately good at sports he also had his father's love for books and music. Tennis to him was just a pleasant form of exercise. It brought him no closer to his mother. It was his grandmother to whom he felt he really belonged and to whom he owed his education and his happiness as a boy.

Now, thinking about these things, Corrie suddenly spoke to Violetta about her daughter.

'Do you think that as this—this awful affair—has been going on for so long we ought to let Vanessa know about it?'

Lady Grey-Ewing took off her horn-rims and considered this point. She began to swing the glasses in her hand thoughtfully, remembering Vanessa as a child. She'd wanted so much to love her and be equally loved but the sweet darling little girl she had dreamed of, longing to be kissed and cuddled, and who Violetta could dress in enchanting frocks, was not the daughter she gave birth to. Vanessa nearly cost Violetta her life and became the type to wriggle out of her mother's arms rather than into them. Once she was in her teens, mother and daughter had clashed. The big, healthy, rather aggressive young girl was a complete puzzle—and disappointment—to the light-hearted ex-actress with her melting eyes and the aura of glamour that still hung around her. Violetta was not surprised that Martin's poor father had died a saddened man. Vanessa was too selfish to make anybody happy, although Violetta had to confess 'Husband Numero Deux', as she called the second choice, seemed to get on with Vanessa very well. He was rich and he could partner her at tennis. They were well-matched. So Violetta hardly ever saw her daughter although they exchanged dutiful letters. But Violetta lived for her grandson once her own adored husband died. This mysterious disaster that had overtaken Martin was a crushing blow.

After a few moments' thought, she answered Corrie. 'I suppose we *ought* to tell Vannie. Yes, dear, she *is* his mother. But she won't worry much about not hearing from him. She never has written to him often. When I feel I *can,* dear Corrie, I'll put a call through to Sydney and break the news. But let's give it a little more time. I just don't yet feel Martin is irrevocably lost to us—do you?'

Corrie felt a curious shiver go through her but mindful of Violetta's feelings she tried to be cheerful.

'No, of course I don't.'

'In any case,' added the older woman, 'Vannie's last letter said that she and Walter were playing tennis in New Zealand as from this month so I can't get her on the phone anyhow for the present.'

After lunch they sat out on the sunlit balcony. Lady Grey-Ewing had been given one of the best rooms in the new wing. It had a glorious view of the sea and the garden that was so full of green trees and vivid flowers. Away to the left lay the little harbour and the dazzling beauty of the mountains against the cobalt sky. Violetta, as was her custom, shaded her delicate little face from the sun with an old-fashioned parasol but Corrie leaned back in her chair and let the golden warmth soak into her. She could stand any amount of it. Even this last two weeks she had acquired a rich tan. But Violetta had found her painfully thin and changed—a bundle of nerves, and no wonder.

Corrie kept her eyes closed. 'I suppose there has been nothing in the papers about this, has there—at home, I mean?' she asked.

'Heavens, no—there wouldn't be. As Sir Paul told us, Scotland Yard and Interpol are not interested in missing persons. There's no crime the Press can write about. Was there anything in your local rag in Madeira, darling?'

'Yes. I've saved all the cuttings for you. The Inspector thought it a good thing to broadcast the story. It might meet the eye of *someone* who had either seen Martin or could help us in some way.'

Violetta took one of Corrie's slender hands in hers. 'Don't lose hope, darling,' she said. '*Please* don't.'

Corrie controlled herself and gripped Violetta's small surprisingly strong fingers. 'I won't. I promise.'

Somebody knocked on the door. A waiter came in to clear away the lunch trays. He also handed Corrie a note.

It was from Hugh Aylmer:

'I know you'll be tied up with Lady G-E but if you'd like it, I'd love to give you both tea on the terrace. Do come down at four.'

At once Corrie felt remorseful because she had been neglecting Hugh—in fact she had forgotten him completely since Martin's grandmother arrived. He had been so good to her. She mustn't ignore him. She didn't want to. She handed Violetta the invitation.

'This is from the brother of my old schoolfriend—I told you about him—he's done absolutely everything he can to help.'

Violetta gave her famous pout. As she had once said to Corrie, laughing at herself, 'My mouth isn't so effective these days what with my false teeth and wrinkles, but I still use the pout—it often gets me places.'

Now she teased Corrie. 'Tall, dark and handsome, eh, this Mr. Aylmer? And in love with you?'

Corrie gave a wan smile. 'You're joking, darling.'

'I didn't say were *you* in love with *him,* you silly girl!'

Corrie's smile broadened. Martin's adorable grandmother was at her best when she was in a jocular teasing mood.

'Well, I assure you Hugh isn't in love with me but he is an extremely nice person and I think you would like him and I *would* like you to thank him for all he's done, darling.'

'Of course I will. Let's go down to the lounge at four o'clock as he asks. I'd like to taste some of that Madeira cake again after all

81

these years. Bill used to love it. I shall put on weight, but I don't care!'

Corrie tried to get a grip on herself and smother some of the intense feeling that was running so high in her at the moment. It was Martin, Martin, *Martin* in her mind all the time. But she fully realised one couldn't go on talking about him every minute of the day— conjecturing—going over and over the same story. It would drive them crazy. She knew perfectly well, too, there was little else on Violetta's mind. But she was a brave old lady and made Corrie feel suddenly weak and stupid. It would be good for them both to go down and talk to Hugh.

Corrie went along to her own room carrying the suitcase that Violetta had brought for her from London. She needed a change and Ann had sent just the right things. It was a relief to get into fresh blue slacks and a crisp shirt and comfortable sandals. During this last fortnight she had walked and walked and *walked* around Funchal, always rather idiotically, she supposed, searching for Martin.

When she rejoined Violetta she noticed that the old lady had also changed and was now wearing a charming pink and white floral dress and jacket; also that she had pinned a pink rose to one lapel. What a splendid coquette she was for an eighty-year-old, Corrie thought fondly. She was quite sure the rose had been put on to impress Hugh. The old lady loved flirting with young men.

It wasn't long before Hugh Aylmer joined the long list of those who adored Violetta. She took off her big glasses, gave him the full benefit of her still beautiful blue eyes, placed her small hand in his and said, 'You've been wonderful to my dear Corrie, I believe. Thank you *so* much—' At once he was at her feet.

They drank China tea, ate the beautiful cake which at Reid's tasted like no other Madeira cake in the world, and chatted. For the first ten minutes Lady Grey-Ewing asked Hugh mostly about himself and his sister, and as happened with people she met, she found out more about him during those few minutes than some people did in years. She was so genuinely sympathetic.

Corrie smoking her after-tea cigarette, watched and listened. She was trying hard to pull herself out of the shadows and join in the light conversation. Violetta glanced at her, read the girl's mind and turned the conversation to Martin. Poor dear Corrie! He was the only thing she wanted to talk about. She was quite sure there was no other man in the world for Corrie *but* Martin. But Hugh was obviously a good type and an excellent friend for the girl just now.

Soon they were sifting over old ground and reaching the usual unhappy conclusion that Martin's disappearance was bathed in a mystery nobody could solve.

'You seem to have been most kind, Hugh—I know I may call you that,' said Lady Grey-Ewing. 'How long are you going to stay here?'

'I meant to go home and get on with my new book at the end of this week, but I feel I just can't leave Reid's at the moment. That is—' He glanced at Corrie's pale young face with the compassion he always felt for her—'there might be something I can do and if you hadn't come, Lady Grey-Ewing, I would certainly not have left Corrie alone.'

'Can you keep your room on?' Corrie asked.

'Well, as a matter of fact, they're moving me because mine is booked but I've been given another.'

'I hope you won't get a less attractive one.'

His dark eyes smiled at Corrie. 'It would be no hardship for me but I think all the rooms here are comfortable. It's just a question of view, and I don't really care whether I have a seaview or not—I'm hardly ever in my room.'

'I'm quite sure that both Corrie and I will be glad for you to stay on with us,' put in Violetta, 'I for one intend to stay just as long as it is necessary. I have a sure feeling that my grandson will turn up, and I want to be here. I couldn't rest in London, anyhow. And if they can't let me have my lovely suite, I'll go to another hotel.'

'I'm quite sure the manager won't let you do *that,*' said Corrie.

She spoke lightly but there was still no

84

lightness in her thoughts. Violetta had just said that she was sure that Martin would turn up. Why was it she, Corrie, couldn't share that optimism?

Corrie kept to herself the fact that last night for the first time for quite a while the dreaded nightmare had disturbed her again. Nowadays it seemed that the whole thing had a prophetic significance. She was seeking for Martin but never finding him. It was never Martin who pulled her out of the darkness into that room where deeper—even more horrifying gloom awaited her.

Suddenly a terrifying thought flashed into her mind. *I'm beginning to wonder if he's dead. Oh God, perhaps he is dead. And perhaps I'll never know how he died or where.*

She heard Violetta say, 'Darling, are you all right? You've lost all your colour.'

Corrie clenched her hands and made an effort. 'I'm fine. Let's go down to the Lido and get some air.'

'Maybe I'll have a swim,' said Hugh, rising.

He went off to get his things. Lady Grey-Ewing took one of Corrie's hands.

'Sure you wouldn't like to go upstairs and lie down? You've been through a great deal, my pet.'

'No, no, I'm fine,' said Corrie and thrust her ugly, awful fears back into the recess of her mind.

'I do like your Hugh Aylmer. He is a
85

charming boy. Tell me why he's limping and has to have a stick.'

Corrie began to enlighten her about Hugh's accident and the loss of the girl he had been going to marry. Then she saw the manager walking quickly towards their table. As he reached them, Corrie introduced him to Martin's grandmother. He bowed and shook hands with her but almost immediately turned to the girl.

'I have some news for you,' he said.

The blood rushed into Corrie's face. She sprang to her feet. 'Oh, you don't mean it,' she exclaimed. 'Good news? Oh, tell me it *is* good!'

'Ah—we cannot take it for granted that it is either good or bad. It is just *news*. The first we have had at all.'

Lady Grey-Ewing stared at the manager, her own heart beating fast.

'Tell me quickly please. What is it, monsieur?'

He sat down and began to talk.

It appeared that the assistant to the Inspector, the young *guarda,* had just telephoned the manager and asked him to pass some information on to the English lady. By the merest chance the *guarda* had taken his wife, on his day off, to a certain restaurant in the *Câmara de Lobos.* They went there sometimes to sit in the sun and eat the big local prawns. All the tables had been full so they had to share with two other people. Naturally they started a conversation and the young *guarda,* an enthusiast in his job, brought up the subject of the missing Englishman. It had, after all, become a focal point of discussion in Funchal. But the two who were sharing their table were not Island people. They came from Lisbon and were just about ending their holiday. They did not know about Mr. Martin Ashley and the queer way in which he had vanished from Reid's. They wanted details and got them. Soon they knew all about the beautiful English girl waiting, sorrowing, in the famous hotel. The *guarda* told them that it was during the late morning of March 19th that Mr. Ashley had vanished and that a search was being made throughout Madeira but more particularly in Funchal at his hotel where he had last been seen. For a few moments the Lisbon couple looked at each other shrugging their shoulders, then suddenly the young man seemed to have a brain-wave, and after some further conversation announced that the *guarda's* description of the English gentleman had reawakened his memory. They believed they had seen the missing man. The couple had wished to visit the beautiful village of Camacha, which was not far from Funchal and was the centre of the all-important wickerwork industry. They were great walkers and went up the mountain on foot. Half-way up the road, so richly wooded on either side, they came upon a magnificent mimosa tree from which there tumbled a cascade of feathery yellow flowers—an exotic, exquisite sight. The young man wished to take a photograph of it. And ahead there was another young man by the tree, admiring it.

The Lisbon boy reminded his wife that they had whispered to each other that he must be an English *senhor.* He certainly did not look Portuguese. He was fair and handsome, and he gave them a smile and said 'Good morning' in a very English voice. He remarked on the warmth of the sunshine for the time of the year, then went his way.

'His description,' the manager told Violetta and Corrie, 'tallies with that of Mr. Ashley. So we could surmise that he walked from Funchal up the Camacha Road that morning.'

Corrie's heart beat violently. She turned large luminous eyes upon the manager and said in a breathless voice, 'What else did they say? Did they tell you what he was *wearing?* Did they give you any details at all? Oh! I am sure that it *was* Martin—even the date is right.'

'We cannot be *sure,* but—' the manager spread out his hands, 'the *guarda* told me that this couple from Lisbon remembered little except his fair hair and skin, and his very nice English voice.'

Corrie started to tremble. 'Martin *has* a nice voice, a particularly attractive one. Did they mention his size? His height?'

The manager eyed her sadly.

'I fear not. Such details would not have been of importance to them. After the few words when the Englishman mentioned the weather, he said goodbye and moved on.'

Now Violetta spoke. Her voice was not quite steady. 'Did they not overtake him further up the route or see him at all in Camacha?'

'No. They stayed behind taking many photographs of the mimosa tree and they were quite certain they did not see Mr. Ashley in Camacha.'

Corrie put a hand to her throat. She felt choked. 'Oh, if we only knew more! Can we meet this couple from Lisbon? Could I speak to them, myself?'

'Alas, they left Madeira this morning. But believe me, they had absolutely nothing else to tell the guard about Mr. Ashley. He is a good lad and he cross-examined the couple expertly—he assured me of this. You must understand the Lisbon people were not on the lookout for a missing person, mademoiselle. With them it was just a question of coming across a young Englishman for a few moments, then—finish! Naturally, the matter had not the importance for them that it has for you.'

Lady Grey-Ewing leaned forward and took a firm hold of Corrie's arm.

'Don't get too excited,' she whispered. 'It isn't much to go on. The fair man wasn't even

89

necessarily our Martin.'

'Couldn't they describe what he was wearing?' Corrie asked pitifully.

'They were questioned on all such details but could say no more,' the manager replied with patience. He was so sorry for the young girl—he wished he could have brought her more definite news. But he pointed out that the very fact this fair Englishman seemed to look like Mr. Ashley appeared to minimise the possibility that he had stayed by the coast and had a fatal, still undiscovered accident—either from the high, rocky cliffs—or in the sea.

Corrie clung to this. 'Then we must go to Camacha at once.'

'The Inspector, himself, has informed me that his men have combed every house, shop or café in the village or thereabouts,' said the manager, and sighed.

The light—momentarily brightening Corrie's eyes—faded. Her colour paled. She looked at Violetta who was tight-lipped, stern, obviously just as disappointed.

Then Hugh came back, wearing shorts and singlet, a towel under one arm. At once he was drawn into the little drama, and had something to say about it.

'I think we should go to Camacha, all the same,' he said.

Corrie leapt at this. 'So do I.'

'I agree.' Lady Grey-Ewing nodded.

'You will speak to the Chief Inspector first, I

am sure,' the manager suggested gently.

'That would be wise,' said Hugh and glanced at Corrie.

This ended in Violetta tactfully withdrawing from the scene. Despite her yearning to be what she called 'in on everything' and young again, she recognised the fact that she was eighty and had not the strength to do what the young people could do and tired more easily than she wished. So she might end by being a nuisance to them.

'I won't take a minute getting back into my clothes,' said Hugh.

'Please do take Corrie to the police station,' Lady Grey-Ewing said to him. 'I shall stay here. And while you change. Hugh, I'll ask the hall-porter to hire a car. It will go down on my account, of course.'

'Please let me—' began Hugh, but she immediately broke in. 'No—really! Whatever expenses there are likely to be during this search will be my affair. After all, I am Martin's grandmother.'

Hugh said no more.

CHAPTER SEVEN

Half an hour later Corrie and Hugh were in one of the big shining taxis which abounded in Funchal, on their way to Camacha from the *Policia de Segurança Publica.*

It was over 2,300 feet above Funchal, up a winding mountain road to the village.

As the chauffeur drove them quickly through the beautiful squares and streets, past the Cathedral and the Flower Market, and turned on to the mountain road, Corrie and Hugh talked animatedly.

Their interview with the Chief Inspector had given them little more to go on than the news they had received at Reid's. They were, however, able to interview the young *guarda* who confirmed all that the manager had said and had only one thing extra to add. It was a slender clue but Corrie grabbed at it with painful intensity.

He had, the *guarda* told them, marked down in his notebook that the *senhora* from Lisbon had mentioned the fact that she particularly noticed that the English gentleman, admiring the mimosa tree, had said these words:

'How lucky you are to have brought a camera. I wish I had brought mine. It's such an incredible mimosa!'

Corrie became madly excited. That remark

was typical of Martin. He was always meaning to take photographs and invariably forgot to bring a camera with him. It was one of the things they joked about. She had, in fact, just before Martin went away, threatened that his next Christmas present would be an empty photograph album which he would never fill. At which he had laughed and said yes he would—and he'd fill it with lovely photographs of her—his wife—when they married.

As they drove away from the *Policia de Segurança Publica,* Corrie had gone on talking about this.

'I know it might be any man—just any fair Englishman. I *know* this, but one or two things have struck me—not only his not having a camera with him but I can just imagine that if he was waiting for me and didn't expect me at the same time that morning, he might have decided to walk up and see Camacha where they say whole families make all this fantastic wicker-work. He's interested in that sort of thing.'

The last thing Hugh wanted to do was to discourage her and damp down her new-found optimism. But in his own mind he doubted if the young man seen at the mimosa tree had been Martin Ashley. Corrie was right when she said that there could be many young Englishmen on a visit to Madeira who might have walked up to Camacha that same morning.

But Corrie talked on and on. Her long slender fingers were locked in her lap convulsively. Her whole being was exalted by the new hope. It was making the blood run fast through her veins.

She didn't care whether or not the police had already combed Camacha—*she* would comb it now with Hugh's help. *She* might hit upon something the Inspector had not thought of, *she* who knew Martin so well. Somebody had only to make the slightest remark and she would pounce on it, recognise that it was Martin they were speaking of.

She noticed little of the fabulous scenery they passed—yet the upward climb through the wooded mountainside was breathtaking. The huge green avocado trees, the scarlet and purple jacarandas, the miles of bright green bushes and red roses. The occasional picturesque house and the old stone walls overflowing with brilliant bougainvillaea.

Such things made the island of Madeira look like one vast lush garden but Hugh could see that Corrie's interest was focused solely and absolutely on her search for Martin. Strangely he found himself suddenly comparing this girl with his poor dead Juliet. Her love for him had been sweet and gentle. She had had none of Corrie's physical or mental strength, or her purposeful character. Juliet had loved him but she would not have been capable of the all-absorbing love this girl seemed to possess for Martin Ashley.

It made a deep impression upon Hugh. But he was afraid for her. To find in the end that Martin had died—to dry up this torrent of feeling in Corrie—could fate be so cruel to allow such things to happen?

So they came to Camacha.

Hugh told the driver to wait and pick them up again where they had stopped, which was in the main square. Facing them was an old convent school. A lovely old white plastered building, with grey decoration over Gothic doors and high narrow windows. It was a charming village and now the sun seemed even warmer up here than down by the coast. The sky above was an infinity of incredible blueness. Hugh wished sadly there had been no tragedy and that Corrie could have enjoyed this. But obviously she was almost blind to the beauty around her.

She stood still a moment putting on her dark glasses. Her eyes ached perpetually these days—not only because of the sun, she knew that—but because she never seemed able to stop crying herself to sleep. She had lost weight and was always tired.

Hugh tried for a moment to divert her attention by pointing to a huge, very old, tree with strange dark-grey bark, looking like a gigantic elephant's leg. The long branches were starred with white fragrant blossom.

Underneath, there was shade and quiet.

'Would you like to sit here a moment and let me get you a drink?' Hugh asked her gently.

'Not yet. You have a drink if you'd like one but I won't.'

'We'll both have one later,' he said, knowing that all she wanted was to begin the search.

The driver, a typically gay, bright-eyed young Portuguese who spoke English, was standing near them lighting a cigarette. He pointed to the tree.

'*Incencio* tree,' he said showing his white teeth in a smile. 'Very nice, very fine. No same in England.'

Corrie dragged her thoughts away from Martin and smiled back at the boy. 'No, nothing like it in my country,' she said, '*Incencio* is a charming name. I wonder if it has a meaning?' and she walked to the tree and put her face against one of the trailing blooms. 'I think it does, actually, smell of incense,' she added.

She looked just for a moment so animated, so beautiful, Hugh wished with all his heart that the moment could last, and that she need not return to agonising uncertainty and grief. This girl with her great luminous eyes and her long hair was made for love and laughter, not for sorrow.

But almost at once, Corrie turned away from the *Incencio* tree and showed little interest when he pointed out the lilies that grew like weeds all round the town, and the great masses of freesias, of camellias and orchids which were astonishingly plentiful up here.

He took her by the arm and led her to the nearest shop. The window was full of souvenirs and toys and magazines on one side. On the other there was a little café, although empty just now.

He said, 'Will you let me help by suggesting an organised search, Corrie? As I promised you in the car just now, every inn, every house, every shop—and I see there are several—we'll make enquiries at them all. There is always somebody who speaks English.'

She agreed and was grateful for his support. Darling Violetta was a wonderful solace down there in the hotel and a tremendous link with Martin. But Hugh was a man. One needed a man at one's side in this sort of affair. Oh, how lucky she was to have found Liz's brother at Reid's!

For an hour they walked around, knocking on doors, speaking to men, women and even children, begging for information. Showing everybody the photograph of Martin. Receiving only the same answer everywhere.

'Alas, *senhor, senhora*—we have not seen this man.'

To one old man with white hair and a face like a wrinkled walnut, Corrie made a special appeal because he spoke such good English. He had once worked in the post office in

Funchal.

'Please, *please* try to remember. The *senhor* might just have walked through Camacha—stopped for a drink—bought cigarettes—anything—but I feel sure he was on the road to Camacha, why wouldn't he have come up here?'

The old man thought hard. It was a little time ago—the 19th March—and every day Camacha filled with tourists of all nationalities. His memory was not good. Besides it was difficult to recall this *senhor* although the old man studied the picture and face long and close.

'I am sorry, I cannot help. Why not go to the place where they make the baskets?'

Then Hugh broke in, '*Obrigado, senhor,* but we have already tried there. They didn't see him.'

The old Portuguese, intrigued by the story of the missing man, had already been questioned by the *policia,* so he knew the story. He would have something to tell his friends over their wine tonight, about the extreme beauty of this English girl who came seeking her fiancé. He had a kind heart and he would have liked to have helped her.

'Tell your driver to take you to the church at Santo da Serra before you descend to the Portela Pass,' he suggested. 'Sometimes there is a priest there—at this time there is likely to be one—who takes confessions. He might have noticed or spoken a word, perhaps, to the *senhor.* That is all I can think of.'

They thanked him. Corrie lapsed into silence. Her footsteps lagged. She wiped her hot face. She felt terrible, but as they walked, Hugh noticed the change which was slowly but surely taking place in Corrie. She had come up here wild with enthusiasm and hope. Repeated failure had driven the colour from cheeks that were pale under the tan which a fortnight of Madeiran sun had painted on them. Her eyes had lost their lustre.

'You're tired, aren't you?' asked Hugh. 'You look as though you need a glass of wine or a cup of coffee. You have been walking for quite a time and all the questioning is very unnerving for you. Let me take you somewhere for a drink. It's getting on for six o'clock.'

She forced her lips to smile.

'I'm okay. But do let's try the church first. Martin rather liked looking at old churches. Maybe we will find a priest who saw him. It's just a chance.'

They walked to the church. It was as the old man had said—the hour for confessions. The priest was busy. Once inside where it was cool and dark, Corrie stood for a moment beside Hugh looking around her. It seemed to her to differ completely from the cool simplicity of a Protestant church. It was warm and welcoming, with candles burning around the

99

shrine of a Madonna. Richly painted carvings of the Stations of the Cross decorated the walls. The odour of incense lingered in the air. Through the dimness there gleamed a red light from the silver lamp swinging on three chains before the lace-covered altar.

This was not her church, her faith, and yet something about it made Corrie kneel down and hide her face in her hands.

'Listen to me, dear God,' she prayed, 'listen, *please!* Let me find Martin. *Please* let me find him!'

Hugh, watching, read her thoughts. He felt intensely sad as he sat in the pew beside her. He found that he, too, wanted to pray.

'Help me to help her find this man. She loves him so much.'

A few moments later Corrie lifted her head. Her golden eyes sparkled at him. She whispered, 'Let's wait. The priest is bound to come out.'

But when he emerged from the confessional—a young rosy-cheeked boy in a black cassock and with a biretta under his arm—it was no use. He could not speak one word of English. It so exasperated Corrie that the tears filled her eyes and began to roll down her cheeks. She shook her head speechlessly. Hugh stood beside her, feeling equally helpless. But the young priest was intuitive. Besides, he could see that the English lady was in deep distress. So beautiful, so sad, she reminded him of the Madonna. His heart warmed towards her.

'*Espera aqui,*' he said.

Instinctively, Hugh realised that this was the Portuguese for 'Wait here'. Gently he took Corrie's arm. He could feel her trembling.

'He asks us to wait. Let's sit down in the pew again, shall we?'

The young priest smiled, nodded, and hurried out of the church.

After what seemed to Corrie a long time, he returned with a man who was a gardener to an English couple living in the district.

The priest led them all out of the church and into the roadway. They stood in the portico while the man, after greeting them, interpreted for the English couple.

But again it was no use.

The young priest had a good memory, but that day, March 19th had been busy with christenings and burials. After which he was engaged in initiating a new organist. Then he had gone home and not returned to the church until the hour for Benediction. But at no time had he seen Martin.

Corrie feverishly asked him a dozen or more questions; Hugh, also. The interpreter shook his head each time, and reiterated that the priest had neither seen *Senhor* Ashley nor noticed him in the village either on that day or at a future date.

Although Corrie knew she had been hoping

against hope, she walked away from the church bitterly disappointed. When Hugh tried to say a few comforting words she shut her eyes against the glare of the sun for a moment, then put on her dark glasses and said, 'What do we do now? What else *is there* to do?'

'I must admit it's a tough business, but you know, I warned you they told us at the police station they had pretty well combed all these villages above and around Funchal.'

'Shall we go back to Reid's then?' she asked in a dull voice.

Hugh pushed his hair back and wiped his face with his handkerchief.

'I know you were saying a prayer just now in that church, Corrie,' he said, 'so was I.' Then as he saw her turn to answer him with new hardness in her eyes, he quickly added, 'No, don't be cynical. Prayers aren't always answered at once. You must believe that.'

Her heart warmed to him. She put an arm through his and tried to smile. 'You are such a comfort. Thank you. But isn't it true that certain prayers are not answered at all?'

He was silent. He could remember how he had felt after poor little Juliet died. He had stopped praying. He had been bitter against God—fate—whoever, whatever was responsible for the crash that had ended that young lovely life. But he also remembered the days when he had lain in bed half-drugged yet still conscious of the pain in his leg, combined with the anguish of his thoughts. Somehow he had regained his faith, courage had returned and the will to go on living.

Feeling intensely for Liz's unhappy friend, he spoke, perhaps more strongly than he had intended. 'You must not be weak and just give up, or believe that prayer isn't answered. It is—often in a most mysterious way, if not always at once. You'll begin to think I am sort of in the pulpit—preaching—which is the last thing I ever do normally. It's just that I can't bear you to abandon all hope, and once you stop praying, you're in danger of doing that. I *know* I almost lost my mind after Juliet died and I was carted off to hospital. Yet I find today I can live and breathe without all that pain—either in mind or body.'

They were walking towards the square and the waiting car. Corrie made no answer so Hugh stumbled on, 'I *am a* clot! Talking as though you had already lost Martin. But you *haven't.* I swear you haven't. Call me psychic—anything—but I just don't somehow feel that fellow has vanished into thin air.'

She stopped and faced him. 'But he *has* vanished.'

'For the moment,' said Hugh stubbornly.

She drew a long sigh. 'Okay. I'll ride it. Perhaps that couple who saw the man like Martin have put us on the wrong track. Perhaps it wasn't Martin after all.'

'Let's suppose it was. We haven't finished

our private detective job.'

Hugh smiled down into those wonderful eyes that gave him such a strong sense of responsibility. He felt the need to protect her—to save her from despair. But privately he was just as flummoxed as she was—as they all were. However, he hadn't really been pretending when he said he had the strangest feeling that Martin Ashley was not dead.

He glanced at a piece of paper on which he had made notes before leaving the hotel.

'Suppose we get the driver to take us up to this place, Poiso, which is four thousand feet farther up. We could ask there—show Martin's photograph, etc.—couldn't we?'

Corrie nodded. She began to feel better. How nice Hugh was. And without being in the least priggish—or pompous—he was such a *good* person. He had managed to instil some of his own courage into her. The darkness of her despair receded. The light returned to her eyes.

A few minutes later they were driving along the winding road up, and up, to the village above Camacha.

In Poiso they called at the factory where so much wicker-work was handled. Great bundles of willows were stacked here, then woven by the natives, some of them only children, sitting cross-legged in the coolness of rooms that rarely saw the sun. In ordinary circumstances Corrie would have been interested in all the baskets, or hampers, and the attractive wicker souvenirs. But just now her only ambition was to question the husband and wife who owned the place.

Their answers were disheartening.

They looked at the photographs and shook their heads. No such gentleman had come in to buy things here, or even to look at them.

Corrie and Hugh repeated the formula questions all through Poiso—at the one little shop, then the cottages wherever the owners could speak English or they could find an interpreter. No one had seen Martin Ashley, besides which most of the inhabitants had already received brief visits from the Funchal *policia*.

Hugh feared for Corrie. The sun was going down. In a moment it would be cooler, and she looked tired and fragile all of a sudden. He suggested that they should go home.

'Can't we try one more village?' she said piteously. He found it difficult to deny her anything.

'I'll ask the driver what he thinks our next move should be.'

The chauffeur smiled, shrugged his shoulders and pointed to the sky. Clouds were gathering. A mist was forming farther down the road. He thought it wiser for them to descend to Funchal. It could get quite thick up here in no time at all, he observed.

Hugh turned to Corrie, 'I'll bring you up

here again tomorrow and we'll comb the other villages.'

'Very well,' she answered in a low voice.

They drove to Camacha again. Now and then they struck a curling mist and Corrie had to agree that the weather looked ominous. But there were breaks in the clouds now and then, when they could see the view again and the enchantment of the apricot and plum blossom already decorating the little trees. When Hugh pointed out these things, Corrie listlessly agreed that it was all marvellous. She forced herself to show an interest in the old roads, made perhaps a thousand years ago. The small stones were like rounded, flattened cobbles, crushed into the ground.

One or two cars passed by but they saw no one save a few shepherds. The road was deserted.

Corrie's mind kept dragging her back to the mystery of Martin. If he had walked up here, where had he gone? *Where was he now?* Had he vanished in one of these mists? Could he have fallen down a ravine? Yet she knew that the police were still searching and had so far found neither a wounded man nor a dead body.

It was the awful *nothingness* that crushed her.

Violetta was waiting for them when the two young people came back, only to tell her it had been no good.

But she was once an actress and a gay one, and old though she was now, she refused to play the part of a desperately disappointed grandmother. She put on a smiling face, took both Corrie and Hugh by the arm and led them towards the bar.

'I'm so terribly sorry, darlings. But what you both need now is a drink. Come and tell me exactly what you did. Corrie, darling, you look all-in. Would you like to have dinner in bed?'

Corrie shook her head.

'Nothing I'd like less, dear Violetta. I'll be all right. Don't for goodness sake worry about *me*.'

'Well, we do worry about you, don't we?' Lady Grey-Ewing gave Hugh one of her coquettish glances. He responded gallantly.

'Seeing you revives us both, I assure you, Lady Grey-Ewing.'

She smiled gaily. 'Violetta—everybody calls me that. Now, children, what shall it be?'

'Sherry for me,' said Corrie.

'Whisky and soda for me,' said Hugh. An unusual drink for him at cocktail time but he, as well as Corrie, was suffering from fatigue. He used to be a chap who could walk ten miles without blinking, he thought somewhat dejectedly. It was this leg that still ached after undue exercise.

Over their drinks, Corrie and Hugh gave Violetta an account of their journey to Camacha and Poiso. Violetta's blue eyes

107

saddened but she spoke brightly, 'Never mind, darlings. We never really had a lot of hope, did we? I don't see how the young man by the mimosa tree *could* have been our Martin. Otherwise you would certainly have found someone in one of the villages who would have seen him.'

Corrie lit a cigarette. She thought of the *Incencio* tree—of the little church—and of her prayers. She knew exactly how deeply Martin's grandmother must be suffering, and she was *so* brave. Not for the first time Corrie was ashamed of her own emotions which too easily weighed her down. She made an attempt to overcome this.

'We are going to have another look round tomorrow morning, Violetta darling. There are two other villages. I seem to have got a taste for private detection. You see—' she gave a little laugh—'these police just don't know enough about Martin—I mean—I can pounce on any details, can't I? I'm dying to get on with more of it tomorrow.'

'If it's a fine morning,' said Violetta, I'll come up in the car with you. I can sit and doze if I want to, while you two young things walk around. I'd enjoy the drive and seeing those mountain villages again. Bill and I used to picnic up there. You find some wonderful places, and fabulous views. In fact, if you like, we'll tell the hotel to pack us up one of their nice lunches and sit on the grass and eat up

108

there, instead of filing into the restaurant down here—particularly if it's a warm fine day.'

'That sound good to me,' said Hugh.

Corrie continued to put on her own little act of being happy and hopeful rather than cast perpetual gloom on the party. How lucky she was not only to have a friend like Hugh but this adorable old lady who was Martin's flesh and blood and so dear to him.

It was only when she went to bed that night that the fog of her despair closed in on her and once alone she turned her face to the pillow, gripping it hard with both hands and at last allowed the hot tears to flow down her cheeks.

'Martin,' she said his name aloud, *'Martin,* wherever you are, come back to me. Come back soon. I can't bear this pain.'

CHAPTER EIGHT

Two weeks later Corrie sat writing a letter to Ann.

Another rather grim week. Still no sign of my darling. He just seems to have vanished off the face of the earth. I feel I've been away from you and the old life at Brabett's Farm for several years instead of only a month. I must say it has been the worst four weeks of my life. I couldn't have got through it but for Violetta—she's been absolutely marvellous and never lets her age get in the way of her helping and cheering me. But I know she is beginning to despair, herself.

Thanks awfully for your last letter. It came today. I'm glad all goes well with the horses and that life at home continues in its own tranquil way.

I am still living, as you can imagine, dear Ann, in my nightmare. We have had one or two clues but they've led to nothing. We put an advert in the local paper offering a reward for any useful information, and got none to begin with. We by-passed the police and toured the mountain villages ourselves. Difficult though the language is, I have learned enough Portuguese to ask one or two simple questions now. But no luck. Hugh Aylmer has been a tower of strength. He was supposed to be out here to convalesce after his accident, but he hasn't spared himself trying to help us. I told you about his tragedy. Thank goodness his leg is better. He's driven us around almost every town and village within miles. We finally decided that Martin hadn't got lost in Funchal. So we have been going further afield. We had one marvellous moment when a farmer turned up and said he had seen Martin in a place called the Pousada Dos Vinháticos which is a rest house about 2,000 or 3,000 feet up. People go there because it has such marvellous panoramic views. The farmer was sure he saw Martin among some other tourists. He spoke English and was fair and from the description the farmer gave we were full of hope. This Englishman fainted. A Portuguese woman told the farmer he was ill and an ambulance came and took him to hospital.

Violetta and I were sure that it was a case of lost memory so we rushed madly to this hospital. Oh Ann! It was such a bitter blow when a nun took me to the bedside and I looked down and found it wasn't Martin at all. His family were staying at Camara de Lobos and they had already seen him and were going to fetch him the next day. Most of the people round Funchal have been wonderful. English people who live out here and who have heard all about our trouble have asked V. and me to drinks and meals. They know the country and the language, and are anxious to help at any time, but they remain as baffled as we are. So it goes on!

Hugh Aylmer has flown back to

England. He didn't want to leave us but he has a book on the stocks that he has got to finish and deliver to his publisher, and other business to attend to. He said on the phone that he had been to see Sir Paul Mullins and how grieved and worried they all are about Martin. V. is now talking of renting a villa for the rest of the spring and summer rather than go home. We would both be so terribly worried, and have to keep communicating with Madeira. If we find a suitable place, I'll phone you at once. Much as I want to see you, dear Ann, I couldn't bear to leave this island for the present. I won't leave till I am *sure* that Martin will never come back. And that would indeed be the end of that long dark corridor in my nightmare, wouldn't it?

She had written this letter in the hotel library. The atmosphere in there was quite soothing and peaceful. Martin's job was in the book world. It seemed a link.

She felt so tired. So changed from the girl she used to be. She sometimes wondered if that Corrie who had set out for Madeira with stars in her eyes, and a being overflowing with happiness, had ever existed.

Perhaps the worst part of the strain was having to put on a good show—in the way that

Violetta seemed able to do more easily. Smile and talk. Talk and smile. It was anguish for Corrie to discuss her fiancé with so many people—virtual strangers. The disappearance of Martin Ashley had by now become quite famous. It was 'news' out here. She had only to enter a shop and some kindly, sympathetic Portuguese would ask, 'Has the *senhor* come back? Have you not heard anything?'

And all Corrie could do was to shake her head and move on. The pain was at times intolerable, although she was a long way past crying in front of strangers.

A week ago Ann had sent her cuttings from two local newspapers. Each had photographs of Corrie and Martin and covered his strange story.

YOUNG ENGLISHMAN'S DISAPPEARANCE IN MADEIRA.

Martin Ashley, aged 25, book-salesman, who had travelled to Lisbon for his firm—the publishing house of Horton & Mullins—arranged to meet his fiancée, Miss Corisande Gilroy, at the famous Reid's Hotel. He was known to have arrived and left his luggage in his room, after which he went out. Since then he has not been seen or heard of. Miss Gilroy arrived a few hours later and has been working with the police in Funchal, trying to trace her fiancé. She is at present staying at Reid's with Mr. Ashley's grandmother, Lady Grey-Ewing, once known as Violetta Maye—famous musical comedy actress of the 20's. The police in Funchal are continuing the search.

There was one more cutting from a Sussex evening paper which printed Corrie's photograph as well as Martin's. Ann had said in one of her letters that she had been asked for it.

Corrie was unable to control her tears when she first looked at those photographs, side by side; both so gay, so radiantly happy. A real tragedy had struck at her life, and Violetta's. But all too well Corrie realised that life must go on. It was useless looking back.

She spent a lot of time answering letters. She had had a particularly nice one from her former employer, Christine Taylor. Everyone at *Green Fingers* sent little notes of sympathy. Gradually there built up in Corrie a kind of resentment that anyone should write this way—just as though Martin had already died—but she had to get over it and reply with thanks and gratitude.

Lady Grey-Ewing, if anything, received more letters than Corrie because of her vast number of theatrical contacts, both past and present. And, after all, Martin was her flesh and blood. Everyone knew what he meant to *her.* She told Corrie that the story of Martin's disappearance had become quite a topic of conversation in London. Anyone who had met him wrote to Violetta. One of his closest men friends—a crime writer—had even offered to come out and help solve this mystery. Violetta consulted Corrie over this and they both agreed they didn't want anyone to take it for granted that a crime was involved—or even an abduction. There was absolutely nothing to suggest either of these things. In the eyes of the law, Martin remained simply a 'missing person'.

Corrie now left the library and took her letters downstairs. She needed some more stamps. It was considerably warmer today than when she first arrived in Funchal. It was so brilliant and beautiful, especially the intense blue of the sea—she could hardly bear it. All the beauty of it meant so little without *him.*

She had arranged to meet Violetta in the main hall They were driving with a local house-agent to inspect a furnished villa with a garden. It had just come on the market, and Violetta could rent it indefinitely.

It was not that Violetta believed it would be too long before they got news of Martin, but she and Corrie agreed that much as they liked Reid's they didn't want to stay at any hotel. They were too much in the public eye. Too many strangers talked to them against their will. They would be better, quieter, in their own home.

Lady Grey-Ewing was all ready and waiting for Corrie—a trim little figure in a white suit and panama hat with a flowing chiffon scarf. She was carrying a pale blue parasol which matched her scarf. As ever, she looked young and elegant. Corrie always felt better just for looking at her.

Lady Grey-Ewing smiled at Corrie. 'Hello, darling. The agent's waiting outside. Are you quite ready?'

'Yes. I'll just get some stamps if I may and post this letter to Ann.'

'It's going to be really hot today,' remarked her ladyship.

'I'll try and get in a swim before lunch,' said Corrie laconically.

They moved out into the sunshine. Corrie put a huge peasant straw hat on her head. She wore a short cotton dress. Her face and arms and throat were brown. She had done a fair amount of swimming and sunbathing. But Lady Grey-Ewing sighed as she looked at the girl. If only she could sleep better and eat more. The suntan didn't deceive the old lady. Corrie's cheeks were hollowed and her eyes were sunken. She had told her last night, gently but firmly, that she mustn't let herself go, she looked too fragile. She must keep well for Martin's sake, if not for her own. He wouldn't want to come back and find a little skeleton, Violetta joked. Which brought a faint smile to Corrie's sad mouth, but she had no appetite and couldn't sleep for more than an hour or two without waking up and finding it difficult to get to sleep again.

She drank a lot of fresh fruit juice these days. She always seemed thirsty—as though she suffered from a kind of strange inner fever. That was how she really felt. She knew it. The tension and fear of losing Martin forever was consuming her.

The Funchal house-agent, a pleasant young man, drove them to a white villa with red tiles about two miles away from the hotel in a less inhabited part of Funchal. The entrance was marked by two stone pillars bearing a plaque with the name *Casa da Turna.*

Violetta had already seen a coloured photograph of the place. It had reminded her of a villa she and her adored husband had once lived in on the Côte d'Azur long ago. Too long, she thought sadly today, although she chatted gaily to Corrie.

'I hope it'll be as nice inside as it looks, darling, and suitable for us. The great thing about it is that the owners are willing to let us have it as long as we need it. *And* they're leaving their Portuguese cook-housekeeper, Maria. Thoroughly recommended.'

'It sounds great,' said Corrie.

But her mind flew to Room 91X at the hotel It had remained locked and uninhabited since the day Martin had left his belongings there

117

and vanished. There was still so much talk about it, that the manager with great delicacy had kept it unoccupied for the present.

The Casa da Turna lay a little farther back from the road than most of them, and one entered it through beautiful wrought-iron gates flanked by oleanders. There were striped blue and white canopies shading the windows. The white walls were embroidered with deep purple bougainvillaea. A lot of thought and taste had been expended here, Violetta and Corrie agreed, and the garden was charming, with long beds of blue and pink hydrangeas, glorious English roses, pale tall lilies, a number of fine tropical trees and bushes, and the inevitable green, feathery palms.

The agent began to extol the beauties of this place. Built, he said, about thirty years ago, the upper windows had remarkable views of the sea. Owned by a French couple, the Comte and Comtesse de Maudlie who were now on a world tour.

Violetta cut short the man's dialogue by announcing sweetly that she was sure that if the inside was as attractive as the outside she would take the Casa da Turna.

Corrie thought what anguish the pin-pricks of memory can become. Mere trifles affecting sight or sound could take one back to a past that was once so precious and seemed now to be fading with terrifying speed into the limbo of lost things.

As they walked up the steps to the entrance of the villa, she noted the fantastic blue of the magnificent agapanthus, growing in great wooden tubs on either side of the portico. She remembered a day when she and Martin had spent a few happy hours at Kew—both of them fond of flowers—and had stopped in front of one of these giant plants. She had asked Martin if he knew what it was called. He had smiled and shaken his head. They asked a passing gardener, after which Corrie had never forgotten the name. *Agapanthus.* Here in Madeira she had grown used to seeing them. They grew so profusely in many places.

She didn't know whether to feel relieved or sad when Martin's grandmother, after close inspection, agreed to take the villa for two months, with the option to continue.

True, the Casa da Tuma was beautiful. Furnished with great taste. Entirely panelled in light-coloured polished wood, beautifully carved, it contained some beautiful French furniture, most of it walnut. The Comtesse's bedroom was glorious. French windows opened on to a flat roof with a marvellous view of the sea. The beautiful four-poster Empire bed, with its long pale-blue silk curtains, enchanted Violetta.

The rest of the villa was in keeping. So (as Corrie mentioned dryly) was the cost of renting this lovely home. But Violetta seemed determined to delve into her income whether the escudoes remained in their favour or not.

'Prices are going up—and who *cares!* I'm eighty-one next year and I want to get rid of some of my money before death duties annihilate it,' she said gaily. 'Besides, you will enjoy it here and so will I.'

Corrie answered mechanically, 'Yes, it will be marvellous. I can just picture you asleep in that gorgeous Empire bed.'

But for herself she wanted nothing in particular.

Somehow she even felt depressed at the thought of leaving Reid's. She clung to this place where she and Martin had arranged to meet. But she said nothing to Violetta who was delighted with the Casa da Turna. The old actress had always enjoyed moving around. Before they left the villa she interviewed Maria—the little apple-cheeked Portuguese woman who was the Comtesse's cook-housekeeper. She seemed perfect. She spoke French. So did Violetta—there would be no staff problem. Even the old gardener had gallantly come forward with a bunch of the special English roses which he grew, and presented them to the sweet petite old English lady before she drove away.

At the end of April they moved from the hotel and took up residence in the Casa da Turna. The manager himself saw them off. He could not have been more sympathetic. He deeply regretted, he said, that their visit to his hotel had been marred by such a tragic occurrence and hoped sincerely that Mr. Ashley would soon be traced. In addition he assured the two ladies that Reid's was ever open to them and he hoped they would come and have a meal there sometimes and use the lido if and when they so desired.

There followed a further fortnight of mingled hope and despair for both Martin's grandmother and the girl he had been going to marry. Life slowed down a bit once they were settled in the beautiful sun-bathed villa. They enjoyed the tranquillity. Violetta also hired a car and chauffeur so that they had daily transport.

Corrie welcomed their excursions. But wherever they went, Martin was uppermost in her mind. She strained her eyes, watching everybody, anybody in the many little villages. They inevitably returned to the Casa with a sense of failure and disappointment. They could not find any trace of Martin, and the police had not been in touch with them lately.

Many letters continued to reach Corrie from friends and distant relatives who had seen the news about Martin. Strangers wrote to her, too. Some of them who had suffered in a similar way after the disappearance of a loved relative or friend. The letters telling Corrie they had never found the missing person, Corrie would half-read, then tear in pieces. She didn't want to know. But one she kept which gave her new hope. It was from a man whose wife had actually vanished during their honeymoon in Switzerland. He had passed through the same anguish of waiting interminably without news—then in the end, she was found

She had gone out alone to find gentian plants, while he wrote letters. She had not returned to the hotel. It appeared that she had a fall, injured her head and temporarily lost her memory. She was discovered by an old woman who was not actually insane but of diminished responsibility. She gave the girl shelter in a remote mountain but but failed to report the fact that she had found the English girl.

Corrie was given a graphic description of the old Swiss woman's kindness to his wife. She had nursed and fed her and seemed to have enjoyed her company. Then suddenly, as often happened, the girl's memory returned. She ran to the nearest village and telephoned to her husband. So the honeymoon couple were reunited. The man finished his letter:

'This could be the case with *your* fiancé. My wife and I both wish you good luck and may your story end as happily as ours.'

At once Corrie showed this letter to Violetta. They rushed down to the police Inspector with it. He examined it closely but shook his head. He was sure the Swiss case was not synonymous with Mr. Ashley's. It was so

122

different here. Everybody for miles around Funchal had been questioned. And the letter said this girl had fallen into a shallow gully and hit her head. She had lain senseless until the old woman found her and dragged her out. The police had never inspected the hut. Often the mad old woman kept her doors and windows locked and barred, and the little wooden chalet was mistaken for one of those ski-huts which are not used at all in the summer. No one had even been near. They might eventually have done so but it was no time, really, before the missing girl reappeared.

Here, this was not at all the case; Funchal had been combed, the Inspector assured both Corrie and Violetta.

It had taken Corrie a long time to recover from that disappointment. Yet the story of the missing bride haunted her. Wasn't it possible Martin, too, had had an accident and lost his memory and that he, too, would be found?

Corrie found it some comfort to write and tell Hugh all that was happening. He always answered her letters—sometimes he telephoned her. She appreciated that. She seemed to feel his quiet strength and sympathy coming across the miles to give her heart. He refused to allow her to give up hope. When she told him about the incident in Switzerland, he agreed that Martin might very well be suffering from loss of memory.

But the fact remained that he did not appear to be on the island—dead or alive.

Hugh always firmly denied the possibility of his death. 'You must never think it, Corrie dear. Go on hoping, for God's sake.'

Immediately after that call, Corrie sat down and wrote a letter to him apologising for her weakness, calling herself a coward. She often felt that she was one. And as time went on, the less did she seem able to believe that Martin was still in this world.

She was now corresponding regularly with Liz, Hugh's sister.

Liz, so happy with her husband and baby, was full of sympathy and concern for her old schoolfriend. She sent Corrie little coloured snapshots of the baby. She tried hard to comfort her—to reassure her that one day she too, would find happiness with Martin.

Sitting in the beautiful shady gardens of the Casa da Turna, a pad on her knee, pen in hand, Corrie often tried to write in a more cheerful vein to Ann, or Christine Taylor, both close friends—nearly always with the same result. She could find nothing to say. She would close her eyes and begin to feel tense and emotional—so much so she could almost feel Martin's hand upon her head and hear his voice calling her name. This, of course, ended in floods of tears which she had hastily to wipe away before she could let Violetta see her. She was so good to her, so generous. Because she

124

was still 'Violetta Maye' in her own mind, she was naturally gay and sociable. She went out to little lunch or tea parties—invited by friends of the Comtesse, who were residents in Madeira, or friends she had made at the hotel.

'You just can't buy Madeira cake like they give you there!' she would say to Corrie. 'Do come with me, darling.'

Sometimes Corrie did so just to please her, but she felt less and less inclined to meet or talk to strangers. There was only one topic of conversation she really enjoyed. In fact, occasionally she even called at the *Policia de Segurança Publica* to have a talk with the gallant, voluble Inspector who was never at a loss for words and who so admired the beautiful, tragic young lady from England. With him she could discuss the mystery of Martin endlessly and it comforted her even though he could give no further information. But at least she was helped by the knowledge that the Inspector and his men were still looking for Martin. He gave her his word that they had not altogether relinquished the search.

CHAPTER NINE

Towards the end of May, Hugh returned to Madeira. His mother was back at her country home and he had spent most of his weekends with her. He had finished his novel. He telephoned Corrie to say that he could do with a change of air and had decided to fly over to the island to see them, whereupon Violetta immediately seized the telephone and insisted that Hugh should stay at the Casa.

'We have five bedrooms, dear boy, and only use two of them. And we have a good maid. No need to spend money unnecessarily. Please be my guest.'

At first he protested—then agreed that it would be delightful.

It certainly gave Corrie a sense of warmth and pleasure to see Liz's brother again. When he arrived, walking with only the smallest limp and without his stick, she gave him both her hands. They exchanged a brotherly-sisterly kiss.

'How marvellous to see you walking like this!' she exclaimed.

'I'm fine. And you look like a little Indian. I can see you have had plenty of sun. It's very warm over here. Your colour makes me feel whiter than white. I can't say that we're any of us sunbathing at home right now, but we are hoping for a fine June.'

Violetta was out. Corrie called to Maria to bring tea. She and Hugh sat and talked together, exchanging news, in the green arbour facing the house. Hugh thought the whole place perfect. And, of course, the look of the countryside was changing now that it was nearly June. On the way from the airport he had noted that there were fewer spring flowers. An English summer had come to Madeira. The long beds, so gaily decorating the town centre, were gay with canna plants-their bright yellow and red and orange flowers nestling between the ornamental leaves. He didn't particularly care for them but he loved the more attractive flowers here in this beautiful garden. The oleanders made a charming background. The jacaranda trees were full out at this time of year; the arum lilies still lifting their pure graceful heads. And he recognised roses from those in his mother's English garden, and a great bed of tall mauve, and pink, and creamy-white stocks, worthy of Kew.

But he was shocked by the sight of Corrie— the girl he had come so far to see again and who for some reason he had been thinking about ever since he left her. It had surprised him, in fact, to find how often her beautiful haunted eyes had looked at him from the pages of his book—how often his proof-correcting had come to a halt because he couldn't concentrate on it. He kept worrying about Corisande (yes, he liked her full name— one day he would ask her if he could call her that, instead of Corrie). Already he was determined that the heroine in his next book would be a lovely tawny-headed graceful creature like this girl and she would be called Corisande.

He was shocked to see her so painfully thin. She looked to him as though she had lost far too much weight and those wonderful golden eyes seemed far too large for her face.

She was fretting, poor sweet. He knew that. He, himself, had in fact come to an end of hope. He tried to avoid the subject of Martin but of course Corrie plunged into it. He listened gravely and sympathetically to the many stories she had to tell. How she and Violetta had often rushed to find Martin here or there. How all the hopes had faded again.

While they were sitting there, smoking their cigarettes, Corrie steered the conversation to Hugh.

'What's the new book all about? And what's the title?'

'The title so far agreed is *Raise High the Banner*. A great deal of it is about Henry V's wife, Queen Catherine. I've always rather fancied her,' he added with a laugh.

Corrie had no time to answer. At this precise moment a car drove in through the gates of the villa. Out stepped the unexpected figure of the Inspector. He came quickly towards the two who were sitting in the arbour, his buttons glittering in the sun. His handsome face was alert and he seemed excited. He saluted them both.

'Ah! Mees Gilroy. Meester Aylmer— pleasant to see you back in Madeira, sir. I am so happy to come with good news. We have a clue—the most important one yet, for it might indeed lead us to the whereabouts of the *Senhor* Ashley, and establish the fact, at least, that he lives.'

Corrie sprang to her feet. She was white under the deceptive brown. Hugh stood close to her, gripping her hand, feeling her trembling.

'Steady,' he whispered. 'Wait for it. Don't be too excited.'

She was speechless for a second, then spoke to the Inspector.

'What—*what* have you heard? For God's sake, quickly, *please!'*

She listened while he told her, holding hard on to Hugh's hand and glad of his presence once again.

The Inspector explained that he had at Lady Grey-Ewing's request, put up notices to the effect that a reward would be paid for any information about Martin Ashley—times, date, anything that could enlighten the police and lead them to the missing man, be he dead or alive.

129

A young shepherd who tended sheep up the mountainside beyond Poiso had come with this story. He went to the wedding of a cousin who lived not far from his village. He had a crippled foot and only watched the dancing, and listened to the local guitarist who sang with romantic fervour. He took no part in the celebration but he said, practically everybody there were friends or relations. Suddenly there passed by him a rather striking young man he did not know with dark longish hair, a nut-brown face and a dark beard. When questioned further about this the shepherd remembered that the stranger was wearing a white vest with short sleeves and red coarse linen trousers. Nothing unusual about that. Most of the young men in the villages went around in native costume. The girls seized the chance to dress up, most of them in wide black skirts with coloured tops and lace-frilled blouses and coloured ribbons. Sometimes they wore their hair with long plaits and put on little tricorn hats with white pompoms. The voluble shepherd had described these girls and Corrie listened impatiently. Then he spoke of the man who walked alone, with a long black cheroot in his mouth. He had obviously intrigued the shepherd. He had eyes of a strange light colour and somehow the shepherd found his features familiar.

When he went home that night, he looked at a news-cutting he had kept, of the police offering a reward for news of the Englishman who had vanished months ago from Funchal. But it was the photograph which intrigued the shepherd. And because he and his parents were poor and needed money he had gone down to see the *Policia de Segurança Publica.*

Corrie listened, her heart thudding. She exchanged glances with Hugh.

'Can there possibly be anything in it?'

Hugh pursued his lips thoughtfully, then shook his head. 'Not in my mind. Your fiancé was—is—fair and this young man was dark, the newspapers can print awful reproductions of photographs. They are always misleading. I don't suppose this fellow really looked like Martin at all.'

Corrie turned to the Inspector. 'Why do you think this such an important clue?' she demanded.

'The shepherd seemed so confident, Mees Gilroy, that the faces—the eyes—were similar. I thought it worth your investigation.'

Corrie nodded. 'Of course. Of course. We will see the boy. You can interpret any questions put to him. We will go to this village—did you say Gerāno?'

The Inspector bowed. *'Sim.'* He forgot himself, saying 'yes' in his own language.

Corrie decided to drive immediately higher up the mountains to Gerāno. It was built like so many of the villages here at the mouth of a ravine.

'A place of no importance,' the Inspector described it.

It was inhabited mainly by men and women who cultivated the vines for local wine. And inevitably also by the many who dry the osiers and sell them to manufacturers who weave them into furniture. They seemed incredibly poor up there.

The Inspector added that although there was so little money in the mountain villages and many of the houses were mere huts— when there was a wedding in the family, relatives and friends contributed and all these escudos, when collected, provided a real feast for the bride and bridegroom.

'This man still doesn't seem to me to resemble Martin, really,' said Corrie, having listened to all the Inspector told her. 'Actually I've seen quite a number of women and children in Funchal with light eyes. That surely is not so rare?'

The Inspector agreed but stuck to his theory that the shepherd's information could prove valuable.

'The average Portuguese,' he said, 'have either fat faces if they have grown old and stout, or angular ones with high cheekbones and pointed chins, when young. The shepherd was insistent that the structure of this stranger's face was similar to that of the missing gentleman.'

Corrie relapsed into silence.

But a few minutes later, in the Inspector's car with the faithful Hugh beside her, even before the new clue had been followed up, her hopes had evaporated. The Inspector and his driver sat in front. Corrie at the back, with Hugh, whispered, 'I'm not going to get too excited today. You see, Hugh, I'm becoming more sensible and I feel it's on the cards that our friend just wants to prove that the police are still making efforts on our behalf.'

'That's the best way to take it,' said Hugh gently. 'Listening to what our "friend", as you call him, has to say, my own conclusion is that this one is a bit of a red herring.'

Feeling lethargic, Corrie sat back and looked silently at the unsurpassed grandeur of the mountain scenery while they climbed the curving road.

For a long time now she had thought how wonderful it would have been to have had Martin with her to enjoy the almost tropical beauty. But higher up still, the scene became less exotic. They passed long stretches of wickedly-spiked, giant cactus, and strange trees with grotesque branches, to which she could not put a name.

They by-passed Gerãno, calling first of all at a neighbouring village—the home of the young shepherd.

This time, Corrie felt extraordinarily lacking in her old fire and verve. She even asked Hugh to do the interrogating.

'Just ask him everything you can.'

'Of course I will.'

And Hugh did his best. But the brown-skinned almond-eyed shepherd was not very enlightening. He talked a lot but what he had to say would be of no real interest to Corrie. However, he struck stubbornly to his theory that the *face* of the stranger could be Martin's.

'But the *senhor* had no beard, remember?' Corrie put in at one point of the conversation. 'You are sure this young man was bearded?'

'Yes. But it was his eyes I noticed. He was not Portuguese,' reiterated the boy and shrugged, realising perhaps that he was not going to get the reward.

The interview ended in the Inspector withdrawing from the scene. He even felt a trifle annoyed with himself because he had raised Mees Gilroy's hopes. Perhaps it was absurd to suppose that a man with dark hair and a dark beard could be the fair-haired Englishman. And as he told the shepherd sharply, there *were* Portuguese with light eyes, blue, and grey. He had wasted the *senhor's* time.

'Maybe I was too anxious to help, Mees Gilroy,' he added apologetically to Corrie, and wiped the perspiration from his handsome face.

'You are very kind. Is this all we can do now we are here?' she asked.

'No, we can go on to Gerão. The shepherd

134

has given me the address of the bride's mother and father. We can ask them if they know the name and whereabouts of this man who had attracted the notice of the shepherd.'

Corrie agreed, but she was inclined now to believe that the whole project was futile.

Hugh thought so but he was impressed by the change in Corrie. Since he had last seen her she had become so much more resigned and philosophic. And, as he well knew through his own bitter experience, the pain and grief of loss does diminish in time. Corrie was learning to live with her pain, which Hugh had also had to do.

Still, the search was not to be abandoned.

They found Gerāno an attractive little village with small pinkish-coloured houses. Outside, women sat stitching at their intricate embroideries and men wove their osiers. Long canopies of green vine gave them shelter from the sun which could at times be too fierce up here for the workers.

The Inspector found the couple whose daughter had just been married. Again the result was negative. They did not even remember having noticed a dark-bearded young man in red and white, and most of the youths walked around smoking cheroots at a wedding party.

The girl's father suddenly said something to the Inspector who turned to Corrie.

'He says he *does* remember one man in red

and white with the dark hair and beard.'

'Can we see him?'

'No. He was a stranger—unknown to them although they think he was related to some girl who danced with him.'

Corrie looked bitterly disappointed. She wanted to see the man. But Hugh gently dissuaded her.

'It will only be distressing for you, and I think we are wasting time. I feel we're being led down a blind alley. It's all rather wishful thinking. Martin is *not* dark or black-bearded. He is fair and clean-shaven, and why would he dance at the wedding unless he knew either bride or bridegroom?'

'I agree,' Corrie nodded, and gave a sigh that seemed to be torn from her very heart. 'It's all become rather ridiculous. I will make no further enquiries.'

The Inspector once more apologised for having dragged her up here for nothing. Corrie thanked him for his concern. They were driven down the mountainside to Funchal again. When they finally joined Violetta at the Casa and recounted the occurrence of the afternoon, she gave Corrie one of her sympathetic little pats on the hand and said; 'It certainly has been another wild goose chase, you poor darling. But at least it shows the police are still working on your behalf. The poor Inspector was a little too anxious to help.'

'Yes,' said Corrie sadly.

Hugh looked at Lady Grey-Ewing. Violetta read his thoughts and clapped her hands for Maria.

'Time we all had a little drink,' she said brightly. Corrie, as always, was ashamed of her despair when she looked at or listened to Martin's grandmother.

'You're so marvellous, darling Violetta.'

'Seconded,' said Hugh.

'And I'm so pleased to have you back with us, dear Hugh,' Lady Grey-Ewing beamed at him 'It will be nice for Corrie to have someone to take her about and not always be with an old lady.'

'Old lady be darned!' said Hugh, laughing.

During the week that followed there was no further mention of the shepherd affair.

It was just a case of mistaken identity. Perhaps, Corrie thought, it wasn't such a good idea after all—offering a reward, for it wasn't the only false clue they followed up. only to see it end in disappointment. And each time Corrie felt the unbearable bitterness of it and wondered if she would ever *ever* reach the end of the night-black corridor. She must return to it again and again.

Martin's grandmother watched Corrie a little more closely than usual during the week that followed.

She could well see that Corrie was strained. Yet beneath the layer of emotion and the occasional display of weakness she was still her old determined self—not likely to crack. Violetta had a great admiration for Corrie as well as warm affection. She had never criticised her in the past because the tears were rather close to the surface. Lately, in fact, she had noticed that Corrie did not cry much. She was making an effort to accept this awful hiatus in her life with more fortitude than perhaps she had shown at first. Violetta, who under her own mask of gaiety might seem a little shallow, was a very real woman who understood the anguish of love—and loss. Never in all the years that she had been a widow had she forgotten Bill—her charming husband. He had made life heaven for her. And also in Violetta's theatrical world she knew only too well how many marital mistakes were made; she understood the suffering because of the decay of passion, the passing of love, and finally, even of comradeship—then separation—divorce—the end of loving. Divorce was so much too easy and frequent in an actor's world. Old though she was now, Violetta still in her heart remained that young beautiful idolised actress who had become a 'pin-up' and a model for thousands of would-be musical comedy stars, and who knew how necessary it was to a woman to love and be loved.

She could realise to the full what this terrible affair had done to Corrie. She, herself, frequently felt as though there was a dead weight on her mind. Martin was her dearly beloved. Vanessa her daughter didn't need her love—had never wanted it. All the maternal warmth in Violetta was given to her grandson. Sometimes when she woke up in the night and thought about him she shed the tears she never allowed others to see. She was not as optimistic now about him coming back as she pretended to be. She had really begun to fear he was dead. Why or how he died, who knew? But one day they would find out.

She was glad that Hugh Aylmer had come back to Funchal and was with them at the Casa da Turna. Obviously he cheered Corrie up—it was good for her to have his youthful company. Violetta thought him very wise as well as attractive. There was no nonsense about Hugh. Violetta was quite, sure, too, that Corrie's feelings for him were on the most platonic level. It would have been impossible for her to transfer her love for Martin to another man—certainly not so soon. But both she and Hugh had suffered a bitter loss, so in a queer way they were linked and a moral support for each other.

Violetta had never liked a trio. She made it her business to be very social and busy for the next ten days while Hugh was around. She encouraged him to take Corrie out alone for several day-excursions to see some of the famous beauty-spots on the island.

So in Violetta's hired car, and while she was

entertaining her friends, Hugh and Corrie went out sightseeing. They enjoyed Ribeiro Frio—one of the most beautiful valleys on the island. From there they walked to the furthermost point where they saw what they thought the finest view in Madeira. On another day they left Funchal for an all-day trip to Porto Santo—the Holy Port—for Hugh, the writer, was deeply interested in the local history. Christopher Columbus had once lived in Porto Santo. He had taken to himself a Portuguese bride and died on the flower-filled island he had discovered.

In order to distract Corrie from her unhappy thoughts, Hugh arranged that she should take a pad and Biro and make notes which he dictated. He decided now that he would write a book about the great Columbus.

Corrie enjoyed this outing particularly, and listening to Hugh as he talked, she understood what had made him a success as a novelist. He had a vivid imagination and an observant eye. She lost herself for a time in the interesting atmosphere of helping him prepare his book.

'I am learning a lot I didn't know before. It's most instructive being your temporary secretary,' she smiled at him as they drove away from the coast that evening.

They had watched the fishing. They had talked to the natives who produced the grapes for which Porto Santo was famous, and interviewed a Portuguese gamekeeper who

140

preserved the wonderful rare birds that abounded on this small island.

As they neared Funchal again, Hugh felt satisfied that this sort of entertainment was really relaxing for Corrie. She seemed almost happy today and there was more colour in her thin tanned face. In one of the villages he stopped to buy her a big spray of orchids. These wonderful flowers never seemed to be out of season. Corrie insisted on going halves with Hugh when he bought some more orchids for Violetta.

Once back at the Casa, she told Violetta how much she had enjoyed the whole day and described the lunch they had at a new big up-to-date hotel in Porto Santo where they were offered special spring-water which had curative qualities.

'There were all kinds of people drinking it. When we looked at them we judged their average age to be about ninety,' Corrie laughed. 'We felt very young and wondered why we were drinking the waters ourselves and what was wrong with us.'

'No doubt it'll prove a preventative rather than a cure and we shall have nothing wrong by the time we leave Madeira,' put in Hugh. He could hardly remember having heard Corrie laugh before. When, for a moment he was alone with Violetta he made reference to that sudden gaiety.

The old lady smiled and nodded. 'My dear

boy, you're so good for her. I do hope you'll extend your visit. If there's no need for you to go back to England, please stay on at the Casa. You can see how much better it is for poor Corrie to have a friend like yourself to take her out and about, rather than be so much alone with me. I can do so little for her.'

'I'll see how things go at home, but it's most kind of you,' he said. 'I can think of nothing nicer than staying here a bit longer. But don't say you do "so little" You do a lot for *everybody.*'

Violetta sighed, her eyes suddenly shadowed.

'Oh, Hugh, are we *ever* going to see my grandson again? It seems so long since he disappeared. What do you really think?'

'I am naturally worried but the only possible thing we can do is to carry on and believe he will come back. We don't *know* that he's dead. Let's try to think of him at least as alive.'

Violetta took off her big glasses and wiped them. Her lashes were wet. Somehow this nice boy reminded her of Martin. He was the same type in some ways, even though physically so different. Hugh, the novelist, was the quieter, more self-contained of the two. Yet there was a gentleness in him that she had always found in Martin—that touch of chivalry—of thoughtfulness.

There was all too little chivalry nowadays. They were living in a harsh, unromantic world, full of violence, of immorality and sudden death. A world in which it was growing too easy to become cynical, to accept what the young people called 'realism'. This was a word which Violetta associated with far too many cruelties and injustices. It made her feel that such young men as Martin and Hugh were rare specimens—to be treasured.

If only, she thought, her dear Martin would walk through the gates and into this sunny flower-filled garden, this very moment. If only she could hear his voice calling 'Hallo there, Gramma', his own name for her.

I would like to hear that name again, she thought, and to see his wonderful smile just once more before I die. At my age you never know . . .

But those were not thoughts Violetta spoke aloud and a few minutes later she was calling to Corrie to come and join them for the usual evening cocktail.

Part Two

CHAPTER ONE

On the morning of the 19th of March, a few hours before the arrival of Corisande Gilroy in Madeira, Martin Ashley walked out of Reid's Hotel with the intention of killing time by taking some exercise.

He was a good walker and rather glad to have this opportunity to stretch his legs after the rich oily food he had had to consume at all those business lunches in Portugal.

The few days he had spent in Lisbon had been more than rewarding. That attaché case he had left on his hotel bed was full of orders. He was pleased with the fact that he had found one or two new and interesting markets for his firm. Success in business of this kind, he had discovered, was due to several factors other than a salesman's initiative. For instance, he had been able to show the Lisbon chaps some new novels by two outstanding authors who had recently left their own publishers to go to Horton & Mullins. Martin could add this on to his success with the crime and detective books which he had sold six months ago at the Leipzig Book Fair.

There was also a new work by one of the most popular romance-writers in England. She would soon see it translated into Portuguese. Interesting, he thought, the change that was taking place in the world of books. There was less demand for the destructive acid of vice and more for the soothing sweets of a tender love story.

Martin, himself, at this particular moment felt much less willing than he had been in the past to scoff at romantic novels. Of course he was aware that Corisande—his Corrie—their personal romance—had brought about the change in him.

During the years at University and for a time afterwards, Martin used to lead the life of the normal young man who was not bad-looking, was good at sports and popular with women. He used to fall in love lightly; take out pretty girls and make love—but never seriously. Only once had he become deeply involved, with the attractive young widow of a friend who had crashed during a motor race at Le Mans. For a few months Martin really believed he might marry her, although his grandmother had liked her least of all the girls he had taken home.

'I'm sure you'll find someone more worthy of you, darling,' Violetta had said affectionately. 'But it's your choice and up to you. Only do remember she *is* older than you. She's beautiful, I admit, but darling, she's a bit shallow, don't you think? That poor boy who was killed has hardly been dead six months. Do you think she is capable of loving in the deep way that *you* would want your wife to love you?'

Martin could remember arguing with Gramma—trying to defend his fascinating widow, yet worried because he knew his Violetta, and how shrewd and observant she was behind that Dresden-china façade. She had been so right in the past about 'the others'. She made him uneasy. Anyhow, the net result was that his widow found a wealthier consoler than himself. It was *she* who eventually made the break after which he was conscious of relief rather than regret.

How lucky he was! For that very next week he had met his Corisande—his ideal—ideal in every way. And this time Violetta was one hundred per cent with him.

Martin walked out of Reid's into the sunshine and out of Funchal town, up the Camacha road leading to the mountains. He felt vital—eager, almost that he was treading on air.

It was a wonderful day. Madeira, vivid with spring flowers, was enchanting. The practical young salesman, bent on business, had been left behind in Lisbon. Now he was the eager lover waiting for his true love. This was the unique prelude to a honeymoon—his and hers—three heavenly days together, then home, and soon afterwards, their wedding.

Love was marvellous. Business was good. He felt immensely happy. He told himself, smiling a bit, that if he'd been able to sing he would have burst into song. And when an old woman carrying a bundle of willows under her arm passed by him, trudging downhill, he waved a hand and called out: *'Bom dia!'* (good morning!), one of the few Portuguese greetings Martin knew. It was one of the most difficult of European languages.

The old crone didn't reply. She didn't hear him. But he had an absurd wish to rush across take her bundle and carry it for her. She was such an old creature. There were an awful lot of old, very poor islanders up in these mountain villages. He had been told that. The lives they lead bore no relationship to the Westernised much more sophisticated existence of Funchal residents.

He could well understand why Gramma loved Madeira. He was going to like it enormously too, and he was quite sure Corrie would feel the same. She was passionately fond of flowers, which reminded him to buy a huge bunch from the old woman at the hotel entrance—freesias, which were Corrie's favourite—to put on her dressing-table.

She ought to touch down in about three or four hours' time. His thoughts raced ahead.

Tonight, they would have a tremendous celebration dinner at Reid's. Then they'd dance. She adored it. He had never been much of a dancer but she was teaching him, and the last time he took her out she had told him he had improved. If she didn't want to stay in the bar at Reid's he'd take her out somewhere else. The great thing was to be together. There would be no need for either of them to say, 'I must get back!' The mere idea of holding Corrie in his arms again and kissing that warm sweet mouth, so generously offered, made his pulses race.

He pulled out a handkerchief and wiped his forehead. It was warm and wet. Quite tough, this uphill climb, but he was enjoying it. Only a slight ache in his leg-muscles shamed him into the admission that he wasn't the walker he used to be. Leading a London life, he didn't have much opportunity for exercise—except in the weekends when he could play tennis. He and Corrie met either at Brabett's Farm or at one of the tennis clubs near Town where they often had a game.

Thinking of tennis, Martin turned his thoughts to his distinguished mother and all her famous exploits on the courts. He recalled the last letter he had received from her, a few weeks ago, after she had been sent the date fixed for his marriage.

'I know I ought to fly over for it, dearest Mart,' she had replied, 'but Walter and I have simply *got* to go to New Zealand, and will be there for some months, including the very date you've fixed for your wedding. Oh dear, I'm so sad! But we're playing in a Doubles and can't back out. Please forgive us, dearest Mart.'

She had enclosed quite a generous cheque as a present, also a small one for Corrie, and promised to come over to London to see them later in the year.

The letter had made him feel a trifle cynical. It was so typical of Vanessa. 'Never a mother—always a wife'—as he had once said to Corrie. But he had lived apart from Vanessa for so long he was indifferent to the situation. His grandmother made up for all Vanessa lacked. He could no longer be hurt by her indifference.

He walked for an hour, taking the route for Camacha. How much further he had to go he did not know, because he had not bothered to ask the hotel porter for a map He also had a vague notion that he should have told them that he was going out and that if Miss Gilroy should by any chance arrive before he returned, they must tell her he would soon be back. On the other hand, he was sure Corrie didn't land at Funchal Airport until 4.15, so he intended to be back at Reid's long before then.

After another half-mile, he came upon one of the most magnificent mimosa trees he had ever seen. The spreading branches were laden with feathery flowers looking as though golden powder had been sifted upon them. At once he remembered and regretted the camera he had left at the hotel. Idiot! he thought. Corrie was

152

always teasing him about this blind spot in his memory. He constantly forgot to bring his camera with him, not being a dedicated photographer.

A young man with a girl on his arm came walking down the road. They stopped also to admire the mimosa tree. They discussed it excitedly in Portuguese. Martin smiled and nodded.

'Good morning!'

'Morning,' repeated the young man with a strong accent. The girl smiled at Martin but remained silent, hanging a little shyly on the boy's arm.

'Very splendid tree,' the young Portuguese added and took hold of the Leica which hung from a strap over his shoulder. Martin looked at it enviously.

'How lucky you are to have brought a camera. I wish I had mine. It's such an incredible mimosa.'

He waited with the couple while the boy took some shots. Then they bade each other goodbye. Martin walked on in the opposite direction.

After another half an hour of climbing, a little hot and breathless, he turned off the main road and took a rough path that led down the mountainside. He thought the surrounding scenery fabulous. The whole area was so vividly green, studded with flowers. It astonished him to see whole stretches of arum

153

lilies lifting their heads in creamy splendour. There were little yellow wild flowers that looked to him like begonias, and huge clumps of red-spiked plants which he did recognise. Children used to call them red-hot-pokers. The wealth of flowering bushes and trees delighted Martin but he could only put a name to a few of them.

The stony path grew narrower and seemed to lead nowhere in particular. It gradually became a mere cutting between the bushes. He shaded his eyes from the sun and stared about him. The blueness of the sky and the sunlight were dazzling. Then, suddenly, in no time at all, he encountered a phenomenon which was totally unexpected although vaguely he had heard that these things could happen up here in the mountains. The sun was completely blotted out. The panorama which had given him such ascetic pleasure, vanished in a kind of thick vapour which descended with incredible speed. It was like a black cloud— and at once he felt the drop in the temperature and the dampness of that swirling mist. It would, he was sure, start to rain in a moment. Anyhow, he had had enough of walking. Why not go back to the hotel? It was at least an hour's walk down the Camacha-Funchal Road.

Martin literally could not see a step ahead of him now. Enveloped as he was in cloud, he lost all sense of direction.

Certainly he was not aware he had come upon a ravine of jagged rock which cut through the coarse green grass directly in front of him. All he knew was that suddenly he slipped and lost his balance. It was too late to correct the fall—a fall that might have been lethal, for the ravines up here were deep. A rocky ledge jutting out from one side broke his fall. The sports jacket he was carrying fell from his arm and vanished. He hit one side of his head and lay face downward spreadeagled on the ledge. He felt neither shock nor pain. The world was blotted out for Martin Ashley.

In less than an hour the black cloud had been swept away by a gust of wind. The mountainside was once more dazzlingly clear and beautiful.

The deep silence was broken only by the occasional sound of a distant car climbing the mountain road several hundred yards away, and by the drone of an aeroplane, so high up that it was out of sight.

The birds began to sing again and the crickets resumed their steady chirping, deep hidden in the scrub.

Later on, down the same path that Martin had taken, there came an elderly man and a girl.

They carried between them a long deep basket on two poles. The man was grey-haired and bearded and wore metal-rimmed spectacles on the end of his nose. He peered over the rims short-sightedly as though the glasses were of little use to him. He was poorly dressed in coarse linen trousers—none too clean—and a red shirt that had shrunk. He limped slightly. The girl walked splendidly, shoulders back, head up. They both seemed undisturbed by the steep incline of the mountain path. They were accustomed to it. Their basket was empty so no real weight.

The girl had a superb figure. Her black hair which had a blue sheen to it, fell in a long thick plait down her back and was tied with a faded ribbon. She wore a huge peasant straw hat on her head. It hid her face from view.

Suddenly she stopped and dropped her two ends of the poles.

'Far enough, Papa,' she said in French. 'We can get what we want and plenty of it right here.'

'As you wish, daughter,' the old man replied in the same tongue. He, too, set down his poles and wiped his streaming face with a scarlet and white bandana. 'Phew! It is hot now that the sun has come through the clouds. The ground is steaming. Lucky we were not caught in that fog.'

'Lucky? No—not us—we have little luck,' said the girl in a bitter voice. 'You may have had some—me none.'

The old man whom she called 'Papa' said nothing. But his pink-rimmed eyes, small and watery, blinked at her over the glasses with

156

sadness. He was perpetually sad about Sanchia—his poor Chia, as he called her. He liked only to see just the fine profile she now turned towards him. But her eyes held a brooding sorrow, deeper far he knew than that which he had felt for her after her terrible accident. The same shock had hastened her mother's death, two years ago.

He was a sentimental old man and he had loved his wife dearly. Sanchia, his one and only child, he loved still more. But what was to become of her? At moments like this when she stood so straight, so graceful, so strong, any father would be proud—feel that she could overcome any of life's difficulties. She had such a fine straight nose and chin, and a noble forehead with exquisite brows. In the old days visiting artists often wanted to paint Sanchia in the striped skirt and lace-embroidered blouse of the native costume she wore for feast-days. Her eyes were wonderful.

The colour of black treacle, her poor mother used to say. Liquid—shot with gold. Oh, she was beautiful standing here today, one brown slender hand with long strong fingers, shading her eyes from the sun.

Then she turned to him. He had long since grown used to seeing her full face—that *other* side—yet it was always terrible to him. *She* poor child thought it terrible. And others shrank from the sight.

One side of that face was a ruin of past

perfection. Her mouth was drawn up into a leer. The skin of the damaged cheek had puckered, and like the forehead, was criss-crossed with scars. At one point so sunken was that side that all shape had gone from it. Even the beauty of her eyes could not make up for the disfigurement. People turned quickly away having once looked at her. But Sanchia did not want the pity of strangers.

Her boy-friend, the faithless Marcello, had been responsible. He had been out riding his motor-bike—going too fast—and Sanchia was a pillion rider. As luck would have it, it was she who had been thrown on to the stones which accounted for the terrible injuries she had received. But the boy, himself, ended in a ditch where mud and water had softened his fall and he had escaped with little more than a broken nose. There had been no question of compensation, the young fool had not renewed his insurance. He lost his licence and was banned from riding his motorcycle for a year. But Sanchia lost her lover and all hopes of marriage.

Her mother had embraced her and kissed those scars before she died. Her father had never shown one sign that he was repulsed by the sight of her. But Marcello had gone to visit her while she was in hospital, muttered a few words of sympathy, then rushed out. He had never come back. He was unable to bear the change in that once lovely face.

The old man hardly dared allow himself to think about Marcella. There had been no wedding. It was a good thing that he and his family had moved to a neighbouring village—better for all concerned. But he had been labelled a coward—and worse. To have deserted his affianced wife when she needed him most, to have shown so clearly that it was her beauty that had enslaved him—little more—that had been an unpardonable insult and the cruellest of blows.

There had been talk at the hospital of Sanchia having plastic surgery, but it would have cost far more money than José could afford. In any case Sanchia had rejected the idea. Even if she recovered her looks and it brought Marcello back, she would not take him. She hated him now. He had broken her heart. But why, old José asked himself vaguely, was he remembering Marcello at this particular moment?

He turned his gaze from his daughter. They had come out with their basket and a spade to dig as much as they could of the peat-like moss that grew on this mountainside. The turf was at its best and thickest at this time of the year. In the winter they used it for the stove to supplement the paraffin, cooked by it, and warmed themselves beside the fire. It was slow-burning and gave out a good glow once it was alight. They were poor—poorer than most of their friends, because old José earned little, and Sanchia nothing. She rarely left the mountain dwelling which they called home. She had never recovered from the shock of the first moment she had looked in a mirror and seen the destruction of her beauty. She would not go out until dark. She talked only to her father, and one elderly woman who had been a close friend of her mother's. And now even she was dead. Sanchia led a lonely purposeless life—embittered by her catastrophe.

At times José feared that he soon would not be active enough to work and buy the food they needed. He was well past sixty and he had aged a lot since the tragedy of his wife's death and his daughter's accident. His failing strength only allowed him to do part-time jobs. For the most part, helping to re-roof cow-sheds, and thatching outbuildings for the farmers. He had mastered the art of thatching when he was a youth.

Sanchia, who had just been speaking to him in Portuguese suddenly broke into French again, '*Mon Dieu!* Must you stare at me, Papa? What's new about my ugliness?'

'Now, now,' he said soothingly, 'you are not ugly, chérie. Hand me the spade. Come—let us get on with our work.'

José was by birth a Frenchman. He came from the Alpes-Maritimes. Forty years ago, as a lad, he had fallen in love with and married a Portuguese girl. To please her, he had left the South of France for ever and gone to live in

Madeira, where Sanchia was born and bred.

In the long run, José became a permanent resident of the island. Sanchia was born in a little house they had once occupied near Camacha when times were good. Both father and daughter were bi-lingual and enjoyed conversing in French more than in Portuguese.

Today they lived in a meagre dwelling near the village of Quintra on the proceeds of the sale of their old home. In their present home they had been reduced to discomfort although never to squalor, because Sanchia had some talent for making a place look nice and had made it her life's work to care for her father. She worked hard—at the cooking, the washing, and the ironing. She was responsible for the vegetable garden, too, and keeping chickens. It was José who went to the village to buy the food. She refused to expose her face to anyone in the shops.

Friends had hinted that she was locally considered to be a little queer in the head. Certainly her father knew she was no longer the gay bright girl who used to sing, play a guitar, and charm all the young men. But she had always longed to be a nurse. After she left the village school she had entered a convent hospital in Funchal as a probationer.

She had been nineteen then. For a year she trained in the wards, and, as everybody knew, she was not only handsome, but a good generous-hearted girl who enjoyed helping to relieve the sufferings of others. José only knew that now she had become little more than a hermit, a nun, shut away from the world. Even her nature had altered. She seemed to enjoy being sarcastic and even rude at times. She had outbursts of rage. She would turn that marred profile to José and scream at him, 'Look! *Look!* Tell me how ugly I am!'

Then, as he denied this, she ended in tears in his comforting arms.

He considered that it was best she should not meet people outside and be subjected to their pity which only fired her fury against the fate that had so brutally altered her whole life, as well as her face.

He began to slide the spade under the turf. Sanchia, hands on her hips, watched for an instant then walked with her unfailing grace a little farther down the slope.

She had calmed down. She looked through half-closed eyes across the rims of the trees to the valley below, thinking not so much of the beauty of the scene as of the town—Funchal. Only at rare intervals, with a gauze scarf over her face and head, she and her father went down there and visited the market.

They lived a life apart from the world outside. Their cottage built half of stone, half of wood, was a mile's walk away from the village of Quintra. There was only one other dwelling within sight of them. This belonged to Pascala, an aged woman reputed to have a

162

witch's powers, and to be able to see into the future. She was semi-blind and partially deaf and because of her great age and mysterious powers was the one person Sanchia liked to visit, and talk to. She never felt she was being stared at or criticised by old Pascala. And Pascala who, herself, had few friends and visitors, was always pleased to see the girl, and called her her little bird, her *pássaro*.

In this hour, Sanchia began to turn her thoughts to clothes. How badly she needed a dress! She would be compelled to go down to the market soon. If only it wasn't for that one devilish side to her face, she could get a job and earn some money. She could work in a hospital again, or in a domestic capacity. In the season there was much work in Funchal for young girls. (A girl such as she *used* to be! Sanchia told herself bitterly.)

She stopped dead on the brink of a small ravine—that very one which an hour ago had been completely hidden from Martin by the dark cloud. She bent over the edge idly and stared down. Then her heart missed a beat. Fifty feet below, she could quite plainly see the body of a man spreadeagled across a broad ledge, his arms clutching at the jagged rock that must have broken his fall.

CHAPTER TWO

Startled and excited, Sanchia let out a scream. It brought old José down to her.

'*Papa! Papa! Mon Dieu! Papa,* come here!'

He reached her. Together they stared, craning their necks to see more clearly. Then Sanchia let out another scream.

'Look—a man's body. I can see blood on his hair. Oh, Papa, he must have fallen and hit his head. He is *dead.*'

'He may not be so. We must get him up.'

'How can we? We cannot reach him.'

'Somehow we must reach him in case he is not dead. Either that or you must wait here, Chia, while I go for help,' said José, adjusting his glasses with shaking fingers.

'If he still has life in him, he will bleed to death unless we are quick. You know I was once a nurse. I know about these things. I must stop the bleeding if it is external and if his skull is injured.'

'Can you see more? My glasses are slipping. I see little.'

'Mother of God! I see quite clearly, how young he is, Papa. And he is not an islander. He is a stranger—English or American, from his clothes. He is fair. I can see that, too. Poor young man!'

José stood up. He crossed himself, like the

good Catholic he was. 'Jesus and Mary, have mercy on him.'

Sanchia turned to him, her eyes flashing. 'Shame on you to pray as though he is already a corpse. We must bring him up.'

'I cannot go down there. My limbs are too stiff,' José whined.

'But I can reach him. I am strong—I have a good head for heights,' she said breathlessly.

'But you might trip and die yourself.'

'I won't trip. Besides, I do not believe he is dead. I will get him up,' said the girl obstinately. 'You are useless, Papa!'

'I can go and find someone in Quintra. It is nearer than Camacha.'

'No, I have a better idea. There is a length of rope in the basket. Fetch it. It is strong. You use it to bind the osiers. I will climb down to him and tie it around his waist. He has fallen only a little way. It is because he hit his head that he is unconscious. Quick, Papa—do as I say!'

José seldom, if ever, refused to obey his daughter. She was totally in command of him. He hobbled over the rough grasses, found the rope and brought it back.

Sanchia was now lying face downwards on the turf. She sprang to her feet as her father returned. Her ruined face was flushed and her eyes full of a light that he had not seen there for a long time.

'I can see plainly that he is young and

165

handsome. If he has a life to save, I will save it.'

'Be careful,' said the old man fearfully. 'Oh, be careful if you mean to go down that ravine. It is a long way to the bottom should you fall, my child, and you are all I have.'

Sanchia gave a scornful laugh and beat her clenched fists against her chest.

'I've always been a good climber. You remember my dear mother, God rest her soul, called me her little mountain-goat because I am sure-footed. And when she was ill, who carried the heavy iron kettle to the fire, or the water from the well? It was me.'

'Oh! all right, all right,' grumbled José.

But he stared over the edge of the ravine with fear in his rheumy eyes and removed his glasses, shaking his head. He knew that she was justified in her praise of her own muscular power. He knew his Chia. Perhaps her mind had been damaged by the frightfulness of her scarring, but not her iron will or physical courage.

Sanchia was as nimble as she boasted once she started to descend the ravine. As she went cautiously, she clutched great bunches of coarse weeds and bushes with both hands. It took her no time to reach the body of the fallen man. His face was still hidden from her, but she could see the blood was oozing slowly from a wound on the left side of his skull. What hair he had, she thought. Dear God, it had lights of bright gold in it—although it tapered to a gentle brown in the nape of his muscular neck. His body was hunched. She was able to slip the rope under him and tie it around his chest with a sailor's knot. He neither moved or spoke but that he was alive, she was now certain. His body was warm and he was breathing. She was doubly glad that she had insisted on coming to the rescue. Who was to know what might not have happened if he had had to wait another few hours before he received aid. *'First Aid'* they used to call it at the hospital. How well she remembered that. But she had got much farther in her elementary training.

She laid her hand gently on the young man's blood-streaked head.

'Be of good heart, *mon brave.* I will save you!' she whispered.

Gripping the bushes, the grasses and the jagged rocks, she climbed up again with the rest of the rope. She looked at her father with eyes that were bright with new spirit.

'He lives, Papa. We will pull him up now. Together—oh, so slowly and gently. I have knotted the rope well under his arms so that we can raise his head. The rest of his body will slide over the ground and come to no harm. Do as I tell you. Together—gently now—*pull!'*

So the weak old man and the strong young girl brought Martin Ashley out of the ravine and up on to the sunlit ground. Sanchia went down on her knees and turned his body over. For the first time she saw his face. He was deathly pale. It would be dangerous to leave him a moment longer but she must first see if he had any papers of identification. To her surprise she found nothing. If he had had a wallet it must have slipped from his pocket as he fell and dropped to the bottom of the ravine.

She examined him closely. Blood had run down his left cheek as well as matted his hair. But he was handsome, there was no doubt of that, and his fairness and youth filled Sanchia with strange ecstasy. Now she had but one thought—she must stop the bleeding. She threw her orders at her father.

'Give me your jacket. I will place it under his head. Go to the basket and fetch our bottle of spring-water, and one of wine. I will tear my clothes and bind him up. Quickly—fetch the two bottles, Papa.'

Once the old man had limped away to her bidding, Sanchia undressed. She wore a white cotton shirt and an unfashionably long skirt of striped blue and black Terylene, tied with a scarf around her waist which was small for her size, and of which she used to be proud. She tore a piece out of the shirt, and folded it into a pad. Another strip, she took from the skirt. Once her father brought the two bottles she wet the pad with the water, then the wine. The alcohol would be a disinfectant. She wiped the blood gently away from Martin Ashley's face.

He was still deeply unconscious but his pulse was not bad. The blow to his skull had obviously knocked him out. Perhaps he would be unconscious for some time. She did not bother with the matted hair. She would see to that later. But now she continued to press the cold wet pad firmly against the jagged cut on the left side of his head. Finally she bound it with her scarf. The pressure would stop the bleeding, which was not profuse. She moistened his lips with wine. To her delight he opened his eyes. Just for one moment she could see that they were grey. His lashes were dark and luxuriant. But he made no effort to speak—only gave a little groan, then his eyelids shut again.

Sanchia turned to her father, her face crimson after her exertions. Once more the sun had come out. It was warm and humid. She wiped her wet forehead with the back of her hand.

'We have saved his life. But he is not yet conscious,' she said.

The old man smiled and crossed himself. 'We must give thanks to God and His Holy Mother.'

Sanchia gave one of her hard little laughs as she rose to her feet. She knew that she must look a sight in her torn skirt and blouse but she was sufficiently covered for the sake of modesty.

'You are always pious, Papa. Always making the sign of the cross. You should be like me, and believe that not only do we receive help from above we benefit on account of the efforts we, ourselves, make to keep God's law.'

José scratched the top of his head. He had no reply for this. Chia was too deep for him. Sometimes he and his wife used to wonder how they had ever given birth to such a clever girl, both of them being such simple folk.

'Listen, Chia,' he said, 'we must get the *Senhor* to a hospital. He is of gentle birth and a foreigner. It can be seen.'

Sanchia put on the expression that her father sometimes dreaded. The once voluptuous mouth thinned and tightened. Her eyes looked suddenly fierce.

'No, we will not take him to hospital. We will carry him to our home.'

'Are you mad?' gasped the old man. 'He may die. Besides, we have no room for him.'

'You are set on thoughts of death,' she said impatiently. 'Please remember that I know something about these things. His pulse is not bad and the bleeding had almost stopped before I put on the pad. I wish to take him home. We will make room even if I have to give him my own bed.'

'But, my daughter, for what reason?'

Her eyes suddenly softened. She took one of Martin's hands and examined it. The long strong fingers were something like her own

170

boyish ones. She remembered even when she was in love with Marcello, she had not liked *his* plump short hands. And she saw that the *senhor* wore a signet ring. Yes, Papa was right. He was a gentleman of some standing. *And she had saved his life.* No one else would have found him. At least perhaps not until he was long past recovery. She had walked to the ravine and seen him. Fate had led her there, for it was off the beaten track, and tourists kept to the picnic places close to the road. He owed his life to her.

She faced her father, hands on hips.

'I have nothing to live for. My life is ruined, like my face. I wish to be of use once more and to have a motive for living. This young man shall be my motive—if only for a little while. I shall nurse him and care for him. You will see he will recover consciousness and be grateful to me. It will bring me *le bonheur.* That would be a change.'

For a moment, José argued, then Sanchia flew into one of the tempers that alarmed him. Much as he adored his Chia he had to confess that she did not behave normally. But, of course, if she wanted to take this stranger back home and nurse him there was nothing really against it, especially if the young man was not dying and speedily returned to his senses, and could tell them who he was and from whence he came. There might be a reward, the old man thought, but dared not voice his mercenary hopes to his daughter.

'How will we get him home?' he mumbled.

'We will place him in the basket. We can carry it with the two poles as our men carry their passengers in the hammocks, down in Funchal.'

'But I am old and weak and cannot hurry—' began the old man fretfully, only to be interrupted by a tirade from Sanchia. He was only in his sixties. He was not a cripple. He suffered merely from rheumatism. Why was he obstructing her like this? Since her accident he had done nothing but pray that she would find happiness again. So why try to prevent what she was doing? She had decided in a lightning flash that it would make her truly happy to take this injured man home and nurse him back to health.

'I have no husband—no child—I am bored and wretched! *I wish to nurse him.* We need say nothing to anybody but keep him hidden until he is well. Stop grumbling at me, Papa!'

The old man shook his head. Chia was truly crazy at times. But he stopped and carried out her instructions.

Slowly and laboriously they lifted the poles, balancing the long narrow basket in which they had placed the young man. Sanchia half-covered his face with José's coat. No one would see what they carried. Nor were they likely to meet a soul. They were more than a mile from the village of Quintra and went by a winding path familiar to them, a short cut to their home. They stopped frequently to wipe the sweat from their faces. The basket was no light weight. But they met nobody during that slow trudge during which old José groaned and complained, following his strong determined daughter with some trepidation.

Home at last. Panting, relieved, José saw the little stone house with its wooden doors and window-frames, half covered by the wild brilliant cerise bougainvillaea which grew out here so plentifully.

Their small plot of land was enclosed by a rough fence, broken in many places. The only flowers to be seen were the masses of vivid glicineas which grew wild almost up to the doorway.

On the whole it was a poor place, with no modern plumbing and only outdoor sanitation. They relied on their own well for drinking water. At the back was a tumble-down hut wherein they stabled their two goats. During the summer the animals nibbled all the coarse grass and kept it down. The chickens ran around a small wired-in yard and laid their eggs in a wooden shelter José had put roughly together.

Sanchia milked the goats and fed the chickens daily and made cheese as well. She also baked the bread. They could scarcely afford meat but a friend often brought them fish. On the whole father and daughter lived a frugal life, and so isolated was this little place that they had no electricity and burned only oil-lamps.

One great plane tree with spreading branches sheltered the house from the sun. A few hundred yards away they could see the equally tumble-down dwelling occupied by old Pascala.

If Sanchia wished to avoid being seen carrying the wounded *senhor* to this place she knew she need have no fears. Seldom, if ever, did callers come. At first, after her accident, friends had offered their sympathy but she so often rejected them and showed such open dislike, neighbours eventually avoided her. They spoke of her as a bit peculiar these days. Sometimes old José went to the wine-shop, met one or two men he had known for years and gossiped with them, but nobody any longer asked after his daughter.

They put the basket down very gently. Sanchia flung open the door.

'Let us carry him in and lift him straight on to my bed.' she said.

José threaded his gnarled fingers through his long white hair.

'*Your* bed! *Mon Dieu!* Where do you think *you* will sleep, my girl?'

'There is the old camp bed that I used as a child,' she said impatiently. 'It is in the hut. It only needs a clean, and one leg for you to mend. It will take you a few minutes. I can put

174

it in the kitchen at nights.'

'Crazy! Crazy!' the old man muttered but once more did his daughter's bidding.

Now they lifted the young man out of the basket. Sanchia took the heaviest part of the burden, cradling his head against her breast. It gave her an almost frightening thrill to feel that beautiful fair head against her flesh. She was like a woman exalted—in love again— determined not to part with this God-given man. He was a treasure *she* alone had found. Nobody should take him from her.

Soon he was lying on her bed—a neat clean bed because Sanchia had never forgotten the lessons she had learned in the hospital which had always been so immaculate. Daily she scrubbed the wooden floor of her own room. She washed the mats, and the curtains that hung at the tiny windows. They were of cheap cotton floral material, always spotless and well-ironed. Over the bed, her father had hung a crucifix, although she followed few of his religious habits. But she had let the crucifix stay there to please him. On the other side of the room there hung a cheap framed reproduction of Lord Lytton's Victorian masterpiece 'The Lovers'. She had not bought it herself. It had belonged to her mother who had picked it up in an art shop in Funchal. It had cost next to nothing twenty years ago. Sanchia had always been fascinated by the Roman lovers—the handsome man and the beautiful girl. His arms around her, one of her hands lifted to his lips. On her face an expression of mingled pain and ecstasy. He had her fingertips between his teeth. She suffered the pain gladly because she adored him. Sanchia always believed she, too, would gladly suffer pain if it pleased her lover. But Marcello had abandoned her. Pain remained—love had gone forever. Yet she could not bear to part with the painting.

The bed had a brass head and foot—this, too, had been her mother's. The only furniture in the room was a wooden chair with a rush seat which her father had woven for her, a wash-stand with a cheap pink, flowered basin and jug that had a broken lip. When she had been engaged to Marcello, he had bought her a dressing-table. On this she used to keep her brushes and some make-up and an occasional bottle of cheap perfume. After he deserted her, she had made José sell the table. She no longer wanted it. She did not care what her face looked like. She only scrubbed it—washed it clean. Many seasons of hot sun had tanned it to a rich brown except for those devastating scars which remained gruesomely white. But she used no creams, no lotions of any kind.

Now she flung more orders at her father.

'Light the stove, Papa. Boil some water. *Dépêches-toi!* I must wash him. Clean him up so that there will be no infection.'

José began to protest. What was her object

in doing this thing? Sanchia, who was unbuttoning Martin's shirt. turned her head over her shoulder and looked at her father, a tigerish gleam in her splendid eyes.

'I've already told you. It will make me happy. Do not question me.'

José scowled. *'Tiens! Tiens!* And how will you account for him being here? Shouldn't we have taken him straight to the police or a hospital?'

'I won't let him go. I want to care for him myself. Besides, nobody ever comes here so nobody will ever know about this.'

For once José continued to argue. 'But, my child, he, himself, may not be pleased once he recovers—*if* he does! You are taking a risk. It may land us both in deep trouble.'

She hissed at him. 'Only if *you* make trouble. For God's sake stop nagging. Wait until he does recover and sees how well I am nursing him. It is sweeter and more tranquil in this little room than it would be in a hospital ward full of the sick and dying. He will be grateful to me.'

The old man stopped arguing. He got the old-fashioned stove alight but worried about Sanchia and her odd conduct. Also if the young man recovered consciousness, which please God he would, and stayed awhile, José would have to try to augment the present small pay which he received for thatching. Maybe Sanchia was right when she reproached him because he complained that he was too old and stiff to do much more manual work. Some said it was good to stretch the limbs and use them if you have rheumatics. But one man at the wine-shop had suggested he might have something else—it began with *arth*—he didn't know what. But his hands were not too bad. He would go alone tomorrow and see old Estalo who used to have a kind of friendship with him when they were young men. Estalo had done well—was foreman in a factory in Poiso. They made baskets there—every kind of wicker-work. José could weave osiers. Why not go up in the evenings which were light at this season and help with the weaving? It would put a few more escudos in his pocket and he could get a bus to and from work. It left Quintra every three or four hours and returned to the village after dark.

Meanwhile, Sanchia faithfully carried out the sanitary methods her former training had taught her. She washed and scrubbed her hands and put on a clean blouse. Once the water was boiled she was quite the efficient trainee-nurse again.

The injured man lay stretched on her bed, clean and tidy. Tenderly she wiped the dirt from his face. She cleaned the jagged cut and the grazes but left the rest of his head alone for the moment. She must not immerse it in water. But she had a pair of her old surgical scissors and with these she cut away a portion of the bright hair directly around the injuries.

She had been right when she had told her father that the bleeding had stopped. There was nothing more to fear now unless there was internal haemorrhage and she was sure that if this had been so, he would be dead by now.

He was, however, too cold, even on a hot day like this. Of course he had been lying down there in that dark ravine, perhaps for several hours. One of the essentials, Sanchia knew, was to keep him warm.

She found the only stone hot water-bottle and put it at his feet. Beautiful feet, she thought. She had admired them when she drew off the socks. Miraculously white, like the rest of his body. Next to her and her father he looked like ivory. There was little tan and practically no colour at the moment on his cheeks. How long and dark his lashes were! She whispered to him as she covered him with José's best pair of pyjamas.

'Open your eyes, *pour t'amour de Dieu,* open your eyes and show me that you live,' she begged him. But his eyes remained shut. Only his slightly irregular breathing told her that he was still alive.

How long could this coma last, she asked herself? She remembered certain casualties in her ward. She used to help the sister-in-charge deal with unconscious people. Sometimes they recovered within a few hours; sometimes not for days, and the worst cases not for weeks.

Sanchia prayed this would not be the case with her patient. He would have to be fed if he remained unconscious and she was not sure whether she could do this properly. And of course, she didn't know bow long he had lain in that ravine.

If you would only just speak to me once, she thought, watching over him like an anxious mother with a sick child.

But he remained unconscious. And as long as he breathed she was not too concerned. There was now even a tinge more colour in his cheeks. She no longer felt him to be anyone near to the death which her father kept harping upon.

Hastily she went out to the yard, caught a luckless chicken, wrung its neck and plucked it. She stewed it, made soup with the bones and chopped up the breast and wings. She felt sure her invalid would need good nourishment soon.

She could get José to buy a few jellies. She would have to dip into her savings, kept in a tin box under her bed. She had always been thrifty and after her accident she had not spent the money meant for her trousseau. She had at least two thousand escudos left. She had religiously put away her salary when she was a hospital probationer, and sold the few treasures her mother had left to her. Besides which, old José had a few thousand escudos left from the sale of their other house in

Quintra. But that must not be touched. They practically lived on it.

How gladly she would use her own savings if necessary to buy what the stranger needed.

She sent the old man to the wine-shop to get another bottle of wine and a small flask of cognac. When he complained it was mad extravagance, she shut him up, so he made his way into the village, pleased that at least he could have a glass of wine with his friends.

CHAPTER THREE

For three days and three nights Martin Ashley lay in a world of darkness and shadow, watched over by Sanchia.

She seldom left his side during the day and she lay on her camp bed at night in the kitchen, sleeping fitfully, waking if she thought she heard a sound. Once he groaned. She lit a candle and rushed to his side, her heart beating fast, hoping desperately that at last the stranger was recovering consciousness. He even opened his eyes once, but he stared at her blankly and closed them again. That next day she kept squeezing a few drops of warm goat's milk, laced with wine, between his lips to ensure that his body received a little nourishment. She dripped albumen water frequently into his mouth and when she felt

181

that his body was too warm she removed the blankets, covered him only with an old light spread and opened the casement windows wide to let in the fresh mountain air.

Then one evening her father returned from the wine-shop to tell her that police notices had been posted up in Quintra and—so rumour had it—all over Funchal—up here in the mountain villages as well. They stated that an Englishman staying at Reid's hotel had been reported missing.

'What else do you know about it?' demanded Sanchia.

'Only that a young *guarda* was snooping around Quintra this morning, questioning everybody, but of course nobody has seen the stranger except ourselves so they could not give any information.'

'*Mon Dieu!*' Sanchia put her hand to her lips fearfully. 'And who is the stranger? What is his name? Do you know anything about him?'

The old man who had been full of forebodings ever since he and his daughter had brought the young man here, pulled a sheet of glossy paper from his pocket and handed it to her.

'Read all this,' he said, 'You will see what a dangerous thing you have done, Chia.'

She snatched the paper and said angrily, 'Oh, Papa, stop behaving as though we had committed a crime!'

He dared to answer her back. 'Maybe the

182

police would think that what we have done is a crime, *mon pauvre enfant,'* then added in Portuguese, 'It's all been madness. A madness, I tell you.'

The police hand-out was in Portuguese as well as English. Sanchia examined it eagerly, fastening her gaze on the photograph. Of course it was *he* who lay in her room. Easily recognisable, but how well and gay and *beautiful* he was in his picture! Now, of course, he was ill, cheeks sunken, eyes under-shadowed and there was a stubble of beard on his chin. But it was certainly *he*. And his name was MARTIN ASHLEY. She repeated the word *Martin* aloud several times as though she liked it.

She read the police information and José told her a great deal more that he had learned in the village. How Martin had walked out from Reid's Hotel and never been seen again. It all tied up—he had come up here, turned on to the scrubland down the other side of the mountain and slipped into that ravine in the fog. So! He was English and on holiday at Reid's and he had been going to meet his fiancée. They questioned her—a Miss Corisande Gilroy. Sanchia experienced the most bitter hatred and jealousy of this girl. Why should she have been loved by such a wonderful young man? Why had *she* had this great good fortune? Why was it that only she, Sanchia, had been repulsed and thrown into a hell of disenchantment and misery? Condemned to live alone once her father died—and unloved for ever?

'Of course we must go now to the police and inform them,' old José muttered behind her. But she swung round on him, her great eyes blazing.

'Never, never! I shall not give up. We will see what happens when he recovers. Maybe he will not know who he is, so he will not try to leave us. I remember hospital cases like this—loss of memory—they call it amnesia. If he has this amnesia he will not know who he is or where he comes from, so I can keep him with me. I shall tell him he belongs here.'

José took off his glasses and blinked at his daughter with considerable alarm in his eyes.

'Truly, my child, you are out of your mind. The police would find him. You cannot do this. It really would land us both in jail.'

Sanchia tossed back her long black hair and gave an hysterical laugh.

'I will take the risk. I have plans. And I tell you I feel that he is my destiny. He has been sent to me by the God you tell me is so kind and good. Call me crazy, anything you want, Papa, *I don't care.*'

'Chia! Chia!' protested José, his eyes appealing to her over the rims of his glasses. 'Use your sense, my child. They say at the wine-shop that every house is to be visited, even ours—and old Mère Pascala's, too. Why not? Oh! what a pity our radio is broken, no doubt we would hear more about it.'

Sanchia, her cheeks scarlet, rushed to her tin box and drew some notes from it.

'Take these and take the radio to Pedro. You told me when you last saw him that he could mend it. I will pay for it.'

José's eyes bulged. 'Where do these riches come from?'

'My own store—money I have earned. I can do as I like with it and I wish to keep in touch with police enquiries about this man. It is bound to be broadcast.'

'I beg you to allow me to inform the police.'

'No. I love him,' she said suddenly, dramatically.

'How can you love a half-dead man who has not even spoken to you? What has got into you? I wish we had never found him. He will bring the *malheur* to both of us.'

'He has brought me the first happiness I have known since Marcello deserted me.'

'But how? How?' questioned the old man. 'He lies like a log and all you do is feed him—'

'I cannot tell you how or why. I only know that when I first held his beautiful bright head against my breast, I loved him.'

'But I have read the notices of the *Policia de Segurança*. The Englishman has a fiancée. She is at Reid's looking for this man. Your madness will only land us behind prison bars, I keep telling you, Chia.'

185

She opened her lips to speak, then shut them. Her eyes widened. She swung round and looked through the door that led into her bedroom. *She had heard a voice.* What it said she did not know. But she had heard it and it came from this wonderful man whose life she had saved.

Martin Ashley had recovered consciousness at last.

In a flash she was at his side. His eyes were wide open. He looked dazed. She wondered whether he really saw her. Then he said, 'Hello!'

She echoed the English word, 'Hello', a feeling of elation surging through her. He was *really* and truly alive. 'Hello!' she repeated.

'Where am I? I don't . . . understand . . .' One hand went up to his head. He touched the bandage which she had so correctly and capably made in the form of the hospital capelline. It had been one of her treasures taken from her box with a red cross on it, and the words *First Aid.* Now she spoke to him in French.

'You are better, *grâce à Dieu.* Oh, how happy I am!' He frowned. It was obvious that he felt unsure of himself and unable to co-ordinate his thoughts.

The dark lashes she admired so much drooped, then lifted. He looked up again.

'Why do you speak in French?' he asked in a puzzled voice, but she was delighted because

186

his accent was not poor like the average Englishman's. It was good and he spoke quite fluently. He continued, 'Where am I? Am I in France? My God, *I can't think straight.* Tell me who I am—where I am. My brain is so foggy. I don't seem to know anything. Nor do I recognise you. Why does my head hurt? Why am I in bed? Who *are* you?'

Her pulses leaped. Her dearest wish was fulfilled. He had lost his memory. She would tell him only what she wanted him to know.

He shot all these questions at her one after another, jerkily, and with an expression of stupefaction on the pale handsome face that she found so fascinating.

Her pulses raced still faster. She breathed quickly. *He didn't know who he was.* That was good. From her point of view, miraculous. Only now, in this moment of time, did Sanchia realise how much she had wanted him to suffer from amnesia. She had suggested to Papa that it might result from a bad blow to the head.

During the long, long months that Sanchia had shut herself away from the outside world and lived steeped in a self-made world of bitterness and misery, she had slipped into a deep secret existence where fantasy and crazy dreams, not far removed from madness, replaced fact. She was feverish with joy. She seized one of the injured man's hands and put it against her cheek—her good cheek—(she had not let him see the other side). Holding it

187

thus, she answered most of his questions but withheld the important truth—that he was Martin Ashley from England and was officially listed by the Funchal police as a 'missing person'. Also that he had a fiancée waiting for him down in Reid's Hotel.

She told him that his name was Jean (she had made that up quickly) and that he lived here in this house—had done so for a long time and that they were lovers.

'Don't you remember me?' she asked him and kissed the hand she was holding. 'I am Sanchia. You call me "Chia". We love each other. You have asked me to marry you!'

Martin Ashley lay still, staring at her. He lived for the moment in a confusion of images, muddled ideas floating foolishly through his mind. But his thoughts remained nebulous. He could not co-ordinate them. Listening to this girl, feeling the cool smoothness of her cheek against his hand, he could deny nothing that she said. He could only suppose that she spoke the truth. Why not? Why else was he here with her like this?

He couldn't see her clearly for the curtains were half-drawn and the little bedroom was dim. Neither could he view her full face. She was in shadow, and had a scarf over her head, drooping across one cheek. What he saw was pleasing. She was attractive. The long satin-black hair, flowing to her waist, was marvellous, and the eyes turned to him, very

188

beautiful. Yet none of this seemed quite right. He didn't recognise the girl called *Chia*. And how his head ached! But he felt a sudden inner void and forgetting to ask more questions, whispered in English, 'God! I'm hungry!'

She kissed his hand again and dropped it.

'Speak in French, *chéri*. *We* must speak French together. Don't you remember? Father is French. You will recognise him, perhaps, when you see him But don't plague yourself now with too much thinking. You have had an accident and been very ill. I will explain more to you when you feel better. Lie still and I will bring you some broth.'

She raced to the kitchen. She had the chicken broth ready to heat on a primus stove. Her father had gone out, for which she was thankful. She couldn't be bothered with his interference and nonsense.

In her mind she had become the leading lady in a play—a fantastic creation, at once grotesque and exciting. She loved every second of it.

Now she took the bowl of broth and a slice of bread to the man she had christened 'Jean'. She continued her dialogue while she fed him, spoon by spoon, savouring every grateful look he gave her, every word of thanks. He was obviously weak for he whispered rather than spoke loudly. Sometimes he uttered a sentence in English—then again in French.

'Merci, merci, vous êtes très gentille.'

189

She corrected hint '*Tu*—with you and me it is *tu* or *toi.*'

'*Thee—thou,*' he whispered, dazed—only half comprehending. He swallowed some of the broth and shut his eyes. Soon he opened them again. She was bending close to him. He noticed the full magnificence of those dark eyes with their golden lights, and the lashes that were longer and much more luxuriant than his own. But still she did not let him see the whole of her face.

'How beautiful you are!' he muttered.

Her heart leapt in her breast. She was filled with a terrible joy. After these two years of isolation from all men and all love, how wonderful to hear this glorious young man call her beautiful.

'You, too, are handsome—*beau-garçon!*' she exclaimed breathlessly.

Martin Ashley struggled with his thoughts. That part of his brain which stored all memory seemed dark and fathomless. Yet here he was in this strange bed and small quiet room. This girl, strong, fine and immensely sympathetic, had just informed him that they were about to be married. For the moment he was too shaken, too shocked by his accident, to worry overmuch. He could not sift truth from falsehood or fact from fiction. He only knew that he was deadly tired and glad of the warm broth she was spooning down his parched throat. He was able, also to roll his tongue around the little bread pellets which she dipped in the broth and placed in his mouth. He felt better for the nourishment—less dizzy. After a few moments he fell asleep again. She seized his pulse and found it stronger. This was a natural sleep. He had come out of the coma that had for so long dulled all his sensibilities.

What if he woke up *remembering,* she suddenly asked herself, and went cold. What if the amnesia was only temporary? So much depended on the extent of the damage to his brain.

While he was in that deep sleep, she changed his dressing. She could see that there had been no more bleeding. The cuts and grazes looked clean and healthy. She put a dry gauze pad across the small jagged wound and replaced the capelline bandage—sad that she must, even for a moment, cover up that bright crisp hair.

She knelt by the bed, lifted his hand and once more kissed it.

'Your life belongs to me,' she said huskily. 'You are mine, *mon très cher.* I shall do everything to keep you with me.'

She found José in the kitchen. Her cheeks were flaming like poppies, her eyes huge and brilliant. The old man peered at her over his spectacles. He was about to question her but she broke into excited speech. What she had to say not only astonished but frightened her father. There began an argument between them fiercer than they had ever had before.

She was not only mad but wicked, he told her. She had no right to keep this young Englishman like a prisoner. It was criminal. He kept telling her that if she was found out she would be put in jail and so would he, her father, as an accessory after the fact. Did she not realise that they were defying the police order demanding that anyone who knew Martin Ashley was to go at once to the *Policia de Segurança Publica* in Funchal? Besides, they were certain to search this cottage, eventually.

At the wine-shop his friend Pedro had already told him that yesterday a young *guarda* who had been going from house to house, making enquiries, had actually knocked on José's door but the old man and his daughter had been out at the time, so the police had not entered. Pedro, himself, informed the *guarda* that José and his daughter, who was an invalid, lived there alone. The *guarda* did not return.

'But he may come again and try to speak to us,' José told Sanchia. 'The police will leave no stone unturned to trace the *Senhor*. Besides, how long do you think he will stay in your room, just at your bidding? He will want fresh air and exercise and—work. All young men want to work unless they are sick. Anyhow, we cannot afford to keep him. He will have to pay his way.'

Sanchia remained obdurate. She could

manage her patient, she declared. Meanwhile she would not allow the *guarda* to enter this house and see the Englishman as he looked now, and it would take some little time before he was well enough to leave the house. She would continue to establish in his mind the belief that he belonged here and was her affianced husband. 'He will replace Marcello in my life, only he means a thousand times more to me!' she exclaimed.

'But his colouring—it will give him away—it's all described on this police declaration.'

Her eyes narrowed and glittered. 'I have plans. I have consulted old Pascala. She will help me dye his hair black. He is growing a beard. I shall not shave him, and we will dye that, too.'

José put his hands to his head. Truly this poor girl was a problem and a danger to herself. Isolating herself here, brooding and grieving over her lost beauty as well as the loss of her lover, her reason had been affected.

Yet she had never looked happier than she did today, José thought, and it was such a wonderful change. Even with that terrible distortion on one side, it could be seen how beautiful she must have been. Her eyes filled with tears and she flung her arms around his neck.

'Papa, do not oppose me. Let me keep him here. I am completely bewitched. I promise you I will not get into trouble and I shall use all the money that I saved for my trousseau, to buy food and clothes for him. Once it is safe to leave my patient, I shall begin to work again. Yes, even if I have to meet people in the village, I will go out. They need extra help at the house of Carmela Dinheiro where they embroider linen for the shops in Funchal. You know—like the Casa da Machino. Carmela sent me a note when I was in hospital telling me I could work for her because my embroidery is so good and she knew my dear mother. I refused then, but to raise money for *him*—' she pointed to her bedroom door—'I will bury my pride.'

José did not speak but pulled at his little goatee beard and shook his head. He was profoundly troubled, albeit he rejoiced that his poor Chia had sufficiently recovered her zest for life to wish to go outside and work again.

She kissed him on both cheeks. 'Leave all to me—but if he speaks to you, and he will speak in French, for he is fluent in our language, you must call him *Jean.* Keep absolute silence about his past.'

'But what if he wants to know why you wish to keep him from the *policia,* and are disguising the fairness of his hair and skin?'

'First of all tell him as I shall, that he came up in the mountains because he was wanted by the police in England for a bank robbery. That the *Policia de Segurança Publica* in Funchal are after him and if he is caught he will be extradited and put in prison in his own country. I will tell him that we pitied him and gave him shelter and that he fell in love with me and decided to stay here with us. Then he went out by himself—got caught in that fog and fell into the ravine, so we rescued him. I can make up such stories, Papa, and *you* must not argue or gossip. You need not enter into any conversation. You will only drop a brick if you do.'

Bemused but weak-willed as ever in the hands of his strong-minded daughter, José said, 'I will argue no more. Do as you wish and be happy. *Mon Dieu!* You deserve it after all you have gone through. I only hope nothing will go wrong and that he will take in all you say.'

'He will—until he comes out of the coma completely—then we will see.'

But now José alluded to the one thing that so far he had not dared mention. 'So you expect him to believe that he wished to marry you in spite of—' he broke off.

'In spite of my face?' she finished bitterly because she saw his gaze upon her. For an instant, like a light suddenly going out, all joy left her face. She put up a hand to her scarred cheek. 'Yes, even in spite of *this,* I shall make him love and need me and be grateful because I saved his life.'

The old man lifted his brows. He did not think she entirely believed what she said, herself. He said no more but hobbled out of the cottage into the sunshine, crossing himself and muttering, 'May her guardian angel protect her, my poor crazy Chia!'

Another week passed. Martin Ashley's mind remained a blank.

With each morning that she woke, Sanchia rushed to her patient's side with the cup of tea that she knew most English people enjoyed. She was wildly relieved every time they spoke, to find that he still remembered nothing.

She would bid him good morning and although she dared not attempt to kiss even his forehead, she always made that tender gesture of putting his hand against her cheek, the one that was still smooth and glowing. He would talk to her in the French language. By now she was aware that his knowledge of it was somewhat limited. But it was enough for her.

She had prepared herself to answer the many questions that he put to her.

'I feel strong enough to get up today,' he said on one occasion. 'The ankle that I twisted when I fell is much better. I would like to take some exercise. Will you help me dress?'

But her answer was, 'No—not yet. You must not leave this room. I will explain later—but first you must be really well, and feel better able to understand and accept what I tell you.'

He was too exhausted to oppose her.

During that next important week, Martin

could carry on only these brief halting conversations with Sanchia. He found himself quite unable to battle against her or piece together the gigantic puzzle of his presence in this cottage—and his past.

He only knew that this strange girl—half French–half-Portuguese—was immensely kind and sweet to him and could not do enough for his comfort. He was grateful and not unaware of her warmth and generosity.

Unknown to him, Sanchia went down to the market with her father and bought the kind of clothes that a young working man who lived up here in the mountains would wear; one or two coloured shirts; some coarse denim trousers; a white vest and red linen jeans; cheap underwear; and a sleeveless pullover.

She had taken care to measure Martin's old things so that the new ones fitted. She had had to burn his trousers because they were so stained and torn. They were not even worth cleaning. Besides which, she did not wish Martin to examine them. They might stimulate his memory. She showed the clothes she had bought to him, but he merely shook his head and gave her an apologetic smile.

'They mean nothing to me. I suppose they are mine.'

'Why, anyhow should he imagine that what she told him was a tissue of lies? What possible reason would she and her nice old father have for giving him sanctuary here, or the girl for saying he was her affianced husband, if it were not the truth? Sanchia had also explained that he used to live and work in London, which was why he found himself automatically speaking English as well as French. Martin had in fact learned to speak French when he was a boy, staying with his grandmother in the South of France. But of Violetta and those days he had no recollection.

'Why did I come to live here originally with you and José?' he asked Sanchia one morning.

In her feverish imagination she had decided what answer to make and came out with it, readily.

'Before your accident, you arrived in Madeira, penniless and wanting work which you found difficult to get. My father met you one day in Funchal and offered you bed and food in return for your help. He does many jobs—mainly thatching, a little carpentry, or weaving of baskets, and so on. He is growing old and he needed an assistant.'

Martin's brows met in a puzzled frown. 'Can I do these things—weaving—thatching—?' he asked in a halting whisper.

Sanchia dared to smooth the thick fair hair back from his brow.

'Yes, yes, of course. But why worry yourself about it now, *chéri?* Just sleep as much as you can and grow stronger every day. Later I will tell you the bad news.'

But the word 'bad' penetrated Martin's

baffled consciousness. He lifted himself up. His grey eyes looked at her intently.

'What bad news? Tell me now. I must know. Maybe it will help me to remember.'

She went down on one knee beside the bed.

'Are you not content just to be with me and forget everything else?' she asked wistfully. 'Have you forgotten that we are betrothed?'

He lay back on the pillow and drew a hand across his forehead.

'Oh God, I remember nothing, not even *that,*' he groaned.

'Lie still, *chéri*—rest,' she soothed him. 'Leave all to me.'

'I suppose I must,' he said slowly and painfully.

With a quick surge of emotion she said, 'Do you recognise *nothing* about your Chia? Do you remember absolutely *nothing* of our— love—' She swallowed and choked a little.

The natural kindness that was his, filtered into Martin's consciousness. He caught at one of her brown strong hands and kissed it, as she had kissed his.

'It doesn't matter. You have been absolutely wonderful to me. But I wish I knew why you are afraid to let me get up and go outside.'

She was so enthralled by his kiss and the sweetness in his voice that she was ready to dance with joy. Still keeping her ruined cheek hidden by her scarf, she sprang to her feet.

'Oh, *chéri*, life begins for me again! Now I

know you are better. Just now you kissed my hand as you used to do.'

'Did I?' he whispered helplessly, and touched his hair. The bandage was off. He felt no more pain except for an occasional headache. But he had dizzy spells which he presumed were the result of his head injury and concussion.

Sanchia started to leave the room. He called to her. 'Chia—please come back.'

Again her whole body seemed to vibrate. She had asked him to call her 'Chia'. Told him that he, as well as her father, was to use that nickname. She adored to hear it from 'Jean'. He had a marvellous voice. It was glorious to see him using her room, her bed; to see his handsome head on her pillow; to feel that at last she had a wonderful man to love and care for.

She turned to him. 'What can I do for you, Jean?'

'Tell me about this *bad* news. No, do not say I am too weak or sick to hear it. I am neither. It will drive me mad if you do not tell me *everything* that I want to know. I am living in a ghastly sort of cloud. It suffocates me!'

She hesitated, and stood by the casement window, staring out, her brain seething with half-crazed thought.

There were many clouds drifting down from the mountains. It was cooler. Sanchia was glad of her white jersey which she had smartened up with a scarlet nylon scarf. Until now it had been put away between tissue-paper. She had worn it only in the old days for Marcello. Once more she took pride in dressing. She had washed her hair and let the blue-black waves flow over her shoulders in modem style. Already she had had the pleasure of hearing Jean remark that she had wonderful hair.

But as yet, she could not, would not, allow him to see that side of her face that had driven Marcello away. The mere idea terrified her. She would want to die if her new love also turned from her. She would not want to live if she read repulsion in *his* eyes.

Again he asked, impatiently, 'Are you afraid for me to be seen around here? For anyone to talk to me? Surely if I meet some of my old friends in the village, it might help to restore my memory?'

She shuddered. Without looking at him, she said, 'The doctor has told me to keep you very quiet. It will be a strain on you to meet people.'

'Somehow I feel there is more to it,' Martin Ashley said slowly, carefully picking his words. 'You mentioned *bad* news. I insist on 'you telling me what it is, Chia.'

She had the story ready but she couldn't bring herself to worry him with it. Once more she tried delaying tactics. He couldn't do anything about the bad news at the moment, she said. In a day or two she would tell him.

She kept repeating that it didn't matter now. Finally he grew weary of questioning her and fell asleep.

CHAPTER FOUR

Another week passed.

At the end of this time Martin was so much better—he had even lost that faint hesitance in his speech, and could articulate more easily. He decided to pay no further attention to Sanchia's efforts to keep him in bed. He was becoming restless and slightly irritable. But whenever he searched his brain, his memories were not of the past. It was still shrouded in a fog of mystery.

He told Sanchia that he would dress and start using his legs again at the end of this week. It was a new, and in his estimation, a strange man who looked at him from the mirror he forced Sanchia to bring him. He hardly recognised himself. Every word that she had said was foremost in his baffled mind. But although he had no reason to believe she lied, he found her story difficult to swallow.

He was a wanted man, she said. If he went to the wine-shop with José he would be reported and the police would come up from Funchal to arrest him.

She had also told him a dramatic story

about his true association with José and herself. Having met José in Funchal he had agreed to accept the offer to stay in José's home for the time being. He—'Jean' as he was now called—had told them he had money and friends in England and had hoped to escape arrest by vanishing up here in the mountains of Madeira. Unfortunately soon after his arrival he had taken the near-fatal walk which had ended in his accident. Sanchia and her father had searched for him, and eventually found him. But while he lay in a coma, she heard that the police were searching for him. So she had conceived this plan for harbouring him. She would help him change his identity, particularly his appearance. They would speak only in French. Nobody would know he was English. She would procure a dye and as soon as the cut on his scalp was completely healed she would disguise the fairness of his hair. Also the beard that he had begun to grow quite thickly. And she could stain his face and neck and hands a rich brown so that he would look like any other Portuguese on the island. She had wanted to do this before but he had refused. Now it was essential. She warned him that for a time he must not leave the cottage, nor speak to a soul. If anyone discovered him she and José would announce that he was a second cousin, Jean, from France where José had lived, who had come to stay with them; that he was for the time being laid up.

All this amazed Martin, but Sanchia had a glib answer to his questions.

As they walked together, he said, 'You tell me we were engaged to be married. Yet we are really strangers, are we not? Why claim that we were lovers? I find it very confusing.'

She turned from him and answered in a strangled voice, 'I admit that I lied about us.'

'Why?'

She hesitated, then gave a bold reply, 'I am frank and sincere—' she tossed back the magnificent hair—'I fell in love with you as soon as we met. After I helped my father pull you to safety I wanted you. For me it was love at first sight.'

That brought the blood to Martin's hollowed cheeks but he felt more embarrassment than pleasure.

'It was good of you,' he muttered uneasily.

'I wasn't trying to be good. I just wanted to save you. I wanted you for myself.'

'Can a girl be so sure of love after so short a time?'

'Yes, she can, and I am that girl!' Sanchia declared obstinately.

Nothing that Martin had to say could make her refute that statement.

Finally she knelt beside his bed, and put her face against his shoulder, weeping.

'I don't often cry these days. I am usually strong and brave, and until you came, I was hard. Today I cry because I see you are not

204

going to love me in return. While I have been nursing you, I have been living in a fool's paradise—a dream that you were the one and only man for me—that you had come into my life in this extraordinary way, and would never leave me. Oh! *Chéri! Chéri!* forgive me if I have been mad but I swear to you that I do truly love you and that I want to save you now from extradition. The English police will come to Madeira and take you back to England, and you will be put in prison—unless you consent to stay in hiding with us.'

Martin argued again. 'But I cannot remember any of these things you tell me about myself. I cannot believe I was a bank-robber. *I cannot!'*

'You were and you suffer from the sickness they call *amnesia* which means that when the left side of your head hit that rocky ledge, a part of your brain was damaged.'

'For good and all?' he asked, sudden fear in his eyes.

'No, no. You *can* recover. One day, perhaps, you will. Then you will understand what a service I have rendered you. Please, *please* stay with us, Jean. until this police search dies down. Let me disguise you—make you look like a Portuguese—a Frenchman—anyone— but do not stay as you are, so fair, so English, so vulnerable!'

He shut his eyes. He was exhausted by the time their discussion ended. And all the time she stayed with one cheek hidden against his shoulder. Automatically he stroked the satin black head. It had a musky fragrance which was very feminine and a little disturbing even to Martin. For he was a man and from all that he had seen of Sanchia she was a truly handsome girl and he could not but be flattered by her open adoration. In the end he had no option but to accept her offer to shelter him here for the time being. What did he care, anyhow, if she altered his appearance and told crazy stories to her friends? Not that he had seen many. He could not remember anybody coming to this cottage.

Oh God! he thought, if only I knew who I really was, and my real name, and what kind of family and home I have, and how I ever came to be a criminal.

He could even be married. *Had* he a wife? He did not know. It was as though the whole of his past life had been blotted out. What course had he to accept this strange girl's story as verbatim? He could certainly speak fluent French. He was a man of culture, that seemed obvious. One of the most puzzling things was his association with these two poor villagers— so different from himself. If he had had a wallet or any papers of identification on him, when he took that near-fatal plunge into the ravine, they must be lost. All he could do now was to thank his lucky stars that it was not his dead body old José and his daughter had found.

At last Martin sighed deeply and said, 'Please, Chia, go and enquire discreetly the name of the man they are looking for. If I could hear my name it might ring a bell.'

He had lapsed into English. She shook her head.

'I do not understand "ring a bell". Please speak in French. Don't let anyone hear your English tongue.' And she resolved that she would never let him know he was Martin Ashley. Nor must he see the police notices and his own photograph—that might certainly lead him straight to the police.

During the three weeks that he had been in this house with her—like a child in her hands—such a violent passion for him had grown within Sanchia's heart that she could not face up to the idea of losing him.

But she apologised for having lied about their engagement. 'I admit I did wrong,' she said miserably.

It was at this point that Martin drew attention to her appearance.

'Why do you put that scarf over your face? Why do you always hide it?' he asked.

He felt a shudder go through her whole body.

'I dare not let you look at me.'

'For heaven's sake, why not?'

She began to cry bitterly.

'Because you will turn from me. Whether

you love me or not, you will never want to look at me again. I will disgust you.'

Martin put a hand to his forehead.

'I fail to understand you, Chia. First of all I am a criminal and must hide—now *you* are afraid to show your face. Please explain.'

She kept her head down a moment longer, helpless with grief and terror. But she had so much to contend with, and had gone so far with this drama that she had woven about Martin and herself, she felt no longer able to conceal her own tragedy from him It was impossible for her to do so permanently. Now that he was recovering, she must act. She stopped crying and said in a voice of despair.

'Very well—I will tell you my story. I was once engaged to a young man named Marcello. Before we married, he had an accident on his motor-bike. I was riding pillion and was thrown on to the road and hopelessly disfigured. He left me. I could see that the sight of me made him sick. That is the grim truth. Now *you* shall look at me, full-face. All I beg is that you do not rush out of the house because you cannot bear the sight of me. For your own safety's sake, please stay with me a little longer.'

'What is all this nonsense—?' he began, but stopped abruptly, for Sanchia had thrown back her head and allowed the light from the casement window to fall full upon her.

He looked in silence for a moment. He

neither flinched nor did his expression change, although he was frankly startled and slightly shocked. It was a fearful disfigurement. Up till this moment he had only seen that one beautiful untouched profile and her glorious eyes. Now he saw the puckered mouth—the drawn-in cheek—the scarred, pitted brow, the disfigured jawbone, giving the once-perfect face a lopsided, even grotesque appearance.

God! he thought. *How terrible!*

Such an injury would have been bad enough for a man, but for a lovely girl much worse. And this young monster Marcello had walked out on her. Deserted her when she needed him most. All that was kind and good in Martin Ashley's nature rose to the fore. In this hour he was himself again, without realising it. He put out a hand and touched the scars. He smiled a slow sweet smile.

'My poor dear Chia, I don't know what you are worrying about. You are scarred, but for heaven's sake it might have been *me*. I could have struck my face against that ledge—injured my whole face instead of my head You wouldn't have turned in disgust from me. Why should I turn from you?'

Sanchia could hardly believe her ears. She stared at Martin incredulously, her fingertips pressed against her mouth. The words he had just spoken sounded like the sweetest music to her ears. She felt an almost unbearable joy. She gasped, '*It isn't true!* It can't be true. You are just saying this to comfort me.'

'If it comforts you I'm glad. But I'm saying it because that's how I feel. I won't be so idiotic as to pretend it hasn't made a difference to you, but you still have your beautiful eyes and hair—your fine figure, and that one perfect side. You have so much else, dear Chia. I can't even begin to understand how your Marcello could have deserted you. Believe me, it was *his* loss, not yours. Never again will he find a kinder, more noble nature than yours. Even in this day and age, when there is so little nobility, and so much egotism, there are still men and women who appreciate the fine qualities of a true woman and put her price above that of mere beauty. Chia, my dear girl, you have been angelic to me. I could never find you ugly or anywhere near it . . . But I would like to ask you why you didn't ask for plastic surgery? Today they can do so much to eliminate scars and such injuries. They can build a new face, in fact.'

'I know, but I couldn't afford such an operation and I didn't care any more once Marcello left me,' Sanchia whispered. She dissolved again into tears, kissing Martin's hand repeatedly. 'Jean, Jean, I loved you before. Now I *worship* you. You don't know what you have done by looking at me so kindly—smiling, as though I were still the Chia I used to be.'

'I can imagine what you used to be, but I

don't object to the Chia I see this very moment.' Martin smiled again.

'Oh, my beloved Jean, please understand how much this means to me.'

Her emotion, her tears moistening his hand, became deeply embarrassing to Martin. He hadn't the heart to say so in this moment but he knew for certain that he could not return her feverish, exaggerated love. On the other hand he was determined to show his gratitude for all that she had done for him. Obviously had he been taken into a hospital, he might well have ended in arrest and prison.

He said, 'Stop crying, Chia. And don't cover your face again. You need never do so because of me.'

Still she could not believe it. She felt almost hysterical with happiness. The awful bitterness she used to feel—the growing hatred of her fellow creatures, and her desperate desire to remove herself from love and life, evaporated as fast as the clouds out there over the mountainside vanished once the sunlight dissolved them.

Whatever happened in the future, she felt a close kinship to this man whom she had christened 'Jean'. She intended to go on loving and serving him.

He, in turn, was persuaded by her to accept the shelter and disguise she offered, for the present anyhow. If indeed he was escaping from justice, he must do as she suggested.

So, that next day, from old Pascala, the local 'witch', Sanchia bought the necessary dye for 'Jean's' hair, and a brown lotion for his skin.

That evening when José came back from work, the pale fair English boy who had become of such vital necessity to Chia, had disappeared. In his place was a brown-faced young man with thick curly black hair and the short black beard that had grown during his convalescence. With this, and wearing the rough shirt and jeans that Chia had chosen for him, Martin Ashley looked indeed like a native of Madeira.

Old José had become so confused and buffeted by his daughter's fantastic behaviour that he had nothing much to say about the amazing metamorphosis. He could only tug at his goatee beard and swear both in Portuguese and French which he did when he was distressed.

'Well?' exclaimed Sanchia, hands on hips, head flung defiantly back. 'Isn't it wonderful, Papa? Would you have known him? Would anyone here think he was a blond English gentleman? No—they'd believe our story that we have a cousin who had just come from France to stay with us.'

José gave a cackling laugh and nodded. He assured her that he would never have guessed Jean's true identity. Sanchia looked with fond, proud eyes at her creation. Martin looked back a trifle uneasily, although with a spark of humour in his own eyes.

'I only want a beret to complete the make-up,' he said. '*Now* will you please stop worrying, Chia, if I wish to go out and take a walk.'

It was the last thing Sanchia wanted him to do. She begged him not to show himself freely in the daylight for the present, or go shopping, or, if it came to that, visit the village. At least not until the hue and cry for him had died down.

'After dark, we can walk together, Jean *chéri*. I will get you some sunglasses so that nobody can even see the colour of your eyes.'

Martin shrugged. He had better play along with this game. Chia had impressed it upon him that he was a 'wanted man' and the confusion in his mind and the blankness of his memory would not allow him to argue the point. Nevertheless he was far from content with the present situation. He kept trying miserably and without success to dig deeper into the recess of his injured mind. He was sure he was not 'Jean'. Nor part of a gang who had robbed a bank. It was a crazy story, yet why discredit it? And he could find no reason to disbelieve this girl and her father who swore that *he* had told them about the robbery before his accident.

During the days that followed, Martin felt no happier. As time went on he grew more restless—mistrustful of everything and

213

everybody. But at least he had something to do now.

José had brought him some timber. He began to build a chicken-hut for the wretched struggling birds Sanchia kept. That he must have liked carpentering in the past and knew something about it, was obvious, for he attacked the job easily and when the chicken-house was completed, both the old man and the girl complimented him on the excellence of his work.

He began to protest about the money Chia was spending on him. He must get paid work, he said, and be able to give them something for his board and lodging.

The old man was on his side about that. But Sanchia still lived in terror of Martin being recognised. Yet up till now things were going well.

Once or twice he had insisted on going just to look at the traffic on the main road. That, she had allowed. It was only in the post office and the inn at Quintra that notices about Martin Ashley were hanging. Besides, nobody looked twice at the dark-haired, dark-bearded young man with his tinted glasses, and the beret on the side of his head. He seemed to belong here. There were plenty like him.

Old Pascala had left a bottle of lotion with Sanchia, so when Martin's hair began to grow she swiftly touched up the roots. These and other ministrations from her, he received laconically—even with a feeling of indifference. That she was genuinely in love with him, he could well believe. She made no bones about it. But he could not return her passion. He was in no state of mind to desire a love affair with any girl. The mental fog in which he was existing left no room for romantic yearnings.

Now and again—especially when he was half-asleep, half-awake—vague phantoms of that lost memory haunted Martin.

On one occasion he seemed to see a girl's face. But it wasn't Sanchia's. It was pale and sweet and strangely familiar. He noted the colour of her hair—tawny, almost golden-red. He wondered who she was—but as he stared the phantom vanished. In another dream he saw a room—a high long room, and on either side tall cases filled with books. *Why books?* What had they to do with his past life? He wondered. What *had* he been before he became involved in this crime? Where, in fact, was his home? London, he supposed. It was the English police who wanted him. And perhaps Interpol were looking for him, too. Who else was looking for him? Supposing he couldn't bear to stay in this place any longer, what chances had he of escaping the law and of getting away from Madeira? Madeira—why had he come to Madeira? Had he landed at the airport or come by boat? Had he no luggage? The more he thought about things,

215

the more depressed he became.

Then his head began to ache. From time to time he suffered from bad headaches and they made him feel sick. This girl Chia, said that the jagged cut on his scalp had healed. But it still felt raw and sore when he touched it, and damn it, when he did try and get on his feet, he had no great wish to remain on them for any length of time. He wanted to lie down again. He seemed to do a lot of sleeping.

Then when he slept, he felt that he had only passed from one darkness into another, and he wondered when the light would break.

CHAPTER FIVE

As each day passed, Martin's unhappiness and irritability increased. He became less sympathetic with the girl he called Chia— despite his deep-down sympathy for her. But he forbade her to go on kissing his hand and sacrificing herself for him.

'I am grateful to you. You have done *so* much for me and you've saved me from a long term of imprisonment, obviously. But all this—' he waved an arm around, 'is beginning to feel like prison to me. I can't continue *ad infinitum*. I must get going and find out more about myself.'

He said all this in English, then repeated it
216

in French, but it did nothing but depress Sanchia profoundly. Her ecstatic joy when she had first found and brought this glorious young man into her life, was slowly dying down—down, until it was replaced by the old feeling of despair. Jean did not return her love. He didn't show distaste when he looked at her but he did not love her. Would never do so. Having achieved her object by getting him to stay here in hiding, she had finally to agree with him that it could not continue permanently. All she could do now was to delay the finale, if she could.

'Lie low for the moment, *chéri, bel-ami*. I implore you! Once the police are sure you are not on the island and the search ends, you will no longer be a marked man, providing you stick to your disguise and remain Jean, a Frenchman. You can move about freely and go where you want.'

Martin was still conscious of the wish to be kind and gentle with this girl, but he could not stand the boredom of his present life. He did not in his heart *feel* that he was a criminal. He was sure there was some mistake. He staked everything on the hope that his amnesia would pass and gradually his memory would be restored.

He told Sanchia so and this sort of talk always brought a flood of tears from her. She would rush away from him and he would feel helpless to comfort her.

He discussed the position with the old man many times, but José was too frightened of his daughter to enlighten Jean—tell the truth. So he did the next best thing and tried to bring more interest into his life. They needed cash—Jean must, indeed, pay his way. So José took him out on the next job he, himself, was given—thatching a big barn. They needed another pair of hands there. Jean learned the job with speed and intelligence and was a willing worker. José's employer who took the 'French boy' on, paid him the usual money that labourers on this part of the island received. It was not much but it was enough for his needs and José was satisfied. He was well aware that his daughter's hoard of savings had dwindled alarmingly during the past two months. For it was indeed eight long weeks now since they had found Martin in the ravine.

Sanchia could manage her father but in time she found she was unable to control Jean. He had too much spirit for that.

He insisted one evening upon going to the wine-shop with José. When Sanchia screamed at Jean that he would be in great danger despite his disguise, he remonstrated with her, gently at first, then more roughly.

'Leave me to manage my own affairs, for God's sake!'

He was beginning to feel safe. Nobody had questioned his presence in the district. The young man with the black beard was old José's relation.

Sanchia hid her face on her arm and left the room, weeping.

This was late one afternoon—an hour before José was due to visit the wine-shop for his nightly glass of Sercial, the sherry much enjoyed by the locals. And on this occasion Martin also insisted that Sanchia should be given a rest from shopping. In the wine-shop they sold eels—the only freshwater fish that could be procured in Quintra. He would buy some eels for Chia to stew, also sweet potatoes, and a small basket of figs—a welcome change of diet.

He told Sanchia she was not to argue.

'So far I've taken everything and given nothing. Now that I have my first week's pay, I intend to make tonight a kind of celebration.'

Chia had been crying and did not look her best. She covered her face with both arms and whispered, 'You are kind and generous but I worry for you! I don't want gifts. At least let *me* go and buy the food.'

'No,' he said stubbornly, 'I wish to do so myself. If I'm never to appear in public, what's the use of my disguise.'

There was nothing she could say to that. So she left the cottage without the two men seeing her go, and ran all the way to Quintra. White and shaking she arrived at the wine-shop, her scarf wrapped about her face as usual. The woman who served in there eyed her inquisitively. It wasn't often these days that poor Sanchia was seen around. But gossip had been rife lately. She greeted Sanchia with reference to their lodger.

'I hear you have a cousin living with you.'

'Yes,' said Sanchia, and kept her face hidden.

'Nice for you, Sanchia,' the woman said.

'Very nice. Jean is a good boy and works hard with my father.'

'It'll cheer you up. You have shut yourself away far too long,' the woman said. She had once known Sanchia's mother. Of course it was rumoured in Quintra that Sanchia's accident followed by Marcello's desertion, had unhinged the poor girl's mind.

Sanchia avoided further gossip. She looked around her with terrified eyes. The police notice—it used to hang behind the counter—but it was there no longer. Search the shop though she did, Sanchia could see no photograph, no police notice concerning Martin Ashley. Fear and despair led her to be less cautious than usual. She said to the woman, 'We were telling Jean about the missing Englishman. Did they ever find him?'

'I really don't know,' said the woman, shrugging, 'but I don't think so. The *guarda* has been up here snooping about many times and told me he found no trace of the *senhor* near Quintra. Why *should* he have come here? It's a foolish waste of time, all this searching.'

'Are they no longer hanging up notices?' Sanchia asked, with a show of nonchalance.

'I couldn't say. Ours remained until it became torn and dirty, what with people knocking against it and so on. The *guarda* said he would send up another but hasn't done so. Maybe they found the English *senhor* and have called off the search.'

Sanchia drew a deep sigh of relief. She had to pretend that she came for a reason, so she bought a packet of cigarettes—the kind she knew Martin liked—and hurried back to the cottage.

There followed a bad hour for her. José and Martin walked with her back to the wine-shop. This time there were a number of workmen in the place, some alone, some with their wives, drinking, smoking and chatting. There was a babel of tongues.

Sanchia kept close to Martin. She had warned him that his safety depended on him not uttering one word in English. Since few of the locals spoke French, he could not have many conversations with them, for which Sanchia was thankful. Only one girl who had known Sanchia quite well in the past came up and greeted her and mentioned the young man in the white vest and red jeans, with the black beret on the side of his dark head.

'He is very handsome. Is he your new fancy, my dear.'

Sanchia's muscles seemed to contract. It

was only in a whisper that she answered, 'No, not at all. Far from it. He—he has a girl-friend in France.'

It was another of her fancies. She thought it best not to reveal her penchant for 'Jean'. After a moment her former friend bade her good night. Poor Sanchia, the girl thought as she went, how hideous that injured face was except when she showed her best side. The young Portuguese girl wished she could have got to know the Frenchman. She didn't much like men with beards but thought José's young cousin fascinating.

Sanchia was not happy until they were all safely back in the cottage, and she was stewing the eels for their supper.

But it was scarcely a gay evening. José did most of the talking. Martin looked surly and lapsed into long silences. Sanchia went down still further into the darkness of the old pain and grief—knowing that Jean, her dream-lover, could never belong to her.

At the end of the month José received an invitation from a cousin of his late wife's to the wedding of her daughter, Martita. The old man became quite excited about this and waved the letter at Sanchia, his glasses falling from his nose. He only caught them just in time and waved them at her as well.

'It is little Martita—you remember when your mother was alive, you used to visit each other. Martita was younger than you but you

222

were fond of her. Do, I beg you, break your vow never to go to a public affair again, Chia *mon enfant*—please! Wear a veil—but *let us go.* We will take Jean with us. It will cheer him up and it will be a good wedding. If I know her father, there'll be plenty to eat and drink. A fine idea—don't you think so, Jean?' He turned to Martin.

Martin glanced at Sanchia. She had folded her arms and put on the expression he was beginning to dread—one of sullen hostility. She could be so amiable—so unselfish—so kind. *And* so difficult! he thought. Her answer was as he expected.

'No. I refuse, Papa. You know how I feel.'

'But *I* would like it,' said Martin, being obstinate in his turn. He was sick of this narrow, boring life. The idea of a visit to José's cousins and a wedding, interested him.

Sanchia turned on him. 'So! You want to be recognised and arrested!'

'Oh, my dear, do you still deny that I look any longer like the man you found and befriended. *Pour l'amour de Dieu!* Look at me, look at me!' he struck his chest with a clenched fist.

From under her long lashes Sanchia studied Martin gloomily. The overall effect of his black curly hair which had grown long and a little greasy, and his stained skin which had naturally tanned from constant exposure to the sun, plus the black beard and side-burns, did completely disguise him. He bore no relationship to the *senhor* the *policia* were supposed to be looking for. Grudgingly she had to grant him that.

And now into her tormented brain there crept a doubt as to her own decision. She began to think of the wedding and what it might mean. It was so long since she had worn her national costume and taken part in the dances of Madeira. So long since she had listened to a guitar, or a voice singing the songs of the country. Looking at Martin, she felt a sudden urge to dance with him—to be close to *him*. He had been so cool, so distant lately. Agonised with longing, she suddenly capitulated.

'Very well. I will go with you. I can wear the Spanish mantilla that belonged to my grandmother. My grandmother came from Andalusia,' she explained to Martin, 'I can hide my face with it and look coquettish!' And she ended with a cynical laugh.

Martin's spirits rose. He held out a hand to her.

'Bravo! Let us all go and celebrate without fear, either of the police, or of people giving you dark looks, dear Chia.'

She placed her long warm fingers in his. She felt the answering warmth, and tears of sheer happiness began to roll down her cheeks. But she stayed dumb. Fear was still in her heart, fear for his safety. And she hardly dared begin

224

to think what he would say or do if he ever discovered the truth. He would, of course, hate her and never wish to see her again. She could be sure of that. Old José hopped from one foot to another like a pleased child.

'*A la bonne heure.* La—di—da—di-da!' And he began to sing in a croaky voice. The other two had to laugh at his capers. So the invitation to the little village near Pioso was accepted. Gaily, Martin offered to supply the money to pay for their transport by bus. He had his pay packet to come. It was not all that far from Quintra to Pioso. They would spend the day there. They began to make plans.

The three of them journeyed to the wedding of Martita on a day of brilliant sunshine and deep blue skies. The tiny village where Martita and her parents lived was *en fête*—crowded with relations and guests. As José had anticipated, his late wife's relatives did things well. Martita's father was in the wine trade and not as old or as poor as José. After the church ceremony a huge lunch was served under the plane trees, then singing, and finally dancing. Even Sanchia began to emerge from her former wretchedness.

She had taken great care with her beautiful hair and dressed it high with combs and ribbons. She held her mother's mantilla across the scarred spoiled side of her face and was conscious that one or two men looked at her with admiration. The national costume suited her fine slim figure.

Martin enjoyed the whole affair. Flushed with wine and once they started modern dancing, he swung Sanchia into the crowd and found her supple and graceful in his arms. He followed her steps and held her as close as she wanted and told her that she was a wonderful partner. She strained near to him and felt the very joy of life and living begin to run through her veins once more. Certainly she was happier than she had been since Marcello went away. She kept whispering Jean's name—the name she had given him.

'Jean, Jean, Jean!'

But she could see—she could sense—that Martin's gaiety and willingness to hold her was all on the surface. Not once did his eyes gaze into hers with any real meaning—or genuine passion. They even had a faraway expression in them from time to time as though he were not with her at all

There came a moment during the dancing when Martin himself, had the queerest feeling that he was with someone else—*somewhere else.* Long, long ago, it seemed, he had danced with a fair beautiful girl with thick tawny hair. He had dreamed about her. Yes, it was that same girl who had haunted his dreams while he was laid up. What was it all about? If only he could remember her name, other memories might follow.

Then once more he became aware that he

226

was holding *Chia.* It was into her magnificent dark brown eyes that he was looking while they danced. He felt a sudden queer faintness. He let go of his partner and staggered.

'The sun is too much for me,' he muttered, 'I must sit down.'

Alarmed, she led him away from the dance which was taking place in the village square. He did look suddenly ill, she thought.

'Oh, Jean, what is it?'

He put a hand to his forehead.

'Nothing—only the sun,' he repeated. 'It's very hot and I've drunk a lot of wine.'

'Let's sit over there—' she nodded towards a Persea tree which spread its glossy leaves just outside Martita's house. The music was loud and there was laughter and singing. The festivities would go on till late tonight.

They passed a shepherd-boy who looked at them rather too inquisitively for Sanchia's liking.

She hurried Jean to a bench beneath the Persea tree. They sat down in the shade.

'Let me get you something cool to drink—' she began.

'No, I want nothing. Just let me rest a moment. It's my head again,' he said.

His head, his memory, Sanchia thought fearfully, maybe his memory is awakening. *Mon Dieu!* I wish we had never come and the sooner we get home, the better.

She left him alone for a moment to go and

find her father, José, who was now a little intoxicated and as happy as a sandboy. He was smoking and still drinking with his cousins. Just before she reached him, Martita's elder sister Pila, stopped Sanchia.

'Hello, Chia,' she greeted her. 'It's good to see you after all this time You must come over to us more often.'

'I don't go out much,' mumbled Sanchia.

Pila glanced towards the figure under the Persea tree. 'You have a fine boy with you. I thought him very handsome when you were dancing.'

And Pila looked again at the lone figure of Martin sitting there. She admired his crisp white shirt, and bright red linen jeans. 'Take me over and introduce me to him, Chia. What's his name? Where does he come from? I haven't ever seen him around.'

'I'm sorry, I haven't time now,' said Sanchia abruptly, her knees knocking. 'My—my friend is from France—a distant relative. He isn't too well. I think he has a touch of the sun. I was just about to tell Papa we must catch the next bus home.'

'Surely you will wait for supper,' said Pita, disappointed, and with a coquettish eye still upon Martin.

But Sanchia waved her aside and called to her father. They must take the next bus to Quintra.

The old man was disappointed, too. He

didn't want to go home but he could see that something had happened to distress his daughter. Reluctantly, he did as she asked. She did not tell him about it until later when they were back in their own cottage. Then she said that she believed that Jean's head was troubling him. She had noticed he had had bad pain lately. He had gone 'queer' she said, while they danced. It was as though she did not exist and that he might have been with another girl altogether.

José shrugged his shoulders. He told Sanchia that he thought she was just imagining things. But he had to admit that Jean did not look well. He would not eat any more and after a cup of black coffee, went straight to bed.

There was something else, Sanchia confided in her father when they were alone again. The shepherd they called Beppo, had stared repeatedly at Jean. *Why* had he stared? There must once have been police notices up in Poiso and the surrounding villages. Not that she had seen one, she admitted that. But she had felt from the start that it was dangerous for Jean to go to a public gathering. José protested. Again and again he reminded Sanchia that Jean bore no resemblance now to the Englishman who was wanted by the police. Besides, interest in him was surely dying down. It was no longer front-page news.

Sanchia shook her head. She was full of

terrors—both vague and wild. Before she slept that night she tiptoed into her old bedroom, holding a lighted candle in her hand and looked long and fixedly at Martin Ashley— alias Jean.

He was fast asleep. But his brows were knit and even on his sleeping face there was a marked expression of intense worry.

What is wrong with him? What is he thinking? What will happen? she asked herself. If his mind does, in fact, become clear again and he realises what Papa and I have done, what will happen? *Mother of God!*

She was filled with a deep sense of foreboding.

Part Three

CHAPTER ONE

One bright afternoon towards the end of July, Corrie left Martin's grandmother to take her usual siesta and made use of their hired car to drive her up to Camacha. She wanted to go to the factory there to buy a very special basket to take back to England. She needed more luggage. She was collecting souvenirs—she had already bought a few at the Maison Blanc which she thought one of the best shops in Funchal; also a heavenly embroidered tablecloth from the Casa Da Turista. She was going to give that to Violetta whose birthday, she knew, was in August. Had darling Martin been here, he would have bought something for his beloved grandmother so Corrie felt she must take his place.

It seemed so very long since she had first arrived in Funchal to meet him. So long since he disappeared. So long since they all started to search for him. It was as though years and years had passed. She felt suspended, as though time itself had stood still and she could neither go back nor forward. Certainly she could never make plans of any importance. Nothing seemed to count very greatly in her life.

Martin had never come back.

Corrie had passed from anguish and despair

into a condition close to resignation. But the thought of Martin, the longing for him, remained vividly alive in her mind. Even though she never saw him again, nothing could kill her love for him. She would adore him until she died. That *he* might be already dead had become more than a possibility in her mind. If he were alive—surely by now he would have returned? She was not like Violetta who was still optimistic. Corrie had almost, if not quite, given up hope.

While she remained on the island of Madeira she still felt in some way close to Martin. But one or two reasons had recently cropped up to make it difficult for her to stay much longer.

The situation at home was not too good. Violetta would have been willing to keep on the Casa da Turna but Corrie's aunt had problems. The girl who had been her invaluable assistant down in the stables had just had an offer to go out to Canada, so she was going. Mrs. May, Ann's daily cook, who always gave her a good midday meal and left something for her supper, was ill and facing an operation. So far, because Ann's house was isolated, she had not been able to find a replacement for either employee. She wrote lightly to her niece about these things but Corrie knew her aunt—she wouldn't want to worry her because of the tragedy in Madeira. Corrie had actually heard most of Ann's news from a mutual friend who lived on the neighbouring estate. She said in her letter that Miss Williams was looking very tired and worried. Corrie felt she ought to go back to Brabett's Farm and lend a helping hand, for a while, anyhow.

She had talked things over with Martin's grandmother. Violetta's reply was, 'Don't rush it, darling. Find out about the situation from Ann, first of all. If you finally decide you must go home, we'll both say goodbye to Funchal—at least for the time being.'

Corrie, with tears in her eyes, said in return, 'I'd hate to stay in England too long. I still feel in some fantastic way that in the end Martin will be found here. So here I must be.'

Violetta patted her hand. 'That's right, my darling, you can come back once you've settled Ann.'

But more than a vague hope of finding Martin had formed in Corrie's mind. A few nights ago she had been plunged just for an instant into the horror of the old nightmare. But the end had been quite different. For the first time she had seen the light, and Martin, himself, had materialised. It was Martin who had drawn her away out of the darkness—Martin, eager-eyed, smiling. He spoke to her, 'It's all right, Corrie, my Corisande. Don't cry, darling. It's going to be all right.'

She had flung herself into his arms. As they closed around her, she woke up, and as after

235

the other nightmares, she found herself bathed in perspiration, her heart thumped feverishly. Yet the depression—the horror—had vanished. She felt suddenly serene and happy. As she flung herself back on the pillow she spoke to Martin as though he were still with her.

'Oh, darling, *thank you* for telling me. I know it will be all right. Yes—yes—oh, Martin, *Martin,* come back to me soon!'

Of course she told Violetta about it.

'It wasn't the nightmare—it was a new wonderful dream. I've always said I was psychic. Tell me you think so, too. Oh, do tell me I'm not just going mad, and that Martin *is* alive.'

Violetta laughed then wept with her.

'My angel, you're not at all mad, and you know I've always believed in dreams. When you first told me about that awful long dark corridor, I worried. I was afraid something was going to happen to you. And it did. Martin vanished. But I'm absolutely thrilled by what you've just told me. It must mean that you're reaching the end of the black tunnel and you're going to come out into the light any moment now.'

Of course their few shared moments of joy passed. Back crept the doubts and the fears.

Corrie went without much enthusiasm to Camacha that glorious morning. As she drove up the mountain road she turned her thoughts to Hugh Aylmer. He had become her greatest friend. He had stayed with them at the Casa until the end of June, then had to return to his home—and his new book. She had found him such a wonderful person. He had given her unfailing support. She missed his company once he left. But yesterday she had had a long airmail letter from him that delighted both her and Violetta.

The tide had turned for Hugh. It was now many long months since his beloved Juliet had met her death in France, and since his accident. He was healed in both body and mind. Having imagined he would never in this life replace Juliet, he had quite suddenly found a girl who attracted him more than he had ever thought possible. He described her to Corrie:

She's about your age, I reckon, and not unlike you to look at in a funny way. You both have that same wonderful burnished chestnut hair. She wears it loose—like you do. Only her eyes are as blue as forget-me-nots and she certainly isn't as slender as you are. She's always having to diet, so she tells me, to keep her weight down. Not that I would mind having more of her, she's so sweet! Her name is Patricia Coombe—known as Pat. Her people come from Devon—Papa has a big dairy farm, and does well, I believe. Pat works as a secretary at the Foreign Office. I met her through the girl who does all my typing. They share a flat. When I got back from Madeira, my secretary gave a 21st birthday party and she asked if she dared send me an invitation. I told her I was the world's worst dancer but I'd be delighted to go to the party. It was there I met Pat, and to cut a long story short we fell in love and we're going to be married on *her* birthday, which is the 1st September. You're one of the first people I want her to meet and I know she'll love you.

I'd like to end this letter, dearest Corrie, by telling you not for the first time, how deeply I have always felt for you in your tragedy, and how much I would give to hear that you had news of Martin—good news! I know that time is marching on a bit too fast, but never lose hope, and please remember that if there is anything I can do for you on this earth, I always will. I've told Pat about you and she is extremely sympathetic. I, of course, look on you as I do on Liz—you're my second sister, in fact.

That letter had given both Corrie and Violetta great pleasure. They were very fond of Hugh and delighted to think that he could at last bury his own sorrows and start a new, full life. Even though he would never forget Juliet, he would obviously find happiness with

238

this girl, especially if she was as nice as he described.

'And I think I trust his taste,' Violetta added, 'I found him a very discerning kind of man as well as an intelligent one. I had an idea, which I see now was a complete mistake, that he was growing rather too fond of you.'

Corrie laughed and shook her head. 'No, I'm sure that wasn't so, and it wouldn't have been any use anyhow,' she added with a sigh, 'because it isn't just idle talk when I say I shall never marry if I don't marry Martin.'

The old lady had no ready answer for that. She steered the conversation back to Hugh and in particular to the P.S. which he had written at the end of his letter.

Needless to say, you and dear Violetta will receive invitations to my wedding. It's going to take place in London rather than Devon because Pat has made so many friends up here and her parents have agreed.

'I'd like to go,' declared Violetta, 'and I'll find him a really nice wedding present.'

Suddenly it was Corrie's turn to be silent. Violetta could go to Hugh's wedding but *she* really wondered if she could bear to do so. She did feel that Liz's brother was like her own. But her emotions were so mercurial. She was up one moment—down the next, and she felt a long way down when she remembered that had things gone right for her, she would have been married to Martin at least three months ago. Even dear Hugh's wedding would upset her.

They arrived at Camacha. She was a little disappointed for as she got out of the car, she noticed that the sun had gone in. There were large black clouds billowing up over the mountains. The air was sultry and she felt hot and sticky in spite of her cool cotton dress. It looked remarkably as though there might be a thunderstorm. One of the sudden storms that blew up so swiftly out here and ended in torrential rain. She'd better hurry into the willow factory and choose her basket.

As she reached the entrance she glanced at the adjoining café. A young man was sitting outside at one of the tables, smoking. As she looked towards him he got up and came across to her.

He spoke in French. 'Pardon, *madame,* but you have dropped your scarf, I think.'

She looked back and saw the scarlet and white scarf which she had been carrying over her arm. It must have slipped down as she walked to the shop and she hadn't noticed it. She said, *'Merci, monsieur.'* There were so many foreign tourists in Funchal at this time of the year. And he was certainly very civil, because he made a dart forward, picked up the scarf and brought it to her.

He was not a very tall man but he was

attractive. She looked up at him, meaning to thank him, then stopped. She stood transfixed. She felt as though there was already a storm and that she had been struck by lightning.

This man had Martin's face.

It was on the thin side, perhaps, and with hollows under the cheek-bones, and of course, he *couldn't* be Martin. He was as dark as Martin had been fair. He had longish black hair and a beard. But it was his eyes that held her spell bound. They were not as might be expected, a dark brown. They were grey. They were also the same shape as Martin's eyes, and he had the same long dark lashes.

He was staring down at her; rather a blank look—without recognition—but Corrie felt positively sick with the tension that was gradually rising in her. It was like a nausea that gave place to a spell of dizziness She swayed and for no reason except that this man with the grey eyes reminded her so ridiculously of Martin—she spoke his name aloud.

'Martin!'

For a second he neither moved nor spoke, but continued to stare down into the beautiful golden eyes of this girl with the tawny hair, falling so silkily down to her shoulders, this girl who called him *Martin* in a very English voice. He didn't understand why, but he, too, felt as though he had been struck by a lightning flash.

Then she swayed and her eyes closed. He saw that she was going to faint. Instinctively his

241

arms went out and he caught her, lifted her off her feet and carried her inside the café. She was so light. He marvelled at her slenderness. Utterly confused, he put her down carefully in one of the basket chairs and arranged a cushion behind her head. Then he clapped his hands for the waiter.

Martin had given poor Sanchia the slip and come alone to Camacha this morning. He had gone into the factory to see if they wanted help there because he still felt he was not earning enough in Quintra. He had lately decided to break away—get out of Madeira even at the risk of being jailed. He couldn't tolerate his present life. He sat outside the café and just watched this English girl walk towards him. He noted with masculine appraisal how gracefully she moved—also that she was exceptionally beautiful. Her colouring, her general appearance, struck a chord of memory somewhere deep down in him, but he was only faintly disturbed. It was like a ripple in still waters. Yet he wondered if he had seen her before, and if so—*where*. He ordered coffee and a cognac for her.

'Brandy first—*madame* has been taken ill,' he told the young waiter, speaking this time in Portuguese.

The boy returned at once with the cognac. Martin put a hand behind the girl's neck, raised her head and lifted the small glass to her lips. For the first time since Sanchia had uttered her grim warnings he forgot himself and spoke in English.

'Drink this,' he said. 'Come on—open your eyes—let me give you a little of this. You will soon feel better.'

Her lashes lifted slowly. Her recovery was instantaneous. She stared up into the man's face. Her heart was pounding. She drank only a fraction of the brandy and then pushed his hand away, spilling the cognac—not caring. She gasped his name again.

'*Martin.* Oh, God, what does this mean? I suppose you *aren't* Martin Ashley. I suppose I'm right off my head.

But you're so like him—*so like him.* And you spoke English just now. You've got his voice. Oh, you *are* Martin, aren't you?' She ended on a note of hysteria.

Now Martin began to shake. The waiter had come back with the coffee and set it down, staring curiously at these two who were so engrossed in each other. He went away, shrugging. Most tourists were strange in his opinion and all seemed to be millionaires, who paid huge prices for things—why, the escudos they wasted would have fed those who lived up here in the mountains for weeks! And what was the matter with the *senhora?* He must admit she looked sick; but *bonito—beautiful.* Like one of those model girls he had seen in pictures.

Martin sat down rather heavily in the chair

beside the girl. *Had* he spoken in English? That was indiscreet. Sanchia had stressed the possibility that anybody at any time might remember the police appeal for information about him and give him away. Yet he felt a desperate wish to go on speaking to this girl. *Why did she call him Martin?* Was that *his* name? She seemed overcome by the sight of him. *Why, oh why?*

He threw caution to the winds. He spoke again in his own language.

'Who is this Martin? What makes you think he's me?'

She shook her head, her pulses were throbbing at a rate that was positively painful. Her head was still spinning.

'You are English. Why did you speak in French just now?'

He was so keyed up that he answered her rather roughly, 'I'm the one who's asking the questions. Who are *you* and why do you think I'm a chap called Martin?'

'You have the same eyes and your mouth's the same, too—what I can see of it with all that beard,' she laughed and stood up—every nerve in her body quivering.

'Okay, what else?'

'How can you be Martin,' she added pitifully, 'You're so dark. Martin's fair.'

He sucked in his breath. God in heaven, he *was* fair! Sanchia had dyed his hair and the beard, once it grew, and until he became

244

naturally brown from the sun, she had stained his skin.

'Who are you? Tell me where you come from, and why you are so sure my name is Martin?' he asked hoarsely.

'I'm Corisande Gilroy. They call me Corrie. Martin called me that, too. Don't you recognise me? I live with Ann at a place called Brabett's Farm.'

He repeated, 'Corisande—*Corrie.*' He said both names slowly several times.

Now she knew. This *was* Martin. Her eyes frantically searched his face, then his hair. She noticed the fair roots. She could at least see that he was not naturally dark. *He was Martin.* A frenzy of excitement brought Corrie near to losing consciousness again but she took command of herself. She seized one of his hands and spread it out. She looked at the shape of the palm, the length of his fingers. She began to sob.

'They're your hands—your nails. Martin—Martin—*Martin!*'

He shut his eyes, struggling with his own haunted imagination, striving to dig down and break through the inferno of his lost memory.

God, he thought, *God!* what a fantastic coincidence that he should have met this girl, Corisande, up here this morning. *She must know him.* It was obvious she did.

Then his heart knocked a bit. How could he be sure that she wasn't in league with the

Portuguese or English police—that she hadn't been sent up to the mountains to snoop around, still trying to trace Martin Ashley. He must be careful. Sanchia had drummed *that* much into him. Yet he was aware that he had never totally believed all that Sanchia had told him about his criminal record.

Corrie began to talk to him. Soon Martin stopped feeling suspicious of her. His brow cleared. A great feeling of relief replaced all doubts. Confused he might be but he was positive that this girl was no detective. She was too genuinely overjoyed to have found him. At last he was hearing all that he most wanted to know. *Jean* was a myth. *He was Martin Ashley.*

Corrie recited the whole dramatic story of the rendezvous which she and he had agreed should take place at Reid's Hotel. Then of his amazing disappearance followed by the complete failure of the police to find him. Corrie omitted nothing. She kept sipping strong black coffee. She needed the restorative. And she kept looking into his eyes as though she could not tear her gaze away. She ended by asking him a heart-felt question.

'What *happened* to you, Martin? Oh, darling, why didn't you come back? Why are you up here in the mountains like this—in this disguise—I don't understand your dyed hair and beard-the way you spoke to me at first in French? None of it makes sense.'

'And do you think your story makes sense to

me?' he asked in a hoarse voice. 'Until this morning I've imagined my name was Jean. I'm supposed to have fallen into a ravine and hit my head. This accounts for the amnesia. The rest is explained by what I was told by the two people who found me.'

'*When* did you fall into a ravine? *Where?* Who were these people? Where have you been living? You must have been completely hidden. The police couldn't trace you. But why did these people keep you hidden in spite of all the efforts that were made to find you?'

Martin fumbled in his pocket for a packet of cigarettes and lit one. He was so nervous that he could hardly keep the match alight. He breathed fast as though he had been running, and, like the girl, kept exchanging long questioning looks with her. The more he looked and listened, the more familiar she became. Everything about her seemed somehow evocative—even her name was no longer strange. The sound of it had vibrated through him like a bell that had been rung against his ear.

'Corrie—*Corisande*, dear God, I'm beginning to remember that name. Go on talking—say some more, for God's sake!'

Now she was weeping. 'You must remember it all, darling. We were going to be married. We were to have met at Reid's for three wonderful days together before our wedding. You flew from Lisbon—you'd been on a job for the firm you work for—a publishing firm. You were their head salesman.'

She began to pour out so much information about him—his work—his grandmother—that Martin could hardly grasp it all. His mind was still in confusion. Yet the touch of her hands so excited and moved him that he could well believe she was speaking the truth. He had loved her. He had been going to marry her, she said. Yes, that was surely true. He'd never seen anyone so beautiful in his life.

They sat there together for an hour talking, talking, talking.

The thunderstorm Corrie had anticipated suddenly broke. The noise was deafening and at times the lightning flashed so brightly that it even drew an exclamation from the Portuguese waiter who was bringing them their third coffee. He kept muttering, *'Deus!'*

Then the rain came down, heavy and noisy, splashing all over the courtyard. The ground outside the patio turned into a swamp within minutes. Corrie's chauffeur sheltered in his car.

Neither of the two people inside the café took the slightest notice of the storm. They went on staring at each other, telling each other all they knew.

Corrie heard how Martin had come out of his coma. But she still did not understand what actually had happened before. She only knew that a girl, whom he called Sanchia, and José, her father, appeared to have rescued him from the ravine into which he had fallen, and taken him back to their isolated cottage. After that he knew only what Sanchia had told him. Corrie was appalled by the fantastic story of the bank robbery—how Martin had need to lie low and keep away from the police. All this was responsible for what had seemed an incomprehensible disappearance.

Again and again, Corrie asked Martin for details that he could not supply. He was still vague and uncertain of his facts. The pieces of the puzzle did not altogether fit. The true picture had yet to be formed. Yet after an hour with him, Corrie had no doubt about his identity. He was Martin. He had lost his memory as she had always believed. This Sanchia must be crazy—the father, too. They had committed a criminal act, ignoring police investigation and keeping Martin hidden from the rest of the world. 'Jean' they had called him. He had been advised to forget his English tongue and speak only in French, to preserve the appearance of a Frenchman who lived in Quintra with his old French cousin.

It seemed almost too much for Martin when Corrie gave him *her* version of what happened in Funchal after he disappeared. He kept burying his face in his hands and shaking his head.

'Incredible—*unbelievable*—it makes sense, yet it doesn't. It's like fiction. My God, I don't understand how Sanchia could have done such a ghastly thing to me. She must have realised I loathed thinking of myself as a man on the run wanted by police.'

Into Corrie's eyes there came the light of a dawning sympathy for the wicked, yet in a way, pitiable girl. Corrie had heard the whole story now. Sanchia was the victim of her accident and a terrible disfigurement. It was not in Corrie's nature to be viciously spiteful and even though the wretched girl had caused her such anguish—and such unending anxiety—she could pity her. She said, gently.

'I think I understand. Sanchia was obsessed by the thought that no man would ever look at her again, so she tried to keep you. She thought up this crazy plan and her father backed her. She must have known it couldn't last and that one day you might start remembering the true facts, but she took the risk. She took what she could—for the time being, poor creature.'

'I can never forgive her,' Martin muttered. 'My God!' He ran a hand through his hair and down his bearded face. 'I can't wait to get this damned dye off. How I long to be myself again, even though things are still so hazy to me. But if all you tell me is true and I'm sure it is, I'm dead certain I want to go back to England—and to be with you,' he added and put a hand out to Corrie and covered one of hers.

She returned the pressure, her face burning, her eyes bright.

'But you still don't remember anything except waking up in that cottage? You're only taking my word that you are Martin Ashley.'

'Yes. But it ties up with quite a few of the things I've been feeling now and then—memories which at moments have crossed my mind, then faded again. But I've always realised I was English and I've frequently doubted that I was the sort of fellow Sanchia made me out to be. Anyhow, if you'll let me drive back to Quintra with you, *you* can tell them that you've recognised me in spite of my dyed hair, and that's something Sanchia can't deny, even though she gave me the wrong reason for wanting it dyed.'

'Let me tell you what happened when I reached Reid's and after your grandmother joined me,' Corrie said.

Martin listened to her attentively. He was deeply interested—especially in her story of the couple who had seen him by the great mimosa tree on the Funchal road and how he had forgotten his camera, and mentioned the fact. He shook his head in a bewildered way. Then he heard about a shepherd who had seen him at a wedding in a village near Poiso. Martin's head shot up and he exclaimed, 'Ah! I *do* remember that I was at some wedding. I was wearing the red jeans and a white shirt, you described. *Why* do I remember about the

251

wedding?'

'It must have happened more recently—after, not before your fall.'

His excitement died down.

'Yes, that's right, that's it.'

'And your grandmother and I thought it couldn't have been you the boy saw, because he said the man was dark and bearded and we knew you were fair, and clean-shaven. Only I'm sure I'd have recognised you anywhere, as I have done today,' Corrie added. 'Your eyes, your hands, the way you smile—' She broke off, choking.

'If you only knew how much I wish I could share what you are feeling now,' he said on a note of pain. 'You're beautiful—wonderful—it's more than I deserve to find that not only am I okay—free to go back to England without fear of trial or imprisonment—but to have someone like you telling me we are engaged to be married. That's fantastically marvellous!'

Corrie gave a laugh that ended on a sob. Tears glittered on her lashes. She held out her left hand.

'Look, Martin, your ring, darling. It's never been off my finger. You remember it?'

He took her hand and stared earnestly at the stone.

'No, it means nothing,' he whispered. 'Please forgive me.'

She tried to laugh, but her voice broke. 'You'll have to learn to love me again,' she said.

'That won't be difficult,' he whispered the words, and felt his heart stir at the look in her warm, ardent eyes.

He searched every feature of her beautiful earnest face. Then he put out a hand and touched a silky lock of her hair.

'I remember you, my dear—yet I don't. I feel I'm still in that damn fog. Yet I can't even remember falling into a ravine.'

'And you don't remember that you were on a business trip to Lisbon selling books for Horton and Mullins? Or that you arrived at Reid's and half-unpacked your case?'

He frowned. 'No.'

'Nor that *in* London you used to live with your grandmother, Violetta—Lady Grey-Ewing—Gramma you called her when you were a boy.'

'Gramma,' he repeated, and his temples throbbed. He muttered, 'I feel I *ought* to know, but I don't quite recall having a grandmother.'

'Or a mother named Vanessa?'

'No.'

Frantically Corrie thought up every name, every person, anything she could think of that might rouse his memory. But it seemed only to disturb him rather than have any other effect.

Just for a few moments Corrie sat staring at him, speechless, feeling almost light-headed with excitement. God alone knew how many days and nights she had prayed to find him again. How many hours she had wept for him—feared that he might be dead. How many times she had discussed his disappearance with other people and tried to share Violetta's unshakable optimism. And how many times she had gone down that long, dark corridor of despair which had become more than a nightmare.

But last night she had reached the end of the corridor. In her dreams she had found him, and here he was, actually with her—altered by his disguise—a victim of amnesia—and worse still, a victim of a scheming crazy girl named Sanchia—but it was Martin and that was all that mattered. Last night's dream had been gloriously prophetic.

She stood up and drew a long breath.

'Martin,' she said, 'the storm's over. The sun's coming out. Drive home with me. I mean to your grandmother's villa in Funchal.'

Once more he covered his face with his hands. He felt physically sick. She spoke again.

'Don't let's go back to this cottage. I don't think I could bear to see this girl—not now. Not until we've got you back with your own grandmother. She may help you to remember things. Oh, please, darling, let me take you home.'

By this time, he was so bemused and exhausted—he did not want to argue.

He let this wonderful girl have her own way. She settled the small bill. His brain wouldn't

254

even allow him to look for change in his own pocket. He only knew that he had no real wish to go back to the cottage where he had been deceived and virtually imprisoned. For it was quite obvious that even though he could not really recognise the girl who called herself Corisande Gilroy, she spoke the truth. What she said tied up so many loose ends. He spread out the hands that she had recognised as *his*— Martin Ashley's, and gave them a long penetrating look. Then he followed Corrie out of the café and into the waiting car.

CHAPTER TWO

Violetta, straw hat on head, gloves on hands and basket on her arm, was strolling around the gardens of the Casa da Turna picking some flowers for the dinner table. She always liked to do that herself, and the gardener had long ceased to argue with her that it was his job. He had found that the petite old English lady had a will of iron behind her Dresden china appearance.

She was just thinking about Corrie—poor little Corrie—up in Camacha buying a souvenir for Ann. What a tragic time she had had! How miserable for us both, Violetta thought, to go back to England afraid that poor darling Martin must be dead. Drowned, she sometimes thought—although she had never distressed Corrie by saying so. But a body could be pinned under a submerged rock and never washed up by the tide. Perhaps Martin had gone swimming that day. They said he hadn't taken his bathing trunks with him. But who was to know that he hadn't climbed down and dived into the water with nothing on? He might easily have done so, thinking he wouldn't be seen. He might not have known about the dangerous currents along this coast. What else *could* have happened? If he had had an accident and lost his memory he would have been found wandering and brought back. No, Violetta greatly feared that she would never see her much-loved grandson again. She had lately felt her age and was more easily fatigued. The anxiety and pressures of the last few months had told on her. It wouldn't be long, she reflected quite calmly, before she joined her Bill in whatever heaven there might be. She was sad to think she would find Martin there, too. He was too young to die. It was poor little Corrie who would go on suffering. That girl had proved beyond doubt that there just wasn't another man in the world for her.

The sound of a car coming through the gates reached Violefta's ears. She carried her basket of flowers to the portico, set it down and stood there shading her eyes from the sun. It was late. The light was still strong. The sun was setting. Corrie had been a very long time

256

in Camacha—much longer than anticipated. She had said she would be back for tea. Perhaps she had had to take shelter from the storm. They had all seen it—the lightning, the torrential rain over the mountain tops—and heard the thunder. Yet it had stayed dry down here.

To her surprise Violetta saw there was someone else in the car with Corrie—rather an odd-looking companion at that! A long-haired, black-bearded fellow. Violetta was very tolerant but she did like the boys to look more conventional, like her darling Martin or that nice Hugh Aylmer. Actress though she was, or had been, Violetta thought the present generation over-acted their parts a little bit. As the two young people approached her, she saw nothing but Corrie's face. A completely changed Corrie from the girl who had gone to Camacha. The Corrie who for so long had been under a strain and whose eyes held such deep sadness. This was a renewed Corrie—starry-eyed, glowing, excited.

Good gracious, Violetta thought, what on earth has happened?

Corrie literally threw herself into the old lady's arms. 'Violetta! Oh, *Violetta*!'

Martin's grandmother blinked and drew herself away from Corrie. Her gaze was drawn to the young man. She took off her hat. She also took off the dark glasses she was wearing (her eyes were not very strong these days and even when the sun wasn't out she felt the need of the tinted glass). She walked a step nearer the young man who at first sight had looked to her like a peasant—one of those long-haired youngsters to be found all over the world these days. She had also thought he looked a little strange—and rather thin and ill in spite of his tan. Now that she was nearer to him she experienced the same sort of shock that had vibrated through Corrie up in Camacha. The shock of recognition which at the same time her brain denied almost as soon as it flashed into being. They were such *familiar* eyes and so curiously light in colour for that dark-bearded face. Violetta put her fingertips against her lips. She turned to Corrie. 'Who is your friend, darling?'

For a moment Corrie made no reply. She was suddenly afraid that the truth would be too great a shock for the old lady. Now Martin spoke to Violetta.

'Who are *you*?' he asked. 'I seem to know your face, *madame*.'

He spoke in French—perhaps because he had done little else during the last few months. But it was enough for Violetta. *She knew that voice*. She would have known it anywhere. She gave a little scream.

'Martin, *oh, my God, it can't be you!*'

'It is, *it is!*' exclaimed Corrie. 'We've found him. *It is Martin.*'

'But it can't be! He doesn't know us. He's

dark. It isn't Martin—' began Violetta incoherently. Then she called out, 'Marty, Marty!' the name she used when he was a little boy.

She was totally unprepared for this moment and strong, courageous though she had always been, it was a little too much for the old lady. So she did exactly what Corrie herself had done up there in the mountains. She just threw up her hands and fainted. But she fell down before either Corrie or Martin could support her.

Now the drama reached its climax. Martin stared down at the old lady. He was rooted to the spot. His heart pounded. He watched Corrie kneel down and cradle Violetta in her arms. He went on staring at the pretty pink-and-white old face—the silver hair—the tiny figure. All so familiar. Like that name. *Marty* she had called him. He felt as though the closed gates of his memory were slowly opening—letting him through into the light— into the knowledge that had been denied to him for so long.

He rushed forward and picked the little old lady up in his strong arms. He carried her through the portico into the house.

'Gramma,' he stammered the name as he went. 'Darling old Gramma!'

Corrie, the tears pouring down her cheeks followed them into the salon and watched Martin lay his grandmother down on the sofa.

When he turned round to her he spoke with a new authority.

'A drop of brandy would be the thing, Corrie,' he said. *So he knew her, too!*

She was wild with excitement—the joy of realising that he was slowly but surely regaining his memory. There had been considerable shocks all round and it had needed a good one, she thought to penetrate the fog in poor Martin's mind. Hearing his boyhood's name—seeing Violetta fall like that—had done the trick.

There was no need to worry about Violetta's heart. The invincible Violetta who had once played to packed houses on nights when she had felt ill, but considered that the show must go on, very soon recovered her senses. She sat up and waved both of them away—swallowing only half a teaspoonful of the cognac Martin lifted to her lips.

Smiling, gasping, half choking, she tapped him on the cheek with one hand.

'Oh, you wicked boy to give us all such a fright! Oh, my *darling* Marty. Martin *darling,* where in God's name have you been? And what is all this horrid stuff?' she tugged at his black beard and giggled like a girl, 'I've never seen such a fright. Go and shave it off at once.'

'I will, I will,' he said and laughed and kissed the top of her head.

They all began to speak at once—to laugh— to joke—to cry.

260

We shall never forget this moment as long as we live, Corrie thought, and once having made sure Violetta was all right, seated on the sofa and holding fast to her grandson's hand, she ran to the telephone. There were two people she must ring at once. The Inspector of Police, and the manager of Reid's, who had been so good, so helpful ever since Martin disappeared. But as the excitement died down she began to think more clearly and she made neither of the calls. She had no liking for the girl, Sanchia, or her old father after the terrible thing they had done in concealing Martin's true identity, both from him and the rest of the world. But at least she could feel grateful because they had saved his life. It was obvious that if they hadn't found him he might have died a slow horrible death. It was so lonely up there—anybody could fall into a ravine and not be found for days, or if they fell deep enough, might never be discovered. She had to leave Martin to deal with his rescuers. If she gave the news to the police they would likely as not charge Sanchia and her father with having concealed Martin and ignored the efforts of the police, or his relatives, to find him. They would be in deep water.

Violetta amazed Corrie. She took everything so calmly. She looked in the pink again, although she actually agreed to have another drop of that brandy. But she was as gay as a cricket.

'Can you *believe* it, Corrie? And he tells me this is all dye—this black on his hair, etc. I can see the fair roots. It's all so plain now.'

'I saw it, too,' said Corrie.

'Isn't it marvellous that one can recognise him in spite of such a disguise?'

'Everything's marvellous,' said Corrie, her eyes shining, 'but wait till you hear the whole story—the fantastic reason why Martin never got in touch with us.'

'Amnesia, of course.'

'But not only that.'

'I haven't quite taken it in yet, my dear. I'm just so glad he's alive and with us again, I don't think I care what happened before today.'

But this was where Martin—struggling with his newly acquired knowledge of the past—began to remember more recent events in his life. He left Corrie to sit beside his grandmother and reveal a few of the facts. And now there was an image photographed on Martin's brain that brought him considerable distress.

Sanchia.

What in God's name was he going to do about Sanchia and José? They would be wondering what had happened to him. He would have to go back and see them—tell them he knew all. As for that business of Sanchia falling madly in love with him and wanting to keep him, he had little sympathy with her except, of course, he was aware that the poor girl was obviously not normal. And she had in her way done her best for him. She couldn't have realised what a terrible thing it had been for his relatives. Martin had never been anything but kind of heart and sympathetic with other people's tragedies so he still felt sorry for Sanchia—for the accident that had robbed her of her future husband and left her with that terrifying disfigurement. Also he could still feel the warmth of her unending care of him from the time that she and her father had taken him to their home. He knew about her poverty and the misery of her life. He knew that she had spent all her savings on him. He couldn't do other than pity her. But the compassion was tempered by the deep resentment he felt against her and the old man for their lies and deception, and most of all having caused his grandmother and his future wife such anguish.

Bit by bit, Martin began to remember so much else—his work in Lisbon—his flight to Madeira, and he could realise what must have happened when Corrie reached Reid's so full of joy at the thought of meeting him—what she must have suffered when he didn't return to the hotel.

He turned suddenly to look at her. She got up from the sofa and came towards him. She was flushed—glowing like a rose, he thought, and so much more beautiful than he remembered her. For now indeed, he knew his

Corisande—everything about her, about their love for each other. Now the pieces of puzzle were fast falling into place. The whole picture was forming and—it was to him as it seemed to Corrie—a miracle.

'Corrie—oh, my darling, my poor darling!' he exclaimed.

She ran into his arms. They clung together. She pressed her face against his shoulder.

'You know me. You know me now,' she whispered. 'You remember—*about us?*'

'I do. If not anything else—at least I remember *you* and Gramma.'

Violetta stole a look at them. She came to the conclusion that it was high time she made herself scarce. She was in tears as she walked through the archway into her own room. There, in spite of her rheumaticky joints, and the difficulty of bending her knees, she knelt down beside her bed and thanked God for this hour.

In the salon, Corrie and Martin sat close, aims around each other, fingers feverishly interlocked. They were hardly able to tear their gaze from one another. It had all been unexpected and so wonderful. Neither of them could really believe they were together again.

'You must have had a grim time, my darling,' Martin said and lifted a strand of her shining burnished hair to his lips, 'I could forgive those people up in Quintra more easily if it wasn't for the pain they caused you—and

Gramma.'

'And everyone else who knows you. Your publishers—why, Sir Paul himself flew over and told us to spare no money in the effort to trace you. He was most concerned.'

Martin shut his eyes, then opened them again.

'None of it seemed possible. Fancy old Paul coming over, but he always was a magnificent fellow—one of the most respected publishers in Great Britain, and such a good employer.'

'And of course my aunt—and dozens of your friends, dozens of people who read about you both over here and in England—they all wrote to me. Honestly it was chaotic for a time. I never stopped answering letters or phone calls. Can't you imagine the bombshell here on the island? How it affected Reid's when an English visitor vanished from the hotel as though the earth had swallowed him up?'

'It very nearly did,' Martin said with a strained laugh. 'It must have caused havoc.'

'They were all so wonderful and helpful at Reid's. The police did everything they could. Interpol were not interested in what they call a 'missing person'. It would have been different if you'd gone off with half the money from the hotel safe, or committed some sort of felony.'

Martin's thoughts swung to Sanchia, and her insane flights of fancy—her frantic efforts to stop him from finding out the truth.

'I must have been truly damaged in the

265

upper storey, darling, to have taken in all the tales Sanchia concocted.'

'Perhaps that's the kindest thing we can say and perhaps that's why I feel sad for her instead of angry. She fell in love with you, darling. I can understand that, can't I? I fell in love with you, too.'

Martin drew her back into his arms and laid his cheek against her soft glowing one.

'Typical of you to be so understanding. Others in your position would find it difficult to forgive her. But I weaken, too, when I think of her poor face. If you saw it I'm sure you'd agree. She can't be all there.'

'No, she can't be,' sighed Corrie.

Martin told her how after he first came out of his coma, he had not noticed the disfigured side of Sanchia's face. She had kept it covered with a scarf. He had for quite a time only been allowed to look on her one perfect side—her magnificent eyes and hair.

'She must have been stunning—that makes it all the worse for her,' he ended.

Corrie was silent a moment, then she looked up at Martin, marvelling yet again that this bearded stranger and her Martin were one and the same.

'Did you ever feel the slightest attraction towards this girl?'

'Quite frankly, no. A certain admiration, yes, and gratitude. I had to believe what she told me at the time, especially as I supposed

266

they were protecting me. Don't forget I thought I was a man wanted for robbery.'

'Oh, God, what a story!' whispered Corrie. She closed her eyes and tried not to remember the long agonising months she had endured of uncertainty and of pain. She must be happy again. It was all over. He was here. She was close to him. She need never shed another tear. And dear little Violetta who had so often prayed to be allowed to see her adored grandson before she died, had most certainly got her wish.

Now Corrie put her face against Martin's shoulder and gave a muffled laugh. 'I can't think what all the papers will say when they hear about you. And we've got to put up with our dark boy for quite a time,' she added, laughing. 'It's obviously a strong dye and won't come out quickly. It's got to grow out.'

Martin gave an exclamation. He ran his fingers through his hair.

'For heaven's sake! I'll have it cut as short as possible, and darling, really I must go and have a bath and get rid of this beard. Would there be such a thing as a razor in the house, would you suppose?'

She raised her luminous eyes to his.

'Yes, darling, your *own*—your own electric razor in your own suitcase, and all your clothes. We wouldn't let the police take them away. They didn't want to anyhow, once the preliminary investigations were over.'

'Good,' he said, and sat back suddenly, releasing her. 'Darling, would I be a bore, but I simply must have a cigarette.'

She sprang to her feet. 'I'll have one with you—I think it will calm our nerves.'

He stood up. She looked at him, her heart racing. She could hardly bring herself to go and find the cigarettes. She could not really bear to let him out of her sight for a single instant. Never, never again, would she walk down the dark corridor of the old nightmares. Never again need she harbour the fear that there was nothing at the end of that corridor but darkness and death.

Then Martin said, 'Something's just struck me—rather a tricky thought. If we tell the police the truth about my being kept forcibly away from them—and you—they'll charge those two, Sanchia and old José with evasion of the law. The police'll know *they* knew who I was. Sancia must have seen my photograph—José, too—on the handout the police circulated about me. I wouldn't like them to be taken off to prison. After all, they did save my life, and did a lot for me, when I was apparently helpless and penniless. The whole thing's twisted, and of course they've done wrong, but don't you agree with me, we've got to think of something to keep them from being arrested?'

Corrie considered this. She bit her lip, nodding. 'Yes, I see what you mean.'

Half of her, the passionate and possessive side that belongs to every woman, wanted to punish the girl who had done this awful thing, but all that was generous and human battled against that emotion—and won. She said, 'The poor creature—I agree, darling. We must think of some way of getting her and her father off the hook.'

Martin fingered his rough beard. 'I'll go and shave, Corrie darling, and get into some other clothes. Then we'll have another talk with Violetta. She often thinks of things. We'll see what she suggests. I *must* also get someone to drive me up to Quintra so I can let those two know that I shall never be going back.'

After he had gone Corrie rushed to the telephone and put a call through to Ann to tell her the stunning news. She felt as though the world was spinning dizzily around her. She was wildly happy and enormously relieved. The sword that had been hanging over her head had been lifted. She wanted to throw her arms above her head and sing—a song of mad triumph (if she knew one, she thought, and laughed aloud).

It was definitely *her* day. Even Ann's news was less worrying. After she had offered her congratulations to Corrie she told her that things were definitely better at Brabett's. For reasons which she wouldn't bother to explain, she said, the stable-girl's trip to Canada had been cancelled. She had returned to work.

Ann wouldn't need to worry about the horses for the moment, or the dog that was such a favourite—the little Schnauzer, Zena. Zena adored her mistress but the stable-girl used to take her for walks and feed her when Ann was away. Zena had been fretting for her, so Ann told Corrie, and barked her head off when the girl came back. Another thing—a woman from one of the council houses near Forest Row had answered Ann's advertisement and offered to help with the housework. Ann was far less harassed all round.

'But your news is really terrific! I'm absolutely delighted Martin has shown up at last. I won't keep you talking, Corrie dear, it's too expensive a call. Write to me, I want to hear exactly what happened to Martin. Will you all be coming home at once?'

'Everything has happened so suddenly, Violetta has had no time to make definite plans,' was Corrie's reply. 'Once the dye's grown out of his hair, my poor Martin will look more like *my* Martin again. But we're sure to be home next week, anyhow. Violetta's got to settle things up at the Casa first and we must book our flight back. You understand, Ann dear.'

Ann did understand.

Corrie hesitated to telephone anybody else—least of all the Chief Inspector at Funchal. He could wait. She dreaded what *he* would say. He'd be glad that the *senhor* had been found, but furious to think that his men were not responsible for the success. Anyhow, she hadn't talked things over with Martin yet. She did realise that he wanted to avoid the girl, Sanchia, or her father getting into trouble. They must invent a story to circumvent the possibility of them being cross-questioned. After all, the poor girl was obviously a psychopath, to say the least of it.

Corrie went back into the salon and saw Martin standing by the window. It made her pulses leap to see that familiar, long-lost figure once again. He was wearing grey slacks and a dark blue sports jacket which he had found in his own case. A well-remembered yellow-spot silk scarf was knotted about his throat. Without the beard he looked much paler, younger, too, and thinner, but it was truly her Martin again. The dyed black hair did not make all that difference. It was the beard that had aged and altered him. She threw herself into his arms. He held her tenderly, passionately.

'Sorry, love, afraid my face is rough. My razor isn't good and I had to hack at the old beard. I borrowed some scissors from Gramma. Oh, Corrie, I'm beginning to remember so much. Things creep back into my brain all the time—seeing and listening to darling little old Gramma has done a lot for me. How I could ever have forgotten her *or* you, I don't know. Amnesia is a terrifying thing. I seem to have been living in a complete fog.'

Corrie looked up at him, her eyes sparkling with tears, although her lips smiled. 'Yes—it has all been terrible, but oh, darling, you look so like your old self now, it's too heavenly.'

'You haven't rung the police yet, have you?'

'No, I've been waiting to discuss it with you.'

'And I've decided I've got to go back to Quintra and face the music with that unfortunate girl. I've been talking about it to Gramma. She says she wants to come with me. You know what she's like—she's fabulous with people in difficult situations. She'll help me tackle the affair in the most diplomatic way—I know it! And in spite of the fact that she found it difficult to forgive Sanchia, she said she was very sorry for her.'

'So am I,' said Corrie in a low voice.

'You're both wonderful, she caused you so much pain—quite apart from the harm she did me with all her pretence—those fantastic lies.'

'But Gramma and I are both women so we understand how a woman ticks,' Corrie said. 'I, for one, take it for granted that the poor girl is a bit demented. And, as you said, she developed a sort of crazy passion for you. Maybe in her place I'd have done the same. *And* lied in order to hang on to you.' She laughed shakily.

'Oh, my darling, my dear darling Corisande,' Martin said. They kissed like the lovers they had always been—arms straining, mouth seeking mouth, heart beating against heart with the wild happiness of their reunion. Corrie knew now that she would never again travel down that long, dark corridor. The old nightmare would never return. That last dream had been prophetic. She had found Martin waiting for her in that dream, and it had come true.

CHAPTER THREE

Up in José's cottage in the mountains the scene with Sanchia took place, yet was not at all the difficult and unpleasant affair Martin had dreaded. He had fully anticipated a storm of abuse from the unfortunate girl, but the Sanchia who finally faced them seemed as though she, herself, had been turned to stone by the day's events.

At first when Violetta's car had arrived, Sanchia had rushed out, confident that it was her Jean who had been brought back, and relieved, because he had been away so very long. She had feared he had been at last recognised as Martin Ashley and taken down to Funchal, or even become involved in another accident.

The sun was setting. Soon it would be dark. José had already lit the oil-lamps. They were in the kitchen when Sanchia's quick ears caught the sound of the car pulling up outside the cottage.

She had been in a black mood since midday. When Jean went out alone she was always in a welter of anxiety. The little radio she used while he was still in a coma had long since been hidden away so that he couldn't turn it on, although he didn't speak Portuguese and it was unlikely he would understand anything that was broadcast, even if they mentioned him. Anyhow, why should the name *Martin* waken a chord of memory in him now? He had accepted the fact that he was Jean. Her father was always telling her that she worried too much.

But Sanchia was a very worried girl once she saw the elegant old lady with a straw hat on her head, who was seated beside Jean in that car.

She gripped her father's arm. José had just been standing at the kitchen sink cutting up a rabbit for her to stew.

'*Deus!* I wonder what has happened?' she muttered. 'Why has he come back with that lady?'

José looked through the window and muttered something unintelligible, crossing himself as he did so. He had never lost his childish belief that the sign of the cross would protect him from any harm that threatened him. But he couldn't help feeling that they had

274

at last been found out—the one thing he most dreaded.

Now he spoke to his daughter, 'What are you going to say if it is somebody who has recognised him?'

It was Sanchia's turn to make the sign of the cross, her huge eyes staring at Jean as he helped Violetta out of the car. *'Mother of God*—he has no beard. He has shaved. It's all over, Papa.'

And then there was no further time for discussion. Martin came into the room and the little old lady, with her ebony walking stick in one hand, followed him.

They stood staring at each other—all four of them.

There was a stony silence. Martin had meant to say all kinds of things, but was tongue-tied. He could only look with deep embarrassment at Sanchia whose face had gone a curious grey colour. She held on to the nearest chair as though in need of support.

Violetta gave a quick look round. Woman of the world though she was and, as an actress, greatly experienced in handling every kind of situation, she, also, was for the moment speechless—but she took in every detail of the shabby, old-fashioned kitchen.

It was dim in the light of the oil-lamps, but she could see at least that the place was spotlessly clean. She thought the man with his white hair and steel-rimmed spectacles looked rather an old dear. As for the girl—Violetta could hardly tear her gaze from Sanchia. Oh, what a *tragedy!* That one perfect side to her face—that other, so freakishly disfigured. She must once have been so beautiful with those huge sad eyes, and that blue-black splendid hair tied back with a ribbon and falling below her waist.

Martin was the first to speak—in French as he had spoken for so long to these two. He addressed himself exclusively to Sanchia.

'You know what's happened, don't you?'

She put a hand up to her throat. She was trembling violently.

'Yes, I know. It isn't difficult to guess. Your face—your clothes—you aren't "Jean" any more.'

'No,' he said quietly, 'I am Martin Ashley.'

The old man swallowed hard several times, then with the inborn courtesy of the Portuguese and the French, which seldom allowed a man to keep an old lady standing, he drew a chair forward and spoke to Lady Grey-Ewing.

'Please do sit down,' he said, also in French. She answered in the same language, surprising him by her excellent accent. He could tell that she was far more fluent and accurate than 'Jean'.

'I am Lady Grey-Ewing. Mr. Ashley's grandmother. He has lived with me since he was at school. I believe you know him as

"Jean".'

Old José, red as a beetroot, mumbled, and even giggled. 'Yes, yes, to us he was Jean.'

Then Sanchia came to life. Hands on hips in her customary way, tragic head thrown back, she spoke in a loud clear voice, 'It was I who decided to call him Jean. None of this has anything to do with my father. He is not to blame. I have done wrong. I don't deny it. I knew who Jean was but I kept it from him. I wanted to keep him here.'

Violetta gave her a long puzzled look.

'My dear, you don't know what pain and grief you have caused us all. We were beginning to believe he had died—that we would never see him again. How could you do such a thing or ever think, you poor child, that you could keep him in this place for always? Weren't you afraid that his memory would one day return—as indeed it has?'

Sanchia bit her lower lip so hard that it drew blood. A drop trickled down her chin. She did not even bother to wipe it away.

'Yes, I knew it wouldn't be for ever but I hoped he would stay with us for a while.'

Then Martin intervened, 'Let's all sit down, Chia. There's much to be talked over. My memory *has* returned and so we've got to be realistic. We've all been living in a kind of mad dream.'

'Mad, yes,' Sanchia nodded and gave a harsh laugh, 'I know I'm mad—Papa has told

277

me so many times.'

'Can't I sit down, Chia? Won't you let us talk it all over?' Martin asked gently.

'Sit where you like,' she said in a sullen voice. 'It is not for me to give orders any more.'

José pushed forward another wooden chair. Martin took it. He also pulled a packet of cigarettes from his pocket and offered them around. But Violetta was the only one to smoke—father and daughter refused, neither would they be seated. Sanchia, whose heart felt near to bursting with the pain of discovery, looked through her luxuriant lashes at Violetta and said, 'So you are his *grandmère*—an English milady. How you must hate me, *madame,* for what I have done.'

'I don't hate you at all,' Violetta said, 'I just want to try and understand what actually happened.'

'There isn't much to tell except that Papa and I found him. He had hurt his head and was sick for a long time. I am semi-trained, *madame,* and I nursed him. That is all.'

'But it's so difficult for me to grasp the reason why you made up this incredible story,' said Violetta. 'You made my grandson believe he was a criminal. He has told us that part of it. But why couldn't you see that you were doing a dangerous thing—from *your* point of view, my poor girl. At any moment he could have found out the truth and you would have had the police here.'

Sanchia closed her eyes and clenched her hands.

'But for a little while I had him to myself,' she whispered, 'I cared for him. I needed him. Someone to love—someone to love me. Of course I knew he would never love me. Even if he hadn't seen—this—' she tapped her disfigured cheek. 'It's enough to put any man off, isn't it?' she ended with a rasping laugh.

Then Violetta held out her hand. 'Come here, my child, I want you to sit down beside me and let me talk to you.'

'No—' began Sanchia and choked on the word, and put the back of her hand against her trembling lips. There was something about the gentleness, the compassion in the eyes and voice of this beautiful old English lady that she found unique and irresistible.

'Come,' repeated Violetta, and kept her hand extended.

Sanchia shook her head. 'I did wrong!' she cried. 'You've come to take us to prison. You will send for the police. I know you will. We shall both be accused of concealing Jean—*Martin*—' she stumbled over the English name and choked.

'I assure you you will not go to prison. We shall see to that,' put in Martin. 'It is the thing we want to talk to you about. We've got to hit on a plan which will save you from the police.'

Sanchia gave him an agonised look, then

279

turned back to the old lady.

'Were you in Camacha, *madame?* Did you find him?'

'No—it was his fiancée. She saw him in a café. After an hour with her, he began to remember things and once he came down to Funchal and spoke to me, he remembered everything.'

'His *fiancée,*' Sanchia repeated the word, and the bitterness in her voice was so intense that Martin and his grandmother exchanged glances. But once more Violetta held out her hand to Sanchia.

'Come, child—won't it make you feel better if I tell you that not only will I try to understand the madness that made you do what you did but Miss Gilroy—the girl he is going to marry—also understands. We all of us forgive you, my dear, and Martin especially is grateful to you. He has told us how good you were to him—how you've sacrificed both your time and savings on him. Besides, the courageous way you climbed down into that ravine and helped your father pull my grandson up was marvellous. He told us what a tremendous effort you must have made, and made it before you had time to fall in love with him and decide to tell all those lies.'

Suddenly something in Sanchia seemed to break. Compassion and understanding were things she had never before received. Her own parents had never understood her. But this little old lady—Martin's grandmother—was like an angel from heaven. Suddenly the tears began to pour down Sanchia's cheeks. She stumbled forward, knelt at Violetta's knee and seized the hand she extended. She buried her drenched face against those surprisingly strong little fingers and wept uncontrollably.

Martin, deeply embarrassed, turned to José who pulled at his beard in an agitated way.

'Come, my friend, if you have even a half bottle of wine, let's share it,' Martin whispered.

'At once, *senhor,* at once.' And the old man tottered to his cupboard, opened it, and pulled out his one treasured bottle of Cercial.

Now Violetta stroked the dark satin of Sanchia's hair. The tears were not far from her own eyes. It really was so pathetic. They were such simple people—they weren't really clever schemers. Sanchia was a wild, untutored creature. Certainly she had no mercenary motive for doing what she had done. She had done it at her own cost and for sheer crazy love. Her accident and the tragic fact that her lover had walked out on her, were responsible. It was quite a Greek tragedy in its way, Violetta thought. As for that ruined face—it could surely be put right. There was little plastic surgery couldn't achieve today. Sanchia had told Martin she couldn't afford the expensive operation at the time of her accident. But with a sudden warmth of

281

pleasure, Violetta went on stroking Sanchia's head and her elastic mind leapt to the great idea of taking the girl back to London and getting that face done at *her* expense. She would feel her money well spent.

While the two men drank their wine and talked at one end of the little kitchen, Violetta went on talking to Sanchia. She said many things—both kind and sympathetic. Sanchia continued to sob, and nodded or shook her head as the case might be. Finally when she found it possible to speak, Sanchia said, 'What are you going to do, *madame?* Even if you and *Mademoiselle* are so forgiving—how can you square the police?'

Violetta thought, a good thing French is my second language. When I lived with Bill down in Cannes he always said I spoke and behaved like a Frenchwoman. Now it's really coming in useful.

'Sanchia,' she said aloud, 'dry your eyes, my child, and sit up. Let's discuss the future. Martin is anxious that you shouldn't be involved with the police. So am I, now that I know a bit more about you. You've obviously got a very inventive mind, my dear. Look at all those tales you made up about Martin—"Jean"—whatever you called him! *Mon Dieu!* Help us think of a way to explain his reappearance without allowing the light to be focused on you or your father.'

'I cannot think,' whispered Sanchia,

282

helplessly.

'Then I suggest you make me a nice cup of coffee—I drink it in spite of my doctor's warnings. Run along, dear—put the kettle on.'

Sanchia, like a child, rose from her knees and obediently carried out the old lady's orders.

Martin talked to the old man and occupied his attention. He knew quite well that his grandmother was working the oracle with Sanchia. He felt immensely grateful and full of love for her. This was the last lap—dealing with Sanchia and her father. Curiously enough Martin felt no personal animosity toward them because of his long imprisonment here. From time to time while he talked to José, Martin glanced toward the two women at the other side of the kitchen. In the gleam of the lamp which José had lighted for them, he saw Sanchia looking back at him occasionally. She seemed even more ugly and undesirable than usual, after her violent weeping. But her beautiful eyes were sad and luminous in the lamplight. He could not help pitying her. He knew that in her wild and uncontrolled way she had fallen desperately in love with him. He would not have been a man if he had not felt compassion.

Finally Violetta seemed to have coaxed the unhappy girl into looking forward to a happier future rather than concentrating on the bitterness of the past.

'After all, my dear,' she said, 'I'm a woman and once I was young and beautiful and a great success on the stage. Then I found a wonderful husband. I have lots to be thankful for, so realise how agonising it must have been for you when you lost this boy, Marcello, as well as your good looks. But now Martin will go out of your life. You knew he was not for you, my child. But you needed someone to love, and you suffered when you looked at yourself in a mirror and felt afraid any man who saw you might turn away. I have plans for you but before we discuss them let us talk to my grandson and your father. The police must be dealt with as soon as possible.'

Sanchia went to her room and splashed her face with cold water. Then she combed back her dishevelled hair and returned to the kitchen. When she had first realised that Martin—(her "Jean")—was going away, and that possibly she would never see him again, she had felt complete despair. She had almost wanted to kill herself. Indeed she had decided that there was nothing more to live for. But Lady Grey-Ewing, this wonderful old lady, who was unlike anybody she had ever known, had helped to change those feelings. To make her believe life held some hope for her yet. It astounded Sanchia that anyone could be so kind. Instead of hating her for what she had done. Lady Grey-Ewing was sympathising with her, and even Martin Ashley didn't want her to be punished. These things thawed the ice that had formed around Sanchia's heart. The wilful passionate girl became a pathetic child, holding on to Violetta's hand, listening while they discussed what was best for them to do.

It was at least decided that on no account must Martin let the *Policia de Segurança Publica* know that he had lived all these months with Sanchia and José. Neither could he leave Madeira at once without being stopped at Funchal Airport where authorities had been on the lookout for him ever since he disappeared. So they must think up another story. But they got little further with suggestions before Violetta suddenly stood up and announced that she wished to take old José and his daughter down to the Casa da Turna. They were to be given a good meal and allowed to relax before they had any further discussion.

Sanchia immediately rejected the idea 'I couldn't. I *couldn't* come down to your house, my lady. I know what I look like!'

But here Violetta took command. She put an arm through Sanchia's and tapped her stick on the floor.

'You're going to do what you're told, my girl. It's time someone took charge of you. You're young and you need help, and I'm going to help you, but I find it a bit too hot and shut-in in this place. I suffer from asthma. I need more air. We'll go down to the Casa da

Turna and later on I'll send you back home in my car. But we have a lot to talk over first of all.'

Sanchia looked at her father, half terrified, half intrigued, and wholly enslaved by this angelic old lady who seemed to her to have been transported here from heaven.

Violetta continued, 'Don't you agree, Martin darling? It would be a good thing for Sanchia to meet Corrie, too.'

Sanchia's face reddened. 'No. I couldn't face the young lady who is going to marry Martin—' she began, but Violetta broke in.

'You will find her charming and most sweet, and she understands the whole position. She's deeply concerned in this affair and I think we should *all* discuss it.'

'I agree,' said Martin.

José, bemused and a little fearful of what his daughter might do or say, remained silent. The whole thing was going over his head like a huge wave. Secretly he was content to drown peacefully.

Sanchia burst into tears, but Violetta—as usual—won the day. She even arranged a long Indian silk scarf which she had brought with her, around Sanchia's head and brought a fold over the poor puckered cheek. 'Now you look fine. Just hold the fringe and it won't slip off. *Pauvre enfant,* you look as though you never eat enough. We shall all have a celebration dinner. I do not forget that without your courage in getting my grandson out of that ravine, he might have bled to death.'

It was a completely dazzled Sanchia who finally drove in the powerful car away from Quintra and down to Funchal. If she looked now and again in Martin's direction, feeling all her hopes in tatters, a new kind of hope was being born in her, for as they descended the long winding mountain road the astonishing old lady talked to her about plastic surgery and a certain famous surgeon who she knew quite well, and who quite definitely could make Sanchia's face whole again.

For the first time since her accident, Sanchia closed her eyes and prayed to the God against whom she had turned.

'Oh, *bon Dieu,* I have sinned. *Mea culpa! Mea maxima culpa!* Oh, dear Lord, what have I ever done to deserve such forgiveness. And now this miracle that the great lady is promising me!'

Corrie was standing in the portico waiting for them. The stars had come out and there were stars in her eyes as she saw Martin walking towards her.

CHAPTER FOUR

Five people sat down to dinner at Violetta's elegant table that night. It was a memorable meal for Sanchia who was struck dumb by the splendour of the house—all the glamour and riches around her—and most of all by the friendliness of the English girl who had shown no animosity towards her whatever. Right from the start she took Sanchia by the hand and said, 'Thank you. Thank you for saving him. He has told me all that you did for him.'

Sanchia had meant to hate Corisande Gilroy. But tonight there seemed no hatred possible—not even envy. It was natural, she thought, that a man like Martin should love such a beautiful girl. There was nothing vain or superior in Corrie's attitude to others, either. She was charming to old José. She treated Sanchia like a personal friend. She had put her at her ease as soon as they met, by admiring the national costume which Sanchia wore for this great occasion—her only party dress. Like one in a dream the girl sat eating as she had never eaten before—iced melon—an exquisite dish of chicken with cream and mushrooms—vegetables cooked as Sanchia had never dreamed possible, with a delicious Portuguese wine. And during dinner because of the Portuguese maid, who cast somewhat shocked glances at the *senhora's* strange guests, they did not discuss Martin. Old José became somewhat flushed and giggly. Sanchia felt worried, but Violetta treated him as though he was the perfect guest. Then—when coffee was served in what Sanchia thought the most elegant room she had ever seen—they made plans.

It was Corrie who came up with the best suggestion.

It wouldn't do, she said, for them to say too much—nothing, anyhow, that could make the police suspicious and lead them into making fresh searches. She wanted the whole matter to pass off peacefully, and for Martin to get away without too much questioning.

'Not only for his sake as he has been through enough—but for yours,' Corrie added, looking towards Sanchia, 'and your father's.'

The dazzled and well-fed Sanchia sat upright in her chair scarcely daring to lean back against the satin. cushions. She was thankful she had been offered a cheroot by Martin which she enjoyed and smoked to calm her nerves. With continual astonishment she regarded Martin Ashley's future wife. Little wonder, she told herself ruefully, that he loved her. She was not only lovely but lovable—a slender graceful girl—her golden-hazel eyes full of sympathy, and her long tawny hair curling down to her shoulders. Even Sanchia, who had at times looked with longing at the fine clothes she saw in the shop windows, admired the simplicity of Corrie's white dress with its scarlet patent belt, and the red patent shoes with their gold buckles and fashionable heels. Sanchia felt that she had emerged from a distorted world into a kind of mysterious paradise. But every now and then she remembered the wrong she had done Martin, and every time she saw his dyed hair, she felt guilty and miserable again.

She listened while Corrie explained what she thought was the best thing to be done.

Tomorrow, early, she would hire a car and drive Martin to Matur, at Agua de Pena, which was not too far from Funchal. They would go together to a coiffeur there. Nobody would recognise them or remember about the missing Martin Ashley. She would tell the hairdresser that 'her husband' wanted to get rid of his dark hair, and to have it bleached back to its natural colour. Even if it came out white what would it matter? The great thing was to get rid of the black dye. Then Corrie and Martin would go together to the police.

Corrie would deal with the Chief Inspector who was on very good terms with her. He had always been sympathetic. She would inform him that that very day she had passed an out-of-doors café in Funchal and seen Martin, sitting alone, drinking coffee. It had been a terrific shock to her, and such a shock to him when she called him by his name, that his memory had been restored.

Once rid of the black dye and beard Martin would bear no resemblance to the 'Jean', the villagers had seen around Quintra—or in Camacha. Nobody would connect the two, nor dream that it was in fact Martin—the fair-haired Englishman who had been living and working with José under the guise of 'Jean'. Doubtless the police would ask Martin where he had been all this time and how he had lived. He must simply shrug his shoulders and tell them he did not remember. He must stick to that whatever happened, Corrie kept repeating. Obviously they would be astounded and question him. He must continue to tell them that he knew little more than that he had wandered from village to village—procured casual labour here and there to earn a few escudos—slept in barns, stables, woods— anywhere, and eaten the local fruit and vegetables, or bought a square meal when he had money to pay for it. But never would he say who had sheltered or helped him. He would stand by this story.

Everybody in the salon listened breathlessly to Corrie's plan. It would, she declared, keep police focus off José and Sanchia and it wouldn't hurt Martin. The Inspector would no doubt be driven quite crazy because he would be unable to make head or tail of Martin's statement, but in the end he would have to accept it. After all he had come back. There

291

had been no foul play. The search was over. Why worry any more?

Violetta took off her glasses and gave an impish smile at Corrie.

'I congratulate you, darling. You'd better sit down once you're home and write a "whodunit" for Martin to publish. You're so full of ideas. Don't you agree, Marty dear?'

Martin's eyes caressed Corrie. 'I do and I think she's wonderful. It all sounds so simple. I'll just have to mind my p's and q's and, as she says, stick to the theme of "I *remember nothing* until I saw my fiancée, and heard her call me by my name".'

Corrie placed her hand in his.

Sanchia whispered to her father, telling him all that Corrie had said 'She is an angel,' Sanchia added. 'We will not go to prison.' José nodded, half asleep, after all the rich food and wine but he was well pleased with the turn events had taken.

José bowed to Violetta. '*Madame,* we owe much to you and to your grandson and his fiancée. We humbly thank you,' he said, his voice trembling.

'Yes, we owe you more than ordinary thanks,' said Sanchia, 'I can see from *Mademoiselle's* plan that it need never be told that I was so wicked.'

'Forget the wickedness,' said Martin, gently, 'I shall always remember that I owe you my life.'

'And now that we've settled that, I shall tell you what *I* am planning,' put in Violetta.

All eyes turned to the little old lady whose bright blue eyes beamed at them through her huge horn-rimmed glasses.

Sanchia and José would be taken back to their cottage this evening. All connection between them and the Casa da Turna must temporarily be severed. Violetta would deal with her maid, Maria. But she understood little that had been said during the dinner either in French or English. Violetta would merely mention that she had given the two humble guests a meal in return for some service that need not be explained. It was not Maria's business.

She would leave money with Sanchia. In due course the girl was to procure passports for herself and her father, also clothes, and luggage. They would shut up their cottage and fly to England. There, in London, Violetta would find them a small hotel, and be responsible for all payments. By then, a certain plastic surgeon well known to Violetta, would have been booked to operate on Sanchia, and a bed would be reserved in a famous clinic. She would stay there for as long as was necessary—until the ruined side of her face had been restored.

'You will soon look like your old handsome self,' Violetta told her. 'I've always been interested in plastic surgery. When I was younger I used to go round the hospital with books for the Red Cross. I have seen some of the results of the operations this great surgeon has done—men and women with terribly injured faces, have left the ward looking fantastically restored. So you will be, Sanchia, and you will go about with your head held high and feel proud again, and some good young man will eventually want to marry you.'

Sanchia gasped. 'It can't be true. Even if it is, why should you do this for me when I was so wicked—?'

'Sshush,' Violetta interrupted her. 'No more allusions to the past. From the time you enter the clinic your real life will begin again.'

'But *madame*—my lady—the cost of this— the terrible cost—' stammered Sanchia.

'My child,' Violetta broke in again, 'I married a man, a very dear man, whom I sadly miss. He was a millionaire. What better could I do with some of my money than the sort of thing I shall do for you? Money can be so horrid—so badly spent. I have a wonderful grandson to whom I can leave some of it—' she cast a fond glance at Martin, 'but I'm still alive and I intend to stay so as long as I can because I think life is good. It will be a rich reward for me to see you come out of the clinic looking quite changed, Sanchia, so much so that you will never again need to wear a scarf across your face.'

Silence. Sanchia's great eyes filled with

burning tears. 'Papa,' she said, turning to her father, 'Papa, do you understand?'

'Of course I do. She speaks in perfect French. Am I not a Frenchman?' José grumbled.

For the second time that evening, Sanchia went down on her knees by the little old lady and hid her scarred face on that kindly lap.

Martin held a hand out to Corrie. He whispered, 'Let's go out in the garden. It's warm and beautiful and the moon is up.'

'Oh, darling,' she whispered, 'what a great idea!'

They sat in Violetta's favourite arbour for a long, long time. Corrie, remembering all the anguish of losing Martin looked now in a kind of ecstasy—first at him—then at the beauty of the night. A myrtle tree, its dark green leaves glossy and scented, was silhouetted against the moonlit sky. The air was redolent with the perfume of all the glorious flowers that graced this enchanted garden. For Corrie it was complete enchantment—holding fast to Martin's hands while they talked.

'There'll be much to attend to, won't there?' Martin murmured, and as he used to do, he let a strand of Corrie's satin bright hair thread through his fingers. 'My mind isn't very clear or active at the moment, my sweet, but I'll have to pull myself together and face up to a bit of publicity. After all, Martin Ashley is still a missing person and the police may still be searching for him,' he finished up with a laugh, shaking his head.

'Shall we stay in Madeira or go straight home as soon as we can book our flight? Violetta wants to.'

'Do you think the police will swallow that story you concocted?'

'I'm sure of it,' she nodded. 'They can't do anything else, if you stick to it.'

'They'll certainly be a bit confused.'

She drew a long sigh, 'Nothing matters except that you're back with me, my darling.'

He put a finger under her chin, lifted it, and gently kissed her lips. 'One of the things that beats me is how I could ever have forgotten you.'

'Darling, that's what amnesia is. That particular part of the damaged brain just doesn't work.'

'How right you are! Mine certainly didn't. But it's lucky there wasn't greater damage. Tonight I keep remembering dozens of things and it's all pretty exciting.'

She sighed again. 'That poor girl, Sanchia—isn't it marvellous of Violetta to want to arrange for plastic surgery for her!'

'Typical of my grandmother—she was always one for the lame dog.'

'And she's one of the few rich people who like to spend their riches in the right way—helping others.'

Suddenly after all the excitement—the

bewildering events of the last few hours, Corrie remembered Hugh Aylmer.

'Do you remember what I told you up at Camacha about Liz's brother, Hugh, who was with us at Reid's, and was so kind and helpful when you first disappeared?'

'I do. He sounds a great chap.'

'He is. He's going to be married soon and has asked us to the wedding. He's still very anxious about us, so I'll send him a telegram and then phone him with details as soon as I get home. He'll be absolutely shaken and terribly surprised. But you must meet, you two. You're both in the world of books and you'll like each other.'

'I bet. When I stop to think about it you must have had one hell of a time, my poor Corrie.'

'It was pretty awful when I first realised you'd vanished and weren't coming back,' she said in a low voice, and put one of his hands against her cheek. She was still hardly able to believe he was here, close to her, mentally closer than he had ever been.

'We must go to Reid's and thank the manager, too,' she said after a pause. 'He was really most kind to us and couldn't have done more.'

'We'll see him as soon as we get back from this place you're taking me to get all this changed—' Martin rubbed his head. 'Not that I suppose it will look like my own colour, but if it's bleached it will be better, anyhow. I can't stand this blackness.'

'Sanchia certainly had a fantastic imagination, to say nothing of a strong will. What she did was incredible.'

He nodded, then kissing her on the lips again he said, 'One thing's definite. There's to be no more waiting for us, darling. I shall get a special licence as soon as we get home. We'll be married almost at once. Never mind white weddings or a trousseau, or any other little thing. I want my wife safely chained to me.'

She laughed and the tears sprang to her eyes. She put her arms around him and whispered, 'I want to be chained. Yes—just let's get married at once and never have to leave each other again.'

CHAPTER FIVE

On a dazzling morning in late August one year later, a taxi deposited two new arrivals outside the door of Reid's Hotel in Madeira—a man and a girl. They walked into the vestibule. A page-boy followed with their suitcases.

The head porter greeted them politely.

'Good morning, sir. Good morning, madam—' Then he stopped. He looked with some surprise at the face of the handsome English gentleman and at the very beautiful, attractively dressed girl. In a changed voice he added, 'Sir—*Monsieur*—*madame*—it isn't—it can't be—?'

'But it is,' Corrie broke in and gave him a dazzling smile, 'we got married and now we've come back to Reid's. We told you we would. And you do remember us, don't you?'

'Of course—of *course, madame.* Welcome back to Reid's.'

The man looked as he felt—astonished and pleased. Mr. and Mrs. Martin Ashley—why shouldn't he remember them? Could any of the staff forget that unhappy time when poor Miss Gilroy had arrived to meet her fiancé and he had gone out and never returned. And then there had been his sensational reappearance last September. Most of them here had taken it for granted the poor gentleman had died in some mysterious fashion. It had been like a miracle when Miss Gilroy brought him back. His hair had turned white with worry, poor soul.

They had booked a room for a fortnight. The Reception expected them. The head porter had the key all ready. Beaming, he handed it to them.

'It is a great pleasure to see you once again, *monsieur, madame.*'

'It's wonderful to be back under these conditions,' said Corrie, 'we want to lay all the ghosts, if you know what I mean.'

'We have reserved a special room for you—

299

up in the tower—it has three windows looking down to the sea, and the harbour.'

'It sounds fabulous,' said Martin.

'If you like to leave your passports with the Reception, I'll tell the page to take you up in the lift.'

'Just a moment,' said Martin. 'Wait here a moment, Corrie darling.'

As he moved towards the front door, Corrie ran after him.

'*Oh* no, you don't. You're not going out of that door without me. I'm not having you disappear a second time. I couldn't take it.'

Martin grinned, and shook his head. 'I don't think you need worry. I'm no longer a free man, darling. I regard myself as a henpecked husband whose wife won't let him out of her sight. But I must just see the old girl with the basket of flowers outside the door. You love roses, don't you?'

She watched him go and her eyes were full of the happiness she had been feeling ever since the day she found him again.

A whole year ago. How quickly the time had gone. So much had happened. First of all what Martin called the 'gefuffle' with the police. A difficult session with the Chief Inspector who had, as anticipated, been furious to think that he and his *guardas* had been outwitted, but he had to accept Martin's story and finally the whole thing had died down. After all, the 'missing person' had been found—it was enough.

But it was the return to England and all that had happened there that had really enriched Corrie's life. It had all been so exciting. First their wedding—Martin had had his wish. No more separations from his Corisande, and for a while no work. Violetta's favourite doctor had given Martin a check-up. He stated categorically that his patient was to have complete rest and peace for at least three weeks before he resumed his job. Martin had very apologetically told Sir Paul Mullins this. Sir Paul at once gave him the holiday. The firm were delighted to welcome Martin back.

'You've been through a tough time and so has your future wife,' Paul had told him. 'You're to take a good three weeks' honeymoon and not dream of turning up at the office until the doctor gives you the all-clear.'

Corrie and Martin decided not to go abroad again. They spent three unbelievably happy weeks in Scotland in an enchanting little hotel on the river. Martin had always liked fishing and it was the one sport the doctor thought good for his nerves. Fishing had a tranquilising effect on any man and Martin found it especially good with his wife beside him. She didn't find it boring. She didn't think she could ever be bored with Martin, and just now, she too, needed complete rest.

After the honeymoon they were busy buying

and furnishing a tiny house near Hampstead Heath. Ideal for Martin once he resumed work, not far from the station. The firm were not sending him abroad for a bit. He was to be given a new job in the office.

Violetta had been busy—occupied with her latest charity—Sanchia. True to her word Violetta had brought the girl and her old father over to England, and because nothing ever floored Violetta she had also ferreted out a French family not too far away where old José was accepted as a paying guest and could be happy amongst his own countrymen.

For Sanchia, it had meant six months of mingled pain and ecstasy. She had had to endure several unpleasant operations but when she had been allowed at last to look in a mirror and saw that her face was almost back to normal, despite a little puffiness and bruising, she had been thrilled to the core. It was all so much more marvellous than she had expected. She came out of the clinic a new Sanchia. A girl whose life was miraculously changed. That dreadful period of her life when she had had to hide her face had passed. She could lift her head and face the world, smiling again. Full of gratitude, she could not do enough to show it to Lady Grey-Ewing.

If ever Violetta had felt rewarded for her generosity, it was on the day that she personally fetched Sanchia from the clinic. She confessed afterwards to Corrie and Martin that although she was well aware that her friend the plastic surgeon was a brilliant man (he had done wonders with the injured face of one of her old actress friends, following an accident)—she was full of admiration for the surgeon now. For Sanchia, it had been a transformation, with the aid of skin grafted from her own body. She had suffered—yes—and at times lost faith, then recovered as she watched the gradual transformation. But when finally she walked into the waiting room, wearing a smart trouser-suit that Corrie had chosen for her, and her satin-black hair piled high on her head in Spanish style, Violetta was dumbfounded. Of course everybody had guessed having seen the good side of her face, that she had been a beauty. Today she was truly beautiful again. There were still many little scars and bruises which would in time vanish completely, but her cheeks were full and firm and her mouth no longer drawn into a sneer. She was smiling. Her eyes looked enormous and bright as jewels. She took Violetta's hand and kissed it humbly.

'You see? You see, I am the old Sanchia! And this miracle is through you, my lady. Oh! do you know what a young house physician has just said to me?'

'Tell me,' said Violetta.

Sanchia tossed her head and laughed. 'He said "I shall go to Portugal for my next holiday. I have friends in Lisbon. I shall fly from there to Madeira to see you. You are quite a girl, and you turn me on,"' Sanchia laughed again—a happy throaty laugh. 'I know—what it is—the English words *"turn me on"*—Oh, my lady, my lady. If Marcello could see me now!'

'We won't think of Marcello, my child. We think of other nicer young men in Madeira who will be "turned on",' said Violetta gaily.

Later that day Sanchia bade goodbye to Martin for the last time and he, too, looked at her with surprise and pleasure.

'You're truly beautiful, Chia.'

'I will always remember that you did not turn away from me when you saw the *other* Chia,' she said, and her eyes filled with tears which were speedily dried.

As for her father, old José made the sign of the cross several times when he looked at his daughter. He kept shaking his head and talking about 'miracles'. He couldn't believe his eyes—or his own luck. The wealthy grandmother of 'Jean' (he could never think of Martin as anything else) had given him enough money as a farewell gift to buy himself many cases of Sercial many times over if he wanted it. There were good times ahead and no more need to think of having to confess mortal sins. The wrongs had been righted and he could sustain himself with the belief that if his daughter had never behaved as she did, this wonder of restored beauty might never have changed her whole life.

Father and daughter returned that next day to Madeira because they wanted to do so. It was their home and Sanchia with a burst of vanity, had said to Corrie, 'I shall use face-cream and lipstick again and the local boys will start to look twice at me, will they not, Madame Ashley?'

'They will indeed,' Corrie had answered.

Poor Sanchia was certainly no longer the half-demented girl who had hidden Martin in her home. In time she found a new boy-friend, and secured a well-paid job in a private villa, as a cook. She became a nine days' wonder in her village. Gossip was rife. A wealthy English lady had paid for Chia's operation, she was no longer a freak to be avoided. Many local doctors came to see the result of the operation—and departed praising the great English plastic surgeon. It was not long before an enterprising young man decided to marry this famous girl, and as far as she was concerned, the crazy passion she had felt for 'Jean' died and was buried.

Corrie and Martin discussed the idea of spending their first summer holiday in Funchal. At first Corrie wondered whether she really wanted to go back to the island after all that had happened there. Then suddenly she had decided she wouldn't be happy until she saw Madeira again.

'It's a beautiful place and it was made ugly only because of your accident,' she told

Martin. 'I'd like to go back now to recap, so to speak—get rid of my nightmares for good and all. I haven't had one since you came back into my life. But I want to carry out the plan we originally made—to meet at Reid's. Do you understand what I mean?'

He did understand. That was one of the most wonderful things about her husband, Corrie decided—he always understood.

So when they reached the beautiful bedroom in the tower, she made Martin stay inside while she went out into the corridor. Then she played a game—with him—and with herself. She had a childish wish to do so. Just for a moment, when the lift had deposited them on the ninth floor she had experienced a thrill of terror. *It was the long dark corridor again*—Martin might vanish. She must hurry up and find him.

Breathlessly she knocked on the bedroom door. Martin said 'Come in'. She closed her eyes and turned the handle. Then she walked in and opened her eyes and saw him standing there, smiling at her. And through three windows she could see blue skies, blue sea and the beauty of Madeira.

'Oh, you're here,' she said. 'You're *here*— *Martin*, my *Martin*. You'll always be here when I call, won't you? You'll never disappear again?'

He shook his head and held her close. He thought it sweet and very moving that she

306

should play this little game and in her imagination obliterate the past finally. He shared with her the absolute joy of their togetherness.

486
455
388
1010

(6)

841